CRE

Gordon Linzner	Christopher L. Bennett
Ian Randal Strock	James Chambers
Robert Greenberger	Keith R.A. DeCandido
Dayton Ward	Russ Colchamiro
Aaron Rosenberg	Judi Fleming
Danielle Ackley-McPhail	Bryan J.L. Glass
Jody Lynn Nye	Mike McPhail

**"Earth is the cradle of humanity,
but one cannot remain in the cradle forever."
Konstantin E. Tsiolkovsky**

FOOTPRINTS IN THE STARS

Edited by Danielle Ackley-McPhail
Series Editor: Mike McPhail

eBooks
Pennsville, NJ

PUBLISHED BY
eSpec Books LLC
Danielle McPhail, Publisher
PO Box 242,
Pennsville, New Jersey 08070
www.especbooks.com

ISBN: 978-1-949691-03-0
ISBN (ebook): 978-1-949691-02-3

Design: Mike and Danielle McPhail
Cover Art: © Tithi Luadthong, www.shutterstock.com
Copyeditors: Greg Schauer
          Danielle McPhail, www.sidhenadaire.com

"One small step for (a) man, one giant leap for mankind."

Dedicated to the memory of Neil Armstrong,
commander of Apollo 11 and the first man on the moon.

August 5, 1930 to August 25, 2012

CONTENTS

ASTRAL ODDS

Gordon Linzner

I F YOU'D TOLD ME A WEEK AGO MY PROBLEMS WOULD BE RESOLVED BY SOME little green men leaving an indecipherable message, well, I am a betting man, which is what put me in the hole in the first place, but only a rank sucker would have wagered so much as an ace on that outcome. Yet here we are.

We start with me sitting at the far corner of the bar in the Happy Harpy on the corner of Eleventh Avenue, near the old Penn rail yards, a spot I chose on account of the weather's exceptionally cold for October, and a freezing wind blows off the river and blasts through every time someone opens the door, which happily for me is seldom. There's this character, Big Abe Grabowsky, better known as Bookie Abe, and even better known as B Abe, the Babe, to whom I owe more than a few potatoes after a streak of bad errors of judgment with the horses, and while he's been patient in the past, times are tight, and he's got his reputation on the street to consider. Rather than hang in my dinky single-room occupancy nest, waiting for a knock on the door, if the Babe's crew even bothered knocking, I prefer someplace more public, with a one-eighty view and a side delivery door a few steps away, just past the men's john and through the kitchen. Should the Babe's boys poke their snoots in here all they'll see is the heel dust I kick up. It's Tuesday, which means happy hour all night. I nurse my house whiskey, a nameless knockoff of Old Crow, barely a step up from the coffin varnish the place down the block sells, and from time to time add a couple drops of water so whenever Gracie the bartender looks at me, she'll think I'm not yet ready for more, and also because it makes the Faux Crow almost palatable, though by now the stuff is so watered-down it's practically clear. To make doubly sure I don't catch her eye, when I'm not glancing up every time I hear the door open, I stare at the newspaper crossword puzzle in my free hand, occasionally inserting whatever letters come to mind at the moment, since I can't be bothered working out the clues, as I'm too busy figuring out how to get enough scratch to bring down my debit and avoid a trip to the emergency room.

Gracie is six feet tall and then some, thick-built, all muscle. Todd Granger, part owner and full-time manager of the Happy Harpy, is too cheap to hire a bouncer except for late Friday and Saturday nights, but when Gracie is behind the bar the place doesn't need anyone else. If she didn't have those weekend wrestling gigs, the Harpy wouldn't need a bouncer then, either.

Even for a Tuesday night, the dive is pretty empty. One couple is busy with a private petting party at the opposite end of the bar, in a corner shielded from that arctic blast whenever the door opens, and Gracie would've long ago told them the bank was closed if there'd been any citizens in there who cared. The only other patrons to stay more than half an hour are a group of four young fellas seated at a table across from me, near the wall, obviously from out of town, who at a casual glance are ignoring each other, playing around with their tablets, except I've been sliding my eyes in their direction on and off long enough to see they actually are involved in some computer game, which accounts for an excited yelp here and a sorrowful groan there. On the off chance any actual gambling is involved, Gracie also throws them an occasional side-eye, but if any money is being exchanged it's very much on the q.t.

Each time I hear the door open, which as I said is hardly ever this night, I raise the crossword puzzle to cover my face while I give the newcomer a once over. I've been perched on my stool for a couple of hours when this skinny character walks in, dragging his feet, dressed real spiffy and looking young enough, despite his pencil 'stache, or maybe because of it, that Gracie feels compelled to ask for proof of age, though strictly as a formality, since her regular procedure is to barely glance at the ID, and this night is no exception. His puffy down coat leaves the lower part of his suit jacket exposed, but he was walking about with it unzipped anyway. He drapes it on a hook by the bar stool two seats away and catty-corner from me, points up at a back shelf toward a bottle of higher class giggle water than I'm nursing, and disappears toward the john.

In the interval, I hear the front door open again. The paper in my hand crumples slightly under tensing fingers, but a middle-aged jane simply peers inside, shakes her head, and vanishes again. Gracie shrugs, fills a new glass and sets it in front of the newcomer's spot, even using a clean coaster instead of a retread. At this point, she no longer bothers glancing at my drink. The new guy comes back, nods his thanks, lays a Jackson on the bar, and downs half the whiskey in a gulp, not even taking time to remove the plastic stirrer. Then he slumps onto the stool and undoes his red-and-black tie, which he leaves hanging loose around his neck like a dead, or at least very sick, snake. A laminated tag with the logo of the computer tech show at the convention center a few blocks away dangles from his suit pocket. His poor little bunny expression tells me his day's gone south.

I see an opportunity to earn points with Gracie without dropping more mazuma on the bar myself, which is a good thing as I've only got a couple of bob left in my worn-out wallet. A citizen putting away the sauce as quickly as this one is doing could become a liability, even on such a slow weeknight, especially on a slow night where his drunkenness would stand out, but if I can pull him into a little friendly conversation, he'll pace himself better, keep from getting too bent, and give the Happy Harpy a warmer, more inviting atmosphere, and maybe the next dame to stick her nose in the door will be more tempted to stay. Plus, if I charm him enough, and I am nothing if not charming when I pile it on, he'll likely spring for a drink or three for me, so the bar gets more profit without adding to my own tab. If I can also cheer him up a bit, that's a bonus for my mood as well.

I make a show of staring at my crossword, give a long sigh, and tap my pencil against my near-empty glass as a sign of frustration. He doesn't look. I sigh louder, slap my hand on the edge of the bar, drop the puzzle, and take another very slow, very small sip of the Faux Crow. He's staring at the bottles shelved behind the bar, or maybe at the flickering television, although at this hour it's tuned to an infomercial with the sound mercifully off and a picture so sketchy the set might as well be a decades-old black-and-white model. Whatever funk he's in, it's deep.

"Hey, pal," I say.

He gulps down the rest of his drink and waves at Gracie to bring another. I wait for her to deliver the goods and take off again, then lean over the empty bar stool between us. "Just a suggestion, pal," I say, "from one weary night tippler to another, seeing as you look all educated and stuff, I figure you might not mind some well-intentioned advice."

He blinks and slowly turns toward me.

"Gracie doesn't like being treated like a servant," I say. "She is a consummate professional and knows when and how best to approach when you are in need. You do not wish to annoy her."

"Do I know you?" The dork grunts, lifting his newly-filled glass. This time, instead of sucking half of it down, he only takes a sip, so I figure my plan is working, and I continue.

I hold out my left hand, the one not clutching the pencil. "Larry Rosen. Lucky Larry, though not so much lately. Some call me Larry the Lump, but I'm getting more exercise, dropped five pounds last week. The babes have noticed, well, a couple, anyway. Welcome to the Tenderloin, Stan. Named for when the bulls could make enough dough under the table to afford..."

"You *know* me?"

I point to the shiny white exhibition badge dangling from his breast pocket. "Your name's Stanley Coogan, right?"

Stan removes his tag, stuffs it in a side pocket. "What is it you want?"

"Some help," I say. I point to the puzzle, quickly skim the clues until one catches my eye. "Time to level scores," I read, putting on a professorial tone.

"You're confusing me with someone else. I've never seen you before. I owe you nothing." He turns away.

"No, it's a clue. In my crossword." I wave the paper. "Seven letters. 'Time to level scores.' Any ideas?"

He takes another sip of whiskey, closes his eyes, then turns to me again. "It's a pun."

That's seven letters. I start filling in blank spaces. "Appreciate the help," I say.

"The answer is evening. Or even-ing."

I finish writing. "That's what I thought. I wasn't sure."

He tries to look at the crossword. I shift my hand, blocking his view. "You're almost done?" he says.

I crumble the page and shove it in my back pocket. "Looks like you've got a bad case of the mopes, Stan, and I'd rather listen to someone else's beefs than my own. What's up?"

"It's complicated," he says.

"I've got all night," I say.

Stan sighs, takes another sip of whiskey. "If you're as good a listener as you are a talker...." He gives in. "Remember that news story this summer, about extraterrestrial technosignatures indicating intelligent alien life?"

To be on the up and up, some days I can't remember what I had for breakfast. If a story's not on the sports page, and sometimes even if it is, I don't go out of my way to lock down the dope, plus he's spewing way too many syllables, but I'm trying to be affable, like I said, so I nod and smile. He goes on about how several groups of scientists have been examining these weird signals from outer space, trying to decide if they're definitely signs of intelligent life, and, if so, figure out their meaning, on the hush, as per some international protocols. The whole 'not understanding messages' gimmick sounds like every one of my relationships with the janes, so I sorta relate.

Stan spews out background like he's lecturing a baby, which he kinda is. Turns out he's a graduate student at Columbia University, studying particle physics, working on his doctorate. His dream is to make some major scientific breakthrough, get a concept named after him, like the Coogan Paradigm, whatever a pair o' dimes is. That afternoon he'd been part of some panel on alien technology, organized by Columbia, at a tech show at the Javits Center nearby, and now he's got the sweats because somebody said the United Nations would announce the message's meaning on Monday. If the aliens're smart enough to communicate over trillions of light years, and plan to share their smarts through some kind of Encyclopedia Galactica, there'll be nothing left for him to discover, which makes him so despondent he won't even hang with his fellow citizens afterward, instead stumbling into the Harpy on his own. "I'll end up like Lisa Meitner and Percy Julian," he says.

"Who?" I say.

"My point exactly," he says.

He's so earnest I can't help getting caught up in this palooka's narrative. I don't understand a tenth of it, but I get enough that, when he buys another round for us both, I figure he's earned a little of my own wisdom.

"Tell me if I've got this straight," I say. "You want to be famous, but everything you hope to do will be static because they'll have already done it all."

Stan grimaces. "A selfish attitude, I know. I think my selfishness depresses me more than my life becoming meaningless."

"Why would they even care?" I say. "Why wouldn't they just take over? Assuming we have anything they want."

"Sharing knowledge is the right thing to do, isn't it?" he says. "Someone needs something, you've got what they need, you share it, help 'em out, bring them up to your level, work together."

"I wouldn't bet on that. Most people I know, if they've got an edge, just exploit it, and...."

I let the thought trail off, mulling over my own words as I sip my fresh Faux Crow. Stan nods, also goes silent, but his drinking is slower. I was accomplishing my job.

Unfortunately, wrapped up in my own thoughts, something I rarely am, it's not until I hear Gracie's hissed warning that I look up, and then it's too late. The Babe is standing just inside the door of the Happy Harpy, one of his goons, Tiger Tommy, at his side, staring right at me. The Babe does not look like any newborn I ever seen, or any hot doll, either, and in fact looks as if he could take down half a dozen street punks on his own, and still, he is puny compared to Tiger Tom, who as I say is standing beside him.

"Excuse me, Stan," I say, "got to see a man about a dog." I start to slide off my barstool, and sure enough, a second goon, who I recognized as the Roach, bigger and tougher than the Tiger, if that were possible, is already blocking the back door. I stay seated. I know the Babe's not gonna start anything in the Harpy, because he knows Gracie, and he knows Todd, and they've got some history, but she also won't stop him from taking our little dispute outside.

I give him my biggest, phoniest smile and point to my new pal, not to get Stan in trouble but to set the groundwork for an idea I just had, and also to make sure Tiger Tom and the Roach see there's at least one witness.

"Hey, Babe! I was just gonna call you!"

"Sure you were." The Babe's voice sounds like a bulldozer backing up. "You got my dough?"

"Something better," I say. "This is my new buddy, Stan."

Stan tentatively raises a forefinger in acknowledgment. He shifts as he sizes up the situation, gives me a what-the-hell side-eye. I widen my smile to assure him he's got nothing to worry about, but my hands are shaking a bit, so I'm not sure the message is getting through.

"Stan has my dough?" the Babe asks.

"We've got something better, like I said."

"He's a doctor, maybe? Fixes broken ribs and fingers?"

"Not a doctor yet," Stan says. "And not a medical one."

"Too bad. For you, Lump. Just keep drinking, Lump's new friend. I gotta have a talk with your pal. Outside."

"Wait! Let me tell you my idea first! Our idea!" I look at Stan, who flinches as if dodging a poison dart. "This guy really knows his onions!"

The Roach leaves the side exit to close in on to me, places a thick paw on my shoulder, cutting off the circulation. I feel myself being lifted off the barstool.

I quickly repeat what Stan told me, but simpler, so the Babe can understand, plus I can't remember it all, about space people contacting Earth and how we don't know what they're trying to say but there'll be an announcement in six days, and nobody knows what the answer is, or if they do they're not talking, so it's open to betting. What I don't say, because the Babe already knows, is that his own pool of regular bettors has been shrinking ever since the Feds made sports gambling legal, and he should expand whenever he can.

"That's total whack!" the Babe says, with a growl. "Who the hell would bet on what little green men do?"

"I might."

All of us, even Stan, who's been trying to figure a way out of this kerfluffle, turn toward the speaker.

Behind the bar, Gracie hovers over the five of us. She's a great listener, but not much of a yakker, so when she does talk even the Babe gives her the benefit of the doubt.

"When did you ever bet on anything, Gracie?" the Babe asks.

"Sports betting's a flat tire. Politics just as boring. But I can see people being keen on this space alien stuff for the novelty. You know who'd really go for it? Those fluky nerds playing with their tablets over there. They were at that tech show this afternoon, and they're staying in town for the comic book thing this weekend, and the Harpy makes for a nicer hangout than their hotel room up the block, you know the dump. I'd bet, but I won't, they'd even put down cash up front. I doubt any of them know how this works. They'd be so excited to bet on space people's motives they probably won't care if they win or lose. One of them is such a self-centered dork he might bet on a losing ticket just to be different."

Those were the most words I've ever heard come out of Gracie's mouth at one time. I see the same impression on the Babe's face, and I'm thinking I might get out of this in one piece, this time, anyway, after all.

The Babe turns to Stan, nailing the poor sap with narrowed eyes. "You wouldn't happen to have any inside dope on this space message, would you, kid?"

Stan shakes his head. "Different groups around the world are studying it. Any results so far are top secret. There have been leaks, but they're so contradictory no one knows for sure." Now that he's talking science stuff again, my new pal becomes more loquacious.

"What d'you think?" the Babe says, pushing.

"There are two major options. Either the civilization that sent the message wishes to help us reach their advanced level, or they want to take over our world and exploit its resources. The first option, as I was telling Larry, puts an end to my career before it begins, since they'll hand us any discoveries I might have made. The second, well, I guess that would put an end to my future, too. Everyone's, really."

"Hmm," the Babe says. "Let's you and me talk to those squares, see which of those outcomes they'd bet on."

Stan gives me a nervous glance, but I nod, force a smile, again so he knows everything's jake. For him, anyway.

"'Scuse me, boys," the Babe says as he nears the table.

One of the gamers, a boney duck wearing a pair of cheaters with frames barely thick enough to hold their lenses in place, raises a hand, without looking, to stop him. This is a mistake. The Babe is not the kind of guy who likes to wait.

The Babe waits.

This night is full of surprises.

"Boom!" another gamer shouts, a moment later. "Got the gold, and the girl, and the scepter! You lose, Ronnie! Next round's on you!"

The Babe clears his throat. Tiger Tom circles to the far side of the table. The Roach remains beside me at the bar, still gripping my shoulder hard enough to leave a bruise, should I try to make a break for it. To my surprise, even I'm too caught up in what's going down to worry about a few broken bones.

The one who'd held up his hand turns. "What did you want, Mister?" he says, and then his eyes go wide. "Omigod! It's you!"

The Babe is pretty well known in certain circles on Manhattan's West Side, but how do these tourists know him?

The speaker adjusts his cheaters and waves at the others. "Guys! It's him!" He points past the Babe.

"Who?" one mutters.

"Stanley Coogan! From the panel on alien artifacts!"

All four goggle at my new bestie.

Stan is obviously not used to being famous, so he steps back a pace, nervous, but then goes all in on his new status, shaking hands, accepting pats on the back, the usual. As a rule, the Babe will not stand for being pushed aside, but he didn't become a top bookie by being a dope, and he clearly sees how this might best go down, so he keeps his lip buttoned, lets Stan take the lead.

The nerds get even more excited. At first, it seems they'd rather continue that panel discussion than talk about the actual bet, and I see the Babe start to fidget, but then they start pulling out bills, and not just aces. Three of them put money down on the space fellas being good eggs. "After all," says the nerd with the cheaters, "if they're that advanced, why would they bother taking over? They'd more likely want company on their own level."

"Hooey!" yells the fourth. He hops to his feet, and his star-covered t-shirt rides up to expose his pale pot-belly. "I, for one, welcome our new overlords!" he declares. Even the petting party at the bar look up, though only for a second.

The shouter throws a bill on the table.

"Oh, come on, Glenn," says the kid wearing a too large fedora. "You're putting down a fifty? You can't really believe we'll be invaded! Why would they warn us?"

"That was half a c-note?" Glenn asks, eyes widening. "I mean, yeah, fifty. I totally meant to do that. They'd want to cause panic, laugh at us. Yeah, it's not likely, but if I'm right, all of you are wrong!"

"The bet stands?" the Babe says flatly. It's more of a statement than a question.

"Hell, yes!"

The Babe grins. Gracie will be getting a very good gratuity tonight.

Fedora Kid starts typing on his tablet. "Awesome! I'm posting this straight to my blog!" He looks up at Stan, then the Babe. "I know a bunch of people who'd love to get in on this. How can they place bets? You have a website or something?"

"Let's keep it low profile," the Babe says, again in a tone that is more than a suggestion, though short of being an actual threat, as he realizes these four will be pretty useful spreading the word.

"You should give these gentlemen your emails," Stan says, after an awkward pause. "That way, they'll know how to get you your winnings, and can forward those betting procedure details for you to pass on."

Tiger Tom pulls out a notepad and hands it to the Babe, who writes receipts for each bettor, which all four insist on having Stan autograph. For laughs, the grad student adds a quick sketch of a flying saucer. He holds one up so I can see it and join in the fun.

Business completed, the Babe and Tiger move back to me. The next question is how to spread the word without attracting attention from the bulls, both local and fed.

"Is there any way people can participate online?" Stan asks. "Maybe you can set up a dedicated PayPal account?"

The Babe grunts. "Tried that once. Didn't go well. The trick is to be obvious without being obvious."

Stan nods. "I might know someone who can help with that. And I still have my pass for the tech show, good through tomorrow. I could put flyers on their info racks, post a few around my campus, in science fiction bookstores, comic shops, whatever. Where's the best place for people to connect with you?"

"Why not here, at the Harpy?" I rise from my barstool, slowly, so as not to upset the gorilla hanging on my shoulder, partly to look more authoritative, but mostly because my right leg is cramping. "According to Stan, we've less than a week before the U.N. makes its announcement, and it looks like most of our marks will be coming from that tech show or the comic convention taking its place in a couple days. That's thousands of live ones right there, just a few blocks away. You could post someone here full-time to collect."

I shut up then because if I keep yakking it'll look like I'm angling for that slot, which of course I am, for both health and financial reasons. Offering outright, though, would guarantee my getting shut out, and maybe a finger bone or two snapped as well.

The Babe looks at Gracie.

She narrows her eyes. "I can't say yes, and I'm not here over the weekend, which is when the comic book geeks arrive, but I don't see Todd passing up a deal like this, given how poor business has been of late. Doesn't sound all that different from the playoff betting pools we run for our regulars, except in this case I couldn't collect on your behalf. None of the staff could."

"Nor would we want you to. Todd does owe me a favor or three, though. I'll talk to him." The Babe turns to Stan. "You can be my agent on the spot, kid. You already got a fan club."

"I know nothing about your business, Mr. Babe."

"It's Mr. Grabowski. But, for you, just Babe."

"I'm worried that getting involved in something illegal might affect my academic standing."

"It's a one-time deal," the Babe says.

Stan takes a breath. I can almost hear the wheels turning. "I have to admit, hanging out in a friendly bar like this for a week, talking science with a bunch of fellow geeks, is tempting. I'd still be really uncomfortable collecting the money, though. Now, Larry, here, he knows the deal. He's a much better choice."

Suddenly, I'm in love with Stan.

The Babe gives me a side-eye, then shrugs. "I may be off my nut, but whaddya say, Lump? Beats spending time in the emergency room."

I flex my digits, wincing at their narrow escape. "Would it make us completely jake?"

"Depends on the take. It'll make a big dent, anyway. Take some of the pressure off you."

"Then it would be my pleasure."

The Roach's paw slides off my shoulder, leaving an indent.

"Good. I'll have Todd comp you food and drinks. You won't be lonely, either. One of my guys will drop by every hour or so to see how things are going. And collect the funds." For which, of course, I cannot blame the Babe, and even welcome his caution, as I would not like him to think there was even a possibility of my skimming.

"You." He turns back to Stan. "I'd still want you here to explain the deal, chat people up. You did aces with those four geeks, got them to loosen up, even over-bet. Todd can cover food and drink for you, too, same deal as Lump, plus a percentage of the vig. And you can spend more time with your new pal."

Stan, feeling more and more jake with all this positive attention, can hesitate no more. "What the hell. I'm between lab projects at the moment. I'll bring my laptop and work on my papers here."

"I still have to figure odds on these outcomes," the Babe says. "Let's talk some more. There are two possibilities, you said? Either the space guys are on our side, or they're mugs who want to take over."

"A bit simplified, but, yes, basically."

The Babe pauses. "I'll add a third option. The bad guys just want to bump us all off for the hell of it. That's complete bushwa, total applesauce, so it gets the highest odds. Gracie! Shots! The good stuff, not that horse liniment Lump is sucking up."

Gracie lets his attitude slide because he is, after all, the Babe, and their plan should bring in a lot more business, and she's also pouring herself a double on his tab.

That's how I end up spending the rest of that week at the Happy Harpy, every day from noon to two am, collecting bets, with Stan at my side most of the time. Gracie makes sure the weekend crew knows the deal.

By Monday evening my debt is paid off, and then some. My digits stay intact. Todd is so happy with the extra business, I've got free drinks for life. My new bestie, Stan, has so much fun talking about this space stuff, he considers changing his specialty to xenoarchaeology. His word, not mine. I can barely pronounce it.

And the big announcement at the United Nations that Monday afternoon? Total rhatz. No Encyclopedia Galactica, no warlords with ray guns and laser swords, just a vague shout-out aimed at no one in particular, an echo millions of years old. As that option wasn't even on the board, Babe Grabowsky gets to keep all the scratch, which makes him *very* happy indeed.

I put nothing in the pot myself, and for the record neither did Stan or Gracie. And, personally, I don't think those green or blue or orange space men ever wanted to make actual contact with a civilization so far behind them, whether it was millions of years ago or last week. I wouldn't, if I were them. What makes the most sense, to me, is they were simply pranking any primitives that happened to pick up their signals, just for a giggle. Just to see how we'd react.

And probably betting on the results.

CREATIVELY IGNORANT

Ian Randal Strock

NEVER HAD I BEEN SO SCARED OF SOMEONE WHO WAS SO POLITE. NEAT suit and tie, aviator sunglasses, impeccable haircut, and wired earpiece. He didn't have to show me a badge for me to know he was Government.

"I'm here about the coins," he said after I opened the front door.

"What coins?" I asked. I'm a writer, but not an ad-libber.

His expression told me he was Serious, and I'd better not screw around.

I stepped back, and he stepped in. Behind him, I saw another fellow dressed just like him, lurking in the shadows on the front porch. And at the curb, a Nondescript car was idling.

The coins. Like most writers I know, I have a wide variety of interests and hobbies. One of them is numismatics, but looking through my pocket change one day, I came across two coins I did not recognize.

I checked online, but couldn't find these coins anywhere: about the size of quarters, silvery color, but no reeding, and the lettering on them was nothing I'd ever seen before.

So I did what I always do when I find a coin I can't identify, or that I think might have some value: I put them aside until the next time I was going to be near Stacks, and then brought them in with me. The staff there are walking encyclopedias of numismatic knowledge, but they managed to surprise me: no one there could tell me anything about the two coins. They photographed them, to share with other dealers. Surely someone would know. Normally, if they can't identify something, they assume it's not a legal tender coin, but just a metal disc with some designs on it. But for some reason, they felt these might be something more. I left them my phone number, in case they turned up anything.

And then Mr. Government knocked on my door.

"Please bring the coins," he said.

And though I might have thought about taking decoys, I looked at him, and any pretense at subterfuge deserted me. I took the coins out of a drawer.

I locked the door on the way out, and when we got to the car, he said, "May I have your cell phone, please?"

Though it was phrased as a question, I knew there was only one answer he would accept, and handed it to him.

He said, "Thank you," and put the phone in a solid-looking little box in the car. Lead-lined, I assumed.

He sat in the back with me, but his manner rejected all conversation. As we pulled away from the curb, I realized I couldn't see out the windows.

Some indeterminate time later, the car stopped, and we got out, in an enclosed, featureless garage. He escorted me—oh so cordially—down a bland hallway to a completely unmemorable room.

"Thank you," said the man sitting at the table. My escort nodded and left, closing the door.

Before I could even begin to ask inane questions, he said, "No, you're not under arrest. You're being held pending determination."

"What determination? Whose?"

"Actually, mine. Determination of... well, to explain your situation, let me tell you about mine first. You're a writer, as I once was, which is why I'm the one conducting this interview. But before we begin, may I please have those 'coins'?"

Looking around the bare room, I knew I didn't have a choice, and handed them over.

He nodded his thanks, stepped to the door, and passed them to someone outside. Then he sat back down. "My story," he said. "I wrote mostly science fiction, but I tried anything I thought could inspire others. No dystopias—they didn't entertain me, and I wanted to entertain my readers, to give them hope and inspiration.

"It wasn't a full-time career; just a paying hobby. I knew I wasn't going to make a living writing fiction, but when people asked what I did, writing was the only thing I mentioned. The other things, the day-jobs, were just to put food on the table and a roof over my head. But when I wrote fiction, that was when I was truly alive.

"And I came to it because that's how I'd grown up: reading and watching it. Reading those incredible word pictures of a future that could be, if only.... I actually started with television. *Star Trek* was the first, the one that made the greatest impression on me. I was so upset when I learned that *Star Trek* was just fiction... that I couldn't travel between planets like that. And yet... it didn't crush me. It was that vision of a future which could be that encouraged me. I began to read. Not only fiction, but science. I learned what we knew, what we could do, and what we'd need to learn to get there. It wasn't too many years before I realized I wasn't going to be the scientist who'd figure out how to get us there — as much as I wanted to be. But I also learned of the vast numbers of working scientists who claimed science fiction had encouraged them to go into the sciences, and that... that was something I could do.

"I started, as most writers do, crafting stories based solely in my imagination. Well, not solely. Some of them were based on my extensive reading. But they were purely imagination.

"Eventually, I got to the point where I wanted to add more verisimilitude to my stories, and I started doing actual research. I found that I enjoyed the research almost as much as the writing. At first, it was tracking down obscure facts. The internet is useful, but there are still undiscovered minutiae lurking in the physical world that haven't — won't — be translated into the electronic... as you discovered.

"I started in used book stores, looking for specific things I needed for specific stories. But over time, I branched out, became a lot less selective. As a writer, you never know what you're going to need or when, what's going to stimulate an idea. We writers are magpies. I bought books that looked interesting, books that looked well-used, and sometimes just the book next to the one I was looking for, for the serendipity of it. Several times, I discovered things on my bookshelf with no idea about where they'd come from or why they'd interested me, but which turned out to be absolutely vital for the piece I was working on.

"That's why one day, as I flipped through a book from my shelf that I couldn't recall ever seeing before, I came across a strange inscription that I couldn't read. But there was something about it that made me think it was important. It wasn't the Voynich manuscript, but it was, as I later learned, a completely unknown language.

"After spending several hours pondering that inscription, I put it aside and finished the story. But that book moved from my stacks of 'someday I might need it,' to 'this is interesting, I'm going to hang on to it.'

"As frequently happens, I soon forgot all about that book. I moved on to other stories, other research, other puzzles. I kept writing, kept acquiring books and reference materials.

"Then I discovered the joy of travel, and of putting real people, real places, into my stories. Many people travel for vacation; writers travel for research.

"Once I found myself on a trip to... well, it doesn't matter where, because the land has since been secured. At any rate, I was walking through some fascinating caves and found carving on a wall. Strange marks, definitely not a language I knew, and yet familiar. I took many photographs, from every angle. I'd originally planned to be there for a few hours; I wound up staying for a week, exploring the entire cave system.

"And when I got home, I realized why those markings had seemed familiar: they were the same as the strange language in that book.

"Well, in addition to being a writer, I like puzzles. And this, I decided, was a puzzle. What could the markings possibly mean? They had to make sense to someone, but they were so alien...

"I spent days working on it, and eventually, sought help. I posted pictures on the web... well, I tried to post pictures. But the system failed each time I clicked 'post.'

"I figured I was tired, doing something wrong, and I'd try again the next day. But the next day came, and I again tried to post them, and the same thing happened.

"I posted other pictures of my trip, no problem. I tried the symbols again, and nothing doing.

"Sometimes I'm a little slow on the uptake, but I do get there eventually. These specific pictures were being blocked. Therefore, there *was* something important about them.

"I puzzled over those symbols from the cave, and the symbols in the book, and eventually, they started to make some kind of sense to me. I could see repetitions, congruencies, and connections, but I just didn't have enough of them to translate. I had a hunch they were a language, so I dug out images of written languages.

"I couldn't find these symbols anywhere.

"I turned it into a methodical search, checking out every language we use on this planet. Still no joy.

"Then I went to dead and extinct languages. Of course, I knew that no one speaks Latin anymore, that Aramaic, hieroglyphs, Cuneiform had eventually been deciphered. And they led me to Linear A, the Cypro-Minoan syllabary, and Isthmian: languages we still aren't able to understand.

"So I went back to haunting used book stores, looking for more of those symbols. But since serendipity had brought me to the first book, I knew a targeted search wasn't likely to bring results, and for a time, it seemed like I'd been right.

"Eventually, I decided there must be other people struggling with the same mystery. Rather than trying to post my photographs, I drew a few pictures that were similar, but not identical, to the photos I'd taken and the book.

"And again, my posts wouldn't go through.

"This time, though, a chat window popped open on my computer. Odd, that, since I never used a chat feature. But there it was: a message about my unpostable pictures. 'Where did you see those symbols?'

"I decided to play along, typing, 'In a cave, and in a book.'

"'Where is the cave?'

"'Why should I tell you?'

"'That's a good question,' my anonymous messenger replied. 'We'll be in touch.'

"A few hours later, just after dinner, there was a knock on my front door, probably just like the knock you got this evening."

I grunted agreement. Then he described a ride almost identical to the one I'd just taken.

"Eventually, we arrived... well... here. And I was escorted into... actually, I think it was this very room, and I had a conversation with Director Smith. He didn't give me a chance to get settled. 'I saw your pictures of that cave. We thought we'd found them all, but apparently not. If you'd be so good as to tell me where it is, we can secure it, as well.'

"'Just a minute,' I said. 'What's going on here?'

"'You'd like me to spell it all out for you? You were already puzzling it out yourself. But if you're the thinker we think you are, you don't need me to tell you.'

"'Well, obviously those markings really are some sort of language I don't recognize.'

"He nodded.

"'And since I've looked at a lot of them, I'm pretty sure it's not a terrestrial language.'

"His eyebrows rose.

"'But if you're so interested in it that you're able to block me from uploading pictures, you already know all about it, and have probably translated it all.'

"No real reaction.

"'And if you have already translated it, you'll let me go once I tell you where the cave is.'

"At this, he finally reacted. Just a slight downturn at the corners of his mouth, but I saw it.

"'I'm not leaving?'

"'That depends on how much you care about humanity, how much you can extrapolate.'

"'I get the feeling you want to tell me something,' I said.

"'Want? No. I'd be much happier if you'd tell me where that cave is, hand me the book, and then decide you hadn't seen anything at all. But we both know that's not going to happen.'

"'We're at an impasse, aren't we?'

"He frowned.

"At the time, I liked to think I was an intelligent, creative person. I could tell he felt trapped by circumstance, but he also felt he was serving a higher purpose, and me, my freedom, my very life, did not carry any weight in his considerations.

"Suddenly, I knew, with absolute certainty, that I was here to plead for my life.

He came out of his reverie, and looked directly at me for the first time in his recitation. "Before I go any further, have I convinced you?"

"Convinced me of what?"

His mouth turned down, but he continued. "'I'm not a linguist,' I said to him, 'but I have to assume that, if that language could have been deciphered, it would have been. And if it was deciphered, I would have found a match somewhere. If it was completely undecipherable, you wouldn't care so much; it would be just another curiosity, like the Voynich manuscript. But since I'm here, I have to assume it's not just a curiosity.'

"'The only reason you would have to know who I am and bring me here is because that language does mean something more to you than just pictures.'

"'That means you have deciphered it. And if you have deciphered it, but it's completely unknown, that means you're keeping it a secret, and such a deep, dark secret that you don't even want me to talk about its existence.'

"He quirked an eyebrow, so I kept theorizing.

"'If it were an ancient language you've managed to decipher, what could it possibly say? "The tribe killed an animal, so we didn't starve"? Doubtful. If that's all it is, you wouldn't care.'

"'But you obviously care, so it's something more.'

"'I've written my share of secret history stories, but I know they're just fiction. So it's not just some ancient language. It's something more.'

"'The carvings I saw in that cave—'

"He interrupted me to note that I still hadn't told him where the cave was.

"This time, it was my turn to nod knowingly. 'My security,' I said. 'Once I tell you, you don't have any reason to keep me alive.'

"He nodded.

"'Those carvings weren't recent, not some secret code that's escaped your control. They have to be something old, really old.'

"'So... old, secret, don't want to share it with the world, not secret history... I'm talking myself into a conclusion I'm having a hard time believing.'

"'Remember Sherlock Holmes,' he said.

"'Have I really eliminated the impossible?' I asked.

"He nodded.

"'Then what does it say?' I asked.

"He sighed, and then became far more loquacious. 'Before I tell you what it says, I want you to tell me what it means.'

I knew he wasn't just playing at words. He didn't mean the meaning of the inscriptions; he meant their very existence.

I must have sat there for two minutes. Unmoving, unblinking, while my mind moved at warp speed.

Again, he focused on me. "So, do you know what I was thinking?"

As he must have done those years ago, I sat there, letting "nah, couldn't be" escape from my mental vocabulary. Eventually, I blinked my drying eyes.

"Fermi," I said.

"Go on."

"Fermi's Paradox, and the time variable in the Drake equation means that, though intelligent life may exist somewhere/somewhen in the time/space continuum, the odds of us meeting that life are exceedingly small. But that life did exist, and even visited."

He nodded.

"The carvings, the language you found—and the... coins... I found, the reason I'm here—are all really ancient, but more than that, their origin isn't terrestrial. Do you know how old?"

"On the order of 100,000 years."

"Right. But just proof of an alien language wouldn't be a cause for all this secrecy. You've actually translated it... And it says something much deeper than 'Joe was here.'"

"Keep going."

"In order to mean anything, there has to have been more than what you found in the cave."

"And in the book," he added meaningfully. "And the coins you found. Yes, much more. We thought we'd found it all. But your coins, and my cave, those are the first new pieces that have been discovered in a very long time."

"So you've been able to read it all translated for... how many decades?"

"Well, no. We were able to get most of the syllables teased out fairly quickly, but the true interpretation has only started in the last two decades, as we've developed sufficient basis in the sciences to understand their concepts."

"So why all the secrecy?"

"'To strive, to seek, to find, and not to yield.'"

"*Ulysses*, Lord Tennyson."

"What does that mean to you?"

"Well, Baum said it was ironic, that Ulysses was a flawed hero, rejecting social responsibility."

"Forget the modern nihilist view. I think the true meaning of that line is exactly what it says: that humanity is a being whose purpose is to grow, to discover, to improve the world around us."

CREATIVELY IGNORANT - Ian Randal Strock

"And what does that have to do with some ancient carvings, some alien script?"

"Remember how excited you were when you learned how to do something? Better, the first story you ever wrote. When you typed 'the end,' you were ecstatic, weren't you? Of course you were. We all were. But when you looked back on that story later…"

"Absolutely dreadful. A retelling of the Bible."

"Just like every other writer since the Bible was first printed. We all do that. And that's human nature. We try to learn, to discover, to create. And we're proud of our accomplishments. But when we realize just how far behind the true wave front of human knowledge we are…"

"We want to quit."

"And it's only when we don't get that crushing blow immediately that we can progress. How long had you been writing when you realized just how horrible that first story was?"

"Probably ten years."

"Exactly. You'd progressed so far beyond that Adam-and-Eve rehash that you were only embarrassed by it, but it didn't crush your dreams of being a writer, because you already were one."

"And you're saying that this language is that far beyond us?"

"Not the language, but the concepts it's communicating. You've watched the progress of science, seen how it moves. Why do we continue to research and discover?"

"Because there's so much left to learn, so many problems to solve."

"And how much research has been done in the field of library science, or the internal combustion engine?"

"Not much lately."

"Nothing at all. People look at them and think they're all tapped out, there are no great discoveries left to be made. Like the false quote attributed to Patent Office Commissioner Charles Holland Duell, who never actually said 'Everything that can be invented has been invented.' But people believe he did. So what would happen if we told the people that aliens had visited Earth 100,000 years ago, and left us plans for how to build an engine that could take us to the stars?"

"They'd be thrilled for the chance to go."

"No. Only the science fiction fans would be thrilled. The scientists working on actually getting us there would be crushed: worked their whole lives to improve propulsion science by a few percent, and along comes this ancient text that makes everything they've done, everything they could dream of their grandchildren doing, completely obsolete. And it's not just interstellar propulsion."

"So you're keeping this knowledge from the public..."

"Not *Star Trek*'s Prime Directive. That's a crock. It's not ruining a society by giving it a great leap forward. It's depressing the members of that society into not bothering to better themselves, because it's already been done."

"So you..."

"We try to nudge scientists in the right direction. Try to give out helpful hints, encourage those on the right track, hope that we can encourage people, rather than discourage them."

"And how long do you think it will take?"

"Conservative estimates say at least four hundred years. But I'm an optimist."

"Four hundred years, you're going to sit on the knowledge that we truly are not alone in the universe?"

"That's what we do. That's why I never wrote another piece of fiction after that night I sat with the previous director."

"And now you're offering me that same chance, that same opportunity for anonymity?"

"Yes and no. Late in his life, Isaac Asimov added to his three laws of robotics. Can you quote the zeroth?"

"'A robot may not harm humanity, or, by inaction, allow humanity to come to harm.'"

"Asimov understood what we're doing, without actually knowing about us. We're not robots, but we're trying to keep humanity from learning just how far behind we are, doing our best to not allow humanity to hurt itself, but instead to continue to strive, to seek...."

"So you expect me to just give up my career? Be an anonymous monk, going through the paces, knowing there's something more that man shouldn't be allowed to know?"

"It's not as bleak as all that. We're a fairly small cadre. The young man who brought you in is just a loaner: he knows nothing of what we are here, just follows orders. But you, I think, have what it takes to be involved. Remember, I did say we nudge research and 'discovery.' But we're still translating and interpreting. And those discs you brought us—"

"Brought you?"

"Semantics. While we've been talking, my staff ran a cursory inspection on them. They're almost certain the coins are data storage devices. Don't you want to help us figure out how to access that data, and interpret it?"

"Are they still out there? Will we meet them?"

"Not us. Our g-g-g-great-grandchildren? Maybe. Like I said, we're not destroying the knowledge — we're letting it out as quickly as we can without crushing the human spirit of invention. But we've also decided to modify our activities a bit. Remember all those scientists who grew up on science fiction? Well, in addition to our internal research, we've reached the point where we need to inspire the next generation of scientists into the next great leap. We need to craft hints into some things they're going to be reading. We're looking to hire a writer or two, and we think you might have what it takes."

CHAINS

Robert Greenberger

"IS IT DONE YET?" DR. BALAKRISHNAN ASKED FOR THE THIRD TIME.

Melanie Katzman nearly spilled her coffee, startled at the nasal voice breaking her concentration. The hawk-faced scientist, with his thinning gray hair, and dark, piercing eyes looked like an angry god. She expected to hear thunder in the background instead of the air conditioning.

"No, it should have been completed by now," she replied, carefully placing the mug bearing the Temple University logo, on the desk.

"So, why isn't it?"

She was an intern, not a super-genius. How was she supposed to know? She opened her mouth to say something, anything to mollify her mentor but he rattled on. "I want you to stay as long as it takes. Have that analysis copied and on everyone's desk before morning."

"Sir, I have plans…"

"Don't care. This is your assignment so complete it. Then you can canoodle all you want."

He stormed off, leaving her wondering what the hell 'canoodling' meant.

There were probably better internships, higher paying ones, maybe with better hours where she actually got to see sunshine. Melanie rolled the absent opportunities in her mind, knowing that her fellow interns were done for the day and most likely getting sloshed at some pub. She, though, was now on the graveyard shift at the lab, waiting for the Approximate Bayesian Computation model completed its work. It really should have been done by now.

She had put it off long enough. With a heavy sigh, she pulled her phone from her pocket and dialed Greg.

"Hey, babe, we have to postpone our canoodling," she said.

"What?"

"I don't know. Something Balakrishnan said before ordering me to work late."

"Why the hell do you have to stay late? It's a lab. Can't it wait until tomorrow?"

"You know that bone fragment analysis I was assigned? We completed our preliminary workup and fed the results into the computer but the report is taking forever," she explained.

"When does forever arrive?"

"Not a clue. Look, I know we had plans but for all I know, this will be done within an hour…"

"…Or six hours from now."

The disappointment in his voice hurt. They'd been together since they hit it off at a spring break warm-up party. They were going on six months now and any time apart felt like an eternity.

"I can say I'm sorry only so many times, Greg."

"You haven't even said it once. Look, I get it, you're low man…"

"…woman…."

"…*woman* on the totem pole. Late nights happen, I get it. I was just hoping…"

"What? You were going to get laid? So noted. I'm disappointed, too. Trust me, I'd rather be anywhere but stuck here all night after a full day. I'm all alone and the cafeteria is closed so I'm stuck with crappy takeout. I'll make it up to you tomorrow. Okay?"

"Fine."

The disappointment remained in his voice as they disconnected, leaving her hungry, tired, and resentful…of Greg not being understanding, and Balakrishnan for being a jerk.

There were few lights on, casting shadows that added to her weariness. She called up the local pizza place and ordered herself a deep-dish pie with onions and peppers, an indulgence since Greg didn't like either.

By the time her tepid dinner arrived, the custodial staff had already been through; and security had done their nightly sweep. It was just her and the computers and she felt as if the universe was tormenting her. As it was, she disliked the weight gain sitting around brought her and that the late hours kept her from the gym.

It was quite a coup for her to get into Temple University's Science and Technology labs, and the stipend was a generous one. No waitressing this summer for a change for which her butt and feet thanked her. She arrived on day one and was given a spot to call her own, a place to plug in her laptop, and directions on how to contribute to the communal coffee pot. A stack of documentation in color-coded folders awaited her as did an inbox full of memos outlining the genomic sequencing she would be performing for the next eight weeks.

She was on week four, already dreaming of the brief break between this and the resumption of her Masters work. The other two interns, classmates she vaguely knew, and a steady stream of professors and vesting researchers normally kept the lab space busy, verging on claustrophobic. Temple had gained a sterling reputation for their fossil research and she recognized she was lucky to be there, helping unlock the roadmap from sea life to Homo Sapiens.

Melanie sighed as the hour crept past nine and she struggled to stay alert. Thumbing the computer to life, she called up the bane of her existence. Well, other than Balakrishnan.

On the screen was a close-up of the fossil, which she had been allowed to handle just once, a grayish fragment of what was believed to be a portion of a tibia. The bone felt lighter than similar relics from her classwork, something that gnawed at her, but she had no way of judging. This was one of several dozen fragments found in Russia shortly after World War II ended and just before the Iron Curtain fell. She enlarged the image, scrolling to examine it for the first time in over a week, hoping she could figure out why it was stymieing the computer, which was, like, a million times smarter than she was. Both edges of the ancient fossil were jagged, deeply pitted in places, vertical cracks giving it an interesting pattern. Still, nothing spoke to her, there was no *a-ha* moment, adding to her mounting frustration with the day.

When Temple first acquired the artifacts decades ago, they were measured, weighed, and photographed before being stored away; bits of mankind's history shrouded in dust. The work done in the 1950s felt positively antique compared with the cutting-edge toys she was being allowed to play with. A year earlier, though, Temple helped determine there was an unusual hybrid fossil found, concluding that Neanderthals and their cousins, the Denisovans, mated and created a new branch on the human tree. This further led to speculation that at least one, if not more, "ghost" hominins awaited discovery.

Prof. Steingart, one of the department's elder statesmen, suggested any older Russian fossils in storage be retrieved and reexamined. When the beauty on Melanie's screen was first found DNA testing hadn't even existed. That meant this artifact still had stories to tell and, with luck, she would be around to hear them.

But, apparently, not just yet. The program still cranked away.

Alone and bored with waiting, Katzman walked the length of the lab just to stay awake. She knew the grunt work was as necessary as it was tedious and boring, but it was worth it. Usually. The human genome had always fascinated her. Ever since she literally tripped over her first fossil on a family vacation, she had been enthralled. While others dithered over which career to chose, she had gone after hers with a laser focus some admired but most snickered at. She'd see who laughed when she made a discovery or got published or won a Nobel or…got a good night's sleep.

By the time the clock neared midnight, she had exhausted her small repertoire of cell phone games. Almost by rote, she checked on the program only to discover that somewhere between Fortnite and Candy Crush, the process had completed and she missed it. Melanie called up the analysis and watched bleary-eyed as it scrolled at speed across the screen. The numbers and symbols didn't make much sense, but she chalked that up to her own exhaustion. She reached for the most recent analysis of the previous fossil and held it up alongside her screen.

There were very few similarities between the two.

Something was off but she had no clue what. Frankly, it didn't matter. It was after midnight and the report was finally done. She printed and collated the required copies and dropped Balakrishnan's on his desk. Let him figure it out in the morning. After all, she was just a lowly intern, right?

It was just after nine when she woke to the sound of a braying donkey—the ringtone she'd assigned to Balakrishnan.

She groaned and buried her head in her pillow. *What now?* "What is this gibberish?" he demanded once she answered.

"Gibberish?" She didn't bother to try and sound like he hadn't woke her up. It was his fault she was so exhausted, anyway.

"Yes, gibberish. Is the word unfamiliar to you? This report makes no sense. What did you do?"

Just my job, she thought, rolling out of bed and scanning for something clean to wear. She'd not had time to do laundry lately. From the sound of it, there'd be no time for a shower either.

"Get in here. You're late." He hung up.

She rolled her eyes and tossed her phone on her unmade bed. Grabbing last night's jeans, fresh underwear, and a button-down blouse that was draped over a chair, she hurried through her basic hygiene, all the while trying to figure out how any of this was her fault. All she'd done was wait for the report, it wasn't like she was responsible for entering the data.

She sprinted across campus so she'd have time to at least grab a cup of coffee from the sidewalk vendor. It scalded as she sipped at it, but at least she had caffeine plus adrenaline to get her moving.

It was nearly ten by the time she entered the lab. The place was busy as usual. A few nodded at her; Brad, one of her fellow interns, said something snarky about her hours. At least he got to go home on time.

At her workstation, the report sat with a bright pink post-it note atop reading: "Make sense of this shit!" *How professional*, she thought.

Finished her coffee, Melanie tossed the paper cup and refilled her travel mug from the coffee station before sitting down. Clearly, she had a very long day ahead of her. After all, if the head of the department couldn't make sense of the report, how could she?

With somewhat fresh eyes, she opened up the copy of the report she left for herself and began to study the results. While last night nothing had made sense, this morning, she recognized at least some of it. There were definitely genetic markers that resembled the Neanderthal/Denisovan hybrids. Prof. Steingart's instincts were spot on, which gave her comfort. There was a definite connection between the previously identified fossils and this bone. But the other markers…those baffled her and clearly pissed off Balakrishnan.

Close but not quite. Was it an error, or the evidence Steingart had sent them looking for? Melanie wanted to believe they'd found their "ghost," but who was she to say? Earlier analysis had already determined a previously unknown and extinct group of hominids existed. Could this be evidence of interbreeding between the ghost race and Homo Sapiens in Asia? It would be unusual to find another race so soon after the Denisovans were identified in 2010, but no one said it was impossible. After all, the discovery of one prompted them to go back look for more.

Still, the mathematical output made little sense to her. She had seen the computer analyze the new fossil against the hybrid model as well as Neanderthal and Denisovan models. It had highlighted the discrepancies using symbols she didn't recognize. How maddening! Either something glitched, or this was the key to something big. She just didn't know enough to tell which.

She was a grad student–what did Balakrishnan expect? How on earth could she "make sense of this shit" without some kind of a reference point?

Not up to dealing with Balakrishnan's bullshit, Melanie grabbed the report and maneuvered through the crowded lab to Professor Steingart's office. His space at least looked lived in, unlike so many of the others. His standard-issue diplomas, certificates, and awards shared wall space with a current Arizona Diamondbacks poster and propped among the academic tomes on his shelves were souvenirs from the archaeological sites he had worked over his thirty-year career. Steingart was now in his sixties, plump with a full head of graying hair and a pair of black glasses that did nothing to hide the perpetual twinkle in his eyes.

The professor was reading a journal, coffee steaming in a mug bearing the label "Radiometric dating said I looked how old? The Nerve!" He looked up with a smile as she entered his domain, and then dropped his curious gaze to the binder in her hands.

"Problem, Mel?"

"Yeah, I can't figure out these introgressions and Dr. Balakrishnan is not happy."

"Pissed him off again did you?"

She sighed, smiling, as she handed the report over to him then sat. "The computer analysis took all night. I was stuck here until it was done."

"So, no fun?"

"No. He said I could 'wait to canoodle,' whatever that is."

Steingart chuckled at that.

Melanie raised her eyebrows in surprise. "You know the word?"

"You don't?"

He grinned as she shook her head. "It's kissing and cuddling. You know, before the good stuff."

That caused her to laugh out loud. It felt good, the first relief she felt since the phone call. "That's good stuff, too."

Steingart nodded, eyes not quite meeting hers. Then he blinked and returned his attention to the report. "Balakrishnan's easily annoyed, but I think you learned that the first day..."

"The first *hour*," she admitted, making him laugh. She sat back and let him silently thumb through the printout. He squinted, flipped pages back and forth, and then ran a finger across the columns of numbers and symbols. She wanted to ask questions but wisely bit her tongue.

After several agonizing minutes of silence, he set the binder down on his desk. He took a sip of coffee and made a face as it had obviously cooled beyond his desire.

"Feel a bit like Viviane Slon, don't you?"

Katzman frowned at the unfamiliar name, sure she should know it.

"She's the one who identified the Neanderthal-Denisovan hybrid," he began.

"That 90,000-year-old fossil?"

"You know another? Really, it's her work that got me thinking about the bones we had in storage. Her colleagues found the first Denisovan bones so she got really lucky. They split from the Neanderthal nearly 400,000 years ago but somehow reconnected. Maybe they used Tinder."

Despite herself, Melanie let out another short laugh.

"Anyway, once they figured out this fragment was unlike the others, they found the hybrid. I was hoping for something similar since that box was found, geologically speaking, not far from Slon's find. But this..." he trailed off.

"It confuses you, too?"

"Yeah," he said, turning around the binder to show her a page. "Look, the protein analysis of the bone's collagen is off. It doesn't match either the Neanderthal *or* the hybrid."

He paused then flipped to check another page. He clicked his tongue a few times as he read, paused, reread, and then sat back in his chair.

"Mel, the mitochondrial DNA shows a Denisovan mother. I recognize the markers."

"But the father…" she prompted him, wanting an answer.

"I don't know."

That surprised her. She expected he knew everything about the subject, but if it stumped him, she had no hope of figuring it out. On the other hand, if neither of them could make sense of it, then that gave her an ally against Balakrishnan, which was another relief. "How could he expect me to know if this stumps you?"

"What did he say it was?"

"Gibberish." Which made Steingart laugh again. It was a warm laugh, a reassuring sound.

"That just means he glanced, didn't see something he recognized, and wanted you to figure it out. Lazy bastard.

"There is a high amount of diversity in this genome overall," he continued. "That much is certain. But something with this heterozygosity is unprecedented. It's almost as if it was…"

He trailed off, leaving Melanie squirming in her seat. She figured he had a clue but didn't want to verbalize it. Could it somehow be a tri-brid?

When the silence grew too uncomfortable, she finally waved her hand before the thoughtful man. He was gazing at the numbers with unusual intensity.

"It's almost as if it was…." she parroted.

"They'll never believe it."

That caught her breath. Was this something new, something momentous, something that would actually not be a mistake? So many thoughts whirled through her mind as part of her mentally urged him to continue.

"Believe what?"

"I don't believe it."

"Believe what?" She grew agitated, fighting the urge to raise her voice. She needed more sleep, more caffeine, and a day off but this was beginning to scare her. The air in the small office seemed to grow still, the ambient sounds fading away. Whatever he said next was certainly going to be of great import.

"We'd need to run it by more than a few people, but who to trust…."

"Trust?"

It was as if he didn't remember she was in the office with him, despite her being there the whole time. He put down the mug, closed the binder, and stared into her eyes. She stared back and caught herself holding her breath.

"We need trust. Mel, what we've got here is something I've never seen before. What no one else has seen before. Balakrishnan was a *putz* not to examine the data for himself, rather than make you do it. No offense, but you, my dear, don't have the training or experience for this."

She blinked at that, paused, and said, "None taken." What on earth had he deciphered from the gibberish?

"All the markers are familiar, yet not quite, even to these tired old eyes. There's Denisovan in there, the mom for certain. But dad, dad's not from Siberia."

"He came from a different continent?"

Steingart didn't answer for a long moment. He scanned the report before him once more, a finger tapping his pursed lips. His eyes darted around the page, as if he searched for something. He settled on one line, stared intently, then put down the paper. His eyes met hers once more.

"More like he came from a different world."

Melanie gaped at him. Was he pulling her leg? Yet...he wasn't known as a prankster and the grave air he was affecting made her pause. Aliens? Mating with an early hominid? Was that even possible? She had to ask.

"It shouldn't be," he said. "Just like a man shouldn't be able to see, let alone hit a 100-mile-an-hour fastball, but it happens."

She tried to process the concept. It felt more like the word ricocheted around her mind until a headache blossomed fully formed. He continued to watch her and she realized her mouth had literally dropped open. She probably looked like an idiot. Forcing it shut, she eyed him carefully, looking for signs of mischief. "An alien?"

"Kind of mind-blowing, right?" He wasn't kidding. If that was the case, this was an historic moment but it felt too surreal to properly process. She found it difficult to think coherently around the headache.

"And you're serious?"

He nodded, his gaze steady and his posture unchanged. He was still, his breathing even.

"How can you be so calm?"

"Look, Mel," he began, relaxing into his chair. She sat back and forced herself to be still. This was his lecturing pose and she wanted to hear what he had to say. She took long, deep breaths, hoping to still the clangor in her head so she could focus. Because if he was right, she was at ground zero at something monumental, something historic, something she could never have dreamed about.

Aliens.

"This is one fossil, one set of results. We have a duty to check the data. Run it against the other fossils recovered at the same time from the same place. We have a responsibility to have it checked at other facilities. Maybe even get Slon and her team involved. I can make some calls."

Aliens.

"But, think for a moment what this means. We now know inter-breeding was far more widespread than we ever imagined. That's why we're looking for the ghost of ghosts. We have gaps to fill, but what if, mind you it's entirely speculative, but imagine…what if we have evidence of something extraterrestrial?"

Yeah, about that, she thought. She was calm, she was calm, she was calm…

"It would mean we're not alone. One of the core cosmic questions that has plagued mankind since we first considered the stars will finally be answered. The dating on the fossil goes back how far?"

Melanie was caught off-guard, her own mind splintering in a million directions. "Uh…I believe it was dated around 87,000 years ago."

"Okay, so, right next door to the Slon hybrid. Good. The world was teeming with life at the time, a perfect opportunity to come and study." He sounded so casual she wanted to shout. After all, this was an emotional moment, not a time for Vulcan stoicism.

"From where?"

"Good question. We need the original notes telling us exactly where this was found. Then we pray to God that the site hasn't been touched since then. The geologists and the astronomers at MIT or Hopkins can play together and figure *It* out. Me, I want to know why the Denisovans and not the Neanderthals or the Heidelbergersis or Homo Erectus. Did they even try?"

"Wow, that's a leap."

His eyes twinkled. "Isn't it, though? Everything from this point is a leap. Maybe there's more evidence out there, waiting for us. I feel so teased. If we're right…"

She let that sink in. He was right, it could be a mistake. They had to show caution and do this right. Otherwise, Balakrishnan would have the last laugh at her expense. Never had she wanted something to be so right. Even her feelings for Greg. This went way beyond a singular relationship. "What do you think?"

"I think we're winning the Nobel for this, but that's the wishful part of me. As your colleague, I've been trained not to get ahead of myself. But unlike your fossil, I'm only human." He chuckled but she couldn't see the humor at the moment.

"You really think there's alien DNA in there?" The throbbing in her head had either settled in for the long haul or was actually ebbing. Either way, she was beginning to feel more…human.

"Well, I'm certainly intrigued. The deep computing wouldn't generate numbers like these if there wasn't something anomalous to analyze. It found the Denisovan side easily enough."

"We really have to corroborate this," Melanie said, a sense of fright building in her. She was a person of faith, not a churchgoer for sure, but someone who did believe in a higher power. This was a fundamental shift in her personal thinking. The sheer enormity of it was beginning to make itself felt. Everything weighed her down. At the same time, her heart rate was up, her mind running faster than light, and her soul shaken to its core.

"Absolutely. But who do we confide in? How many copies did you make?"

"Five."

"Okay, step one is to retrieve them, even Balakrishnan's. Tell him what he wants to hear: it *was* gibberish, a programming error. You'll be rerunning the complete analysis from scratch. First, we reweigh and remeasure everything. We also take some scrapings and do additional chemical analysis. Everything. We do it here. Now. With all the modern tools at our disposal."

"I can get started," she said, beginning to rise, the sense of purpose making her feel a little more…grounded.

Steingart shook his head. "It's what, Thursday? Better to start Saturday when everyone is gone. Got plans this weekend?"

"I had planned to go to the movies…" she admitted.

"Ah, that can wait. Join me here and we can begin together, record everything for posterity." He made it sound so easy, but blowing Greg off again was not going to go well, especially since she couldn't share any of this.

"You're taking this way too seriously," she said, almost regretting it.

"We have to, Mel," he shot back. "We can't tell the world E.T. really visited us without concrete, verifiable proof. I want this in the *Times,* not the *Weekly World News.* This will cause a ripple in expected ways."

"The world will..." Mel hesitated.

"'Plotz' is the word you're searching for. No matter how verified this gets, there will be fundamentalist wackos out there who will want us dead for shaking their reality. We'll be lauded..."

"Vilified."

"Questioned."

"Doubted."

"Locked up."

"God, I hope not. Prison colors don't work for my skin tone," he quipped, making her laugh once more. Why couldn't Balakrishnan be like this? His arrogance hid his brilliance while Steingart was far more self-effacing. Why couldn't he mentor her? *He* was the one she looked up to, the role model she wanted to emulate. Unless, of course, they were tarred, feathered, and burned as heretics...

"Seriously, Professor Steingart, how do we broach this to anyone else without sounding like we're pranking them?"

He considered that for a moment, picking up his mug, then putting it down with a face. "We duplicate our results here. We corroborate the results by having another team replicate our study. We test more samples. And we do it all without whispering a word." He fell silent, processing the steps. After all, if someone slipped, if someone tried to steal their research and claim it as their own...so many possibilities for disaster, her head began to throb anew. "I would think whatever that fossil once was, it would be sterile. One of a kind, perhaps. That makes it all the harder to prove."

"So, we keep it to ourselves?"

"For now," Steingart said solemnly. "Trust but verify. Something of this import..."

"What's the harm if a secret remains a secret?" she blurted, interrupting his thought.

"Who are we to suppress such knowledge?"

"We just touched on why keeping it a secret is important. We'll be world-famous, yes, but also targets," she said. Unfortunately, this was an era where school shootings were an all-too-common occurrence. Melanie had participated in more than her fair share of lockdown drills. Mosques and synagogues had become shooting galleries because of ideologies. Tell one of those whackos mankind was not alone in the universe and that would incite even more violence. The idea of being a real target, not collateral damage, frightened her. If this was fame, maybe she didn't want it.

"Fair point," he conceded.

"Do you want to be like Galileo?"

"Remembered? Sure. Tortured by the Inquisition? Not so much."

"Me either."

That sounded final but Steingart didn't look like he was done. Then again, with something like this, would he, or they, ever be done?

"But, Mel, we have a responsibility. The truth wants to be free." He let that hang in the air for a moment as Melanie took it in. The pressure in her head built with his growing list of implications and possibilities.

"You mean you think we were meant to discover the fossil and its secrets?"

"You don't think the hand of the divine is behind this?"

That brought her up short. She and Steingart had never spoken of personal matters despite their easy rapport. After all, she reported to Balakrishnan. In her mind, she now automatically added 'the putz'.

"I've been thinking about it, but it's one of a thousand things on my mind right now," she admitted.

"Okay, so what do *you* want to do?"

"Collect the reports. Back everything up to multiple sources. Then come in Saturday and do as you suggest. Start over and see if the results match."

He nodded. "If they do?"

"Get them verified." He nodded in agreement.

"In house or not?"

"Don't you trust Dr. Balakrishnan and the others?" This could be a trick question, but she knew it wasn't. Not now.

"To a degree, of course, I do," Steingart said. "But I don't know the other interns too well, can they be trusted not to freak out?"

"I really don't know them, either." Despite being a small department in a relatively small building, there was little collegiality. Everyone worked their own project,

As if reading her mind, Steingart interrupted with an answer.

"Well, Balakrishnan will be insanely jealous and want to corroborate the study then insist he put his name on our paper. He's thorough so his word would be good, but I can't stand the thought of his head getting any bigger off our discovery. Hmm, we'll need to rearrange funding, tap the surplus, find an office we can lock…Mel, can you take a semester's leave and work on this full time with me? It's the only way we can ensure privacy while we replicate the analysis. If we're right, we'll know in the fall then seek independent verification."

"Out of house?" She didn't answer the question about her future because suddenly it felt small and inconsequential. She needed to process the bigger issues and then think about her personal reality. A different part of her mind knew she'd do it, especially if it meant really learning at Steingart's side.

"I have contacts, of course. But yes, I think replicating the results here first works. Are you ready for that?"

She sat in thought, chin resting on her hands. Finally, she looked up, feeling a growing sense of alarm.

"This is federally funded…"

"Yes, we'll have to notify the Office of Science and Technology, even if its director is not someone I respect."

"Won't they swoop in and take over?"

"Maybe if this was a movie produced by Paramount, but this is beyond their scope. Do you know how many people they have?"

She shook her head.

"Fewer than four dozen. They're not equipped for this. It'll be easier for them to throw money at us, which means I can afford to keep you, and they'll want it verified here in the states. For 'National Security' reasons they may want this bottled up."

"Even if the fossil comes from Siberia?"

"That means ceding first contact to the Russians. We will want bragging rights."

"And if they don't want us publishing this news?"

He eyed her, a mischievous smile crossing his face. "What, you've never heard of leaks?" If they really did store the Ark of the Covenant in a warehouse, I think we'd know today. You can't keep news like this under wraps, no matter how much they try. We won't tell them officially until we make sure other teams beyond our borders have copies of the research and results."

She nodded at that, feeling somewhat spent by the conversation.

"This is a lot, Mel."

"If we're right."

"If we're right."

She sensed he believed they were, which added to the tension she was feeling. Rising, she took the binder from his hands and walked back to her own space. There was so much to do in the next few hours, much to think about before returning to the lab on Saturday to start anew.

At her desk, she called up the picture of the fossil, enlarging it to 400%. It had felt different, lighter, could that be because of the alien DNA? Did she want to believe? She studied the small bone, wondering at its secrets, trying to imagine the life it led as a mutant, the first and likely last of its kind.

It stared back, refusing to give up its story so easily. Melanie Katzman would have to work to earn the right to that story.

LOST AND FOUND

Dayton Ward

LOST AND FOUND

Dayton Ward

NOW

"HAPPY ANNIVERSARY, DEE."

Of course, there was no answer. Just like each of the past twenty-five years when Alex Casey broke away from her work to observe her little ritual, the only reply to her comment was the litany of sounds emitted by the medical monitoring equipment arrayed around DeShawn Boyd's bed. Respiration, pulse rate, and body temperature, all were within acceptable tolerances. Other monitors and sensors reported normal brain activity. For all the obvious visual evidence, Dee looked every bit a healthy, physically fit man of forty-one years. Shirtless and with a clean-shaven head and face, electrodes and leads attached to various points along his skull, torso, and extremities. His dark skin offered a sharp contrast to the bed's stark white linen.

According to everything communicated by the devices around him, and in the opinion of every doctor who examined him dating back more than two decades, she should be able to rouse him from sleep and leave this place. She so badly wanted to take him away from here, whether home or literally anywhere in the world that wasn't this damned room. All Dee had to do was wake up.

Instead, he remained unconscious, and all anyone knew was his current condition was somehow connected to and dependent upon the eight-foot tall, black cylinder sitting on the other side of the room's transparent north wall.

THEN

Maybe it was just a small portion of a much larger object buried deeper within rock face, Alex decided. With its smooth, gleaming surface there could be no denying the thing, whatever it was, had no business being buried at the bottom of the abandoned quarry.

"What the hell is it?" Dee Boyd asked. Alex heard her boyfriend's voice raise an octave in surprise. "How long do you think it's been here?"

Alex pointed to the assortment of rubble lying on the quarry floor. "It looks like a lot of new stuff broke away after that last quake." She indicated the jagged rocks in various shapes and sizes near the object, and visible cracks in the bedrock she did not remember from her last visit. "Lots of new damage."

"Come on," Dee said, heading for the worn path which once served as a road for trucks and heavy mining equipment. "Let's check it out."

"Hold up a second." Alex put a hand on his arm. "Are we sure it's safe?"

Dee smiled, and his brown eyes seemed to twinkle. "You sound like my mom."

"I'm just saying, and speaking of moms, mine's going to start wondering where I am if I'm not home soon." Alex still had homework and an evening studying for a test ahead of her. Her first quarter of tenth-grade algebra was already stressing her out, and she was not looking forward to her eyes glazing over as she confronted the problems on tonight's assignment.

And yet, she could not resist the urge to get a better look at their unexpected find. Still, she remained cautious, surveying the area for signs of danger. The quarry, abandoned years earlier, was a popular hangout for local kids despite the occasional tremors which seemed to be occurring with greater frequency. Despite the chains and fences blocking off access and signs declaring the area off-limits, police had long ago given up trying to keep people out. Though there was some trash scattered around the site and blown up against the fence or larger pieces of rubble, the area was mostly clean. Perhaps an attempt to avoid giving the police or anyone else an excuse to crack down on trespassers. The deep pool at the center of the artificial canyon was a big summer draw. Dee and Alex came here every so often after their dates. Everyone had a theory about what lay at the bottom; everything from missing cars to dumped bodies and even a crashed alien spaceship. So far as Alex knew, nothing like that had ever been discovered.

Until now?

Dee gestured for her to follow. "Just a quick look. Sooner or later, someone else will come down here and then who knows what'll happen? We may never get another chance like this." He flashed that wide grin she was hopeless to resist. "What if it's buried treasure or an ancient pyramid or something?"

Alex's laugh echoed off the surrounding rock. "You watch too many movies." She disregarded her initial hesitation and followed him to the quarry floor. Dee pushed through the lone unlocked gate which stood as the last halfhearted line of defense against intruders. Once inside, they skirted the larger boulders, taking care to avoid slipping on the fresh rubble littering the ground. Staring up at the rock face, it was easy to pick out the most recent damage. Newly revealed surfaces glinted in the afternoon sun, free of dirt or fading or other signs of long-term exposure.

She said, "The news said yesterday's quake was minor, barely registering on the Richter scale." Looking at all the stuff on the ground, she frowned and shifted nervously. Maybe it wasn't such a good idea to be down here after all.

Upon closer inspection, the object was even more impressive. From what she could tell, it appeared to be fused directly with the bedrock rather than occupying a space carved out for it.

"How long do you suppose it's been here?" Dee asked.

Alex shook her head. "No idea. It almost looks like it's been here forever, like the rock itself, but that's impossible."

"Is it?" Dee smiled when he saw her roll her eyes. "How old do you think this rock is? Millions of years?" He gestured to the quarry around him. "Buried deep down. If the mining company hadn't gone under, they'd have found this thing, and if not for the quake, it'd still be buried. Somebody put it here."

"Somebody?" Alex knew where this was going. "You mean space people or something?"

They moved closer and she now saw rows of tiny markings etched into the dark material. Instinct told her it had to be some kind of language, but like nothing with which she was familiar.

Alien? Alex grimaced at the idea, but she could not deny their discovery appeared to defy other, easier explanations.

So caught up was she in trying to make sense of their find that she did not notice Dee moving closer to the object until he reached out to touch it.

"What are you doing?" she snapped, lunging forward and grabbing his other arm. The frantic motion was not enough to stop him before he laid his right palm flat on the object's smooth surface.

Nothing happened.

"Cool to the touch," Dee said, running his hand along the object's face. "You'd think the sun would warm it. I guess I thought—"

A low, rumbling hum filled the air, emanating from the object, which now emitted a blue glow. It was strong enough to make her exposed skin tingle. Flinching in response to the unexpected change, Alex pulled on Dee's arm, trying to drag him away from the thing.

"Come on!"

He said nothing, and moving him proved impossible. The hum grew louder and the glow brighter as she yanked on his arm again, and now Alex saw his eyes were closed and his right hand remained in contact with the object. She moved around him, grasping his wrist and trying to pull him free, but it would not budge.

"Dee!"

Bright blue light clouded her vision, drowning out everything. A wave of nausea washed over her and she released her grip on Dee's wrist. Stumbling backward, she threw out her hands and tried to steady herself. The effect was fleeting. Within seconds, her vision returned, leaving only a lingering churning in her stomach which was already subsiding. Shaking her head to throw off the last effects, Alex returned her attention to Dee. He still stood with his hand on the object.

Then the hum faded and the glow disappeared, and Dee fell limply to the ground.

NOW

Standing next to Dee's bed, Alex divided her attention between his unmoving form and the medical monitors. Like the rest of the surrounding facility, this room and everything in it was dedicated to the express purpose of caring for him and housing the people tasked with studying him and the object responsible for his condition.

Not just for causing it, Alex reminded herself. *Maintaining it.*

Theories abounded as to what was behind all of this, most harboring the common theme that Dee's condition was not an accident but instead the result of a deliberate agenda. This, of course, prompted still more questions about the cylinder. Books and documentaries, more than Alex could remember, devoted themselves to examining the issue from every conceivable perspective. Who or what was behind it all? What did it mean? Would answers ever come?

With a start, she realized her hand rested on Dee's bare right arm. He was warm to the touch, and she felt the muscles beneath his skin. She watched his chest rise and fall in a steady rhythm, breathing on his own rather than with the assistance of a respirator. To the casual observer, he was the picture of perfect health. Despite his only nourishment being the intravenous fluids provided by his caregivers, Dee's body had continued to grow and mature as one might expect of a normal sixteen-year-old male human who followed disciplined diet and exercise regimens into adulthood while avoiding disease or injury. The simple, obvious answer was that the Obelisk was somehow behind it all, but how it did so was just one of a long list of unanswered questions.

"Twenty-five years."

Smiling at the sound of the familiar voice behind her, Alex turned to see Colonel Erica Ribeiro standing in the doorway, regarding her with a maternal expression the younger woman had come to know all too well. Dark hair with only the faintest hints of gray rested on the shoulders of the long white doctor's coat Erica wore over a set of dark maroon surgical scrubs. The coat bore her name and rank stitched over the left breast pocket, offering no other outward sign its wearer was a career officer in the U.S. Air Force.

"Hello, Erica," she said, extending her arms in greeting.

Stepping into Dee's room, Ribeiro accepted the warm embrace. "It's good to see you, Alex. I knew I'd find you here."

"I've become that predictable?"

Ribeiro offered her own smile. "That, and I have a reminder set in my calendar. Not that I really need it, of course."

"Of course." Breaking from the hug, Alex patted the colonel's arm. Of the more than one hundred people currently assigned to oversee, study, and care for Dee, Ribeiro was one of the few who had been with him since day one. As time passed and more information was collected—bit by agonizing bit—about his condition and the object responsible for it, Ribeiro passed up several promotions and assignment opportunities to stay with him. Her superiors soon realized her subject-matter expertise, gained over years of direct contact with Dee and the Obelisk, could not be easily replicated or replaced. To that end, Ribeiro and a handful of others were permanently assigned to this project.

"I know it's silly to think like this," she said, "but every year on this day, I keep wondering if something different will happen. I tried to stop after the tenth year, then the fifteenth, but by twenty I admitted to myself I'd been doing it subconsciously the whole time."

Alex replied, "Me, too. We're just hardwired for that sort of thing, I guess."

As though responding to their musings, a familiar low hum began permeating the room. She spun away from Dee's bed to face the Obelisk, which now emitted a warm blue glow.

THEN

"Alex, you need to stay here. Let them do their jobs."

Yanking her arm from her mother's grip, Alex ran back to the fence blocking access to the quarry. The pitiful, useless barrier against unwanted visitors was now blocked by a pair of bulky green military Hummers sitting before the gate she and Dee had used to enter the site. Six Air Force guards with rifles stood near the vehicles. One of them moved to intercept her as she approached. Instead of aiming his rifle in her direction, he merely raised a hand.

"Miss, I know he's your friend, but I can't let you in."

Holding up her hands to show she offered no threat, Alex replied. "I want to stay with him. I was with him the whole time, so I'm the only one who saw what happened. I've tried to tell other people, but no one will listen to me."

"Alex."

It was her mother, running to catch up and now slightly winded from the exertion. At age thirty-nine, Jessica Casey was essentially an older version of her daughter down to her long blonde hair and fierce jade green eyes. She placed a hand on Alex's shoulder.

"We shouldn't be here. They need us to stay out of the way."

Ignoring her mother's plea, Alex directed her attention to where a massive transparent plastic bubble had been erected around Dee and the mysterious object still embedded in the rock face. The bubble's edges were affixed to the stone itself. Inside it moved a team of four figures. They each wore bright yellow suits covering them from head to toe. All of them stepped around Dee's still unmoving form, though Alex saw her friend now rested atop a drab green stretcher. Two of the group draped a piece of clear plastic over Dee, and she realized they were preparing to move him.

"Where are you taking him?" she asked.

The guard, wearing a nametag on his uniform identifying him as Williams, shook his head. "I'm sorry. I can't answer that." He sounded sincere enough, but that did little to ease Alex's mounting concerns.

Standing next to her, her mom said, "Honey, they know what they're doing."

"How can they possibly know what they're doing?" Alex pointed to the object. "Do they have any idea what that is? How can they?"

Inside the bubble, the four figures each took a corner of the stretcher. They lifted it along with Dee and stepped toward the temporary shelter's single entrance. Outside, another pair of guards, wearing green containment suits and carrying rifles slung over their shoulders, opened the flap. Exiting the bubble, the group walked with their charge toward another Hummer. This one was configured differently from the other vehicles. To Alex, it looked like a military ambulance.

Still ensconced within the transparent shelter, the object in the rock face emitted a harsh crimson glow. It began humming again. Lower and more ominous, it echoed through the quarry.

On the stretcher, Dee's body twitched and convulsed.

Watching all of this, Alex staggered as a new wave of nausea gripped her. Her mother grabbed her around the waist in an attempt to hold her steady. Alex gasped as her vision clouded. Although she could still see, everything was veiled by a red haze. Her mind screamed a single word.

Alex.

"Dee?" Warring against the vertigo doing its best to ensnare her, she waved her arms in a frantic signal for attention.

Alex.

"Don't move him! It doesn't want him to go! You're hurting him!" Alex had no idea how she knew this, but there was no question; no doubt. It was simply fact.

Beyond the stunned guards, she saw one member of the group carrying Dee raise a hand. The others stopped moving. The figure looked in her direction and Alex pointed to the object in the rock.

"Take him back!" It was all she could get out before nausea overtook her and her legs buckled. She fell to her hands and knees, retching as her mother dropped to her side.

"Alex?"

Wiping her mouth, Alex looked up to see the four figures now scrambling back to the containment bubble. The figure who had seen Alex waved toward the guards standing at the shelter's entrance, and within seconds the flap was open and the stretcher carriers had Dee back inside. In response, the object's red glow faded along with the accompanying hum. Alex's queasy stomach subsided.

Only after her mother and Williams helped Alex to her feet did she realize one of the figures in the yellow containment suits had made their way from the bubble to the gate. Another guard moved to open the gate, allowing the figure to exit. The suit's oversized helmet with its black hose connected to a small pack strapped to the wearer's back made it difficult to identify the person within. Then the figure removed the helmet, revealing the face of a young dark-haired woman.

"Are you Alex Casey?" she asked.

Struck by abrupt nervousness, Alex nodded. "Yes. Is Dee okay?"

The woman replied, "We don't know. That's what we're trying to figure out." She pointed over her shoulder toward the bubble. "You knew something was wrong. How?"

Glancing at her mother and Williams, Alex frowned. "I don't know. I just...felt something."

Williams added, "She became nauseous at the same time you were moving the boy, ma'am. When you took him back, she got better." He snapped his fingers. "Just like that."

Her gaze never wavering from Alex, the woman said, "I'd like you to come with me. You and your mother. I have some questions."

After a nod of approval from her mother, Alex replied, "Okay. Do you think it'll help Dee?"

"It's possible." Shifting the helmet to rest under her left arm, the woman extended her right hand to Alex. "Maybe we can find out together. My name's Erica. Lieutenant Erica Ribeiro."

SIX YEARS LATER

The more things change, the more they stay the same.

"You look pretty good, babe," Alex said, taking in the sight of Dee lying in the hospital bed. He looked much the same as during her previous visit five months earlier. While his head was shaved clean for the benefit of the electrodes and other attached leads monitoring his brain activity, someone — a nurse or maybe even his mother — was going to great lengths to maintain his beard and mustache. The dark, closely groomed whiskers traced the lines of his jaw and chin.

Looking away from Dee, Alex turned her gaze to the Obelisk sitting within its protective enclosure. In the six years after falling into his coma, Dee had not been more than fifteen meters from the object, with any attempt to exceed that distance triggering the same debilitating effects he experienced on that first day. The troubling revelation set into motion all manner of activities, the first of which was to cordon off the quarry followed by weeks of careful excavation to remove the Obelisk from its tomb. Dee experienced two more abrupt seizures during this process, accompanied by the object glowing red as though offering a warning, before he and it were transported to their new home at Wright-Patterson Air Force Base in Ohio.

"There she is."

Startled by the unexpected intrusion, Alex turned from Dee but relaxed when she saw Major Erica Ribeiro entering the room.

"Congratulations on your graduation," Ribeiro offered as they embraced. "And Dean's list? Somebody's been busy."

Alex pointed to the patch on the other woman's uniform. "Somebody else has, too. When did you get promoted?"

"Two months ago." Shrugging, Ribeiro added, "Time flies, and all that." She put her hands on her hips, giving Alex a long appraisal. "So, you're back for good. Finally."

"Looks that way, with no small thanks to you."

Ribeiro waved away the notion. "You did all the heavy lifting. A degree in molecular science? Yeah, we're going to put that to work here."

It was the major who convinced her superiors Alex was an important piece of the puzzle that was the Obelisk and its inexplicable hold on Dee Boyd. Despite the incident never being repeated, the girl's reaction as he was moved away from the Obelisk was all the proof Ribeiro required. She made sure Alex was never far from her and her team as their work with Dee and the object continued to expand. When it became obvious no easy or short-term solution was forthcoming, Ribeiro oversaw the relocation of Dee's family, along with Alex and her family, to Dayton, Ohio. The U.S. Government picked up the tab for Alex's college studies at Ohio State University with the understanding the newly minted graduate would come to work with the team.

As for Alex, the past six years were a whirlwind. Finishing high school under the guidance of a tutor at Wright-Patterson, she kept apprised of Dee's condition and maintained a vigil over him whenever possible. She attempted a few awkward dates with other guys while in college, feeble efforts to achieve some semblance of a normal life. They failed in spectacular fashion but she harbored no resentment. Dee remained her focus, driven by the love she still felt for him but even more so by the desire to understand what had happened to him, to identify who or what was responsible, and determine what it all might mean.

"Do people still come around? You know, reporters or curiosity seekers? Whatever?"

Ribeiro grunted. "Not as much as they did in the beginning, but your hometown paper and TV stations still do follow-ups, and the topic pops up on conspiracy websites and talk-radio shows from time to time."

While it proved impossible to keep quiet the object's discovery or its immediate effects on Dee, over time the Air Force and the government crafted a web of disinformation and secrecy that seemed to satisfy all but the most ardent, self-appointed truth seekers. The main exceptions were the clusters of fanatics, some of whom even formed their own pseudo-religious sects with Dee at their center. Was his situation a precursor to the arrival of God or some other deity, or the prologue to some as yet unimagined global calamity? Such questions fueled websites, radio and television programs, and no small number of hucksters, who made comfortable livings traveling the world and spreading their respective versions of "divine prophecy."

Easier to sidestep was Alex's own connection to the entire affair, aided in large part by her family's relocation from Oklahoma to Ohio. A thorough examination six years ago followed by regular check-ups revealed no obvious signs her lone tangential encounter with the Obelisk left any lasting effects. The nausea and the odd sensations she felt that first day had never again manifested themselves, leaving her own possible connection to the object an open question for many, including Alex herself. This as much as anything had motivated Ribeiro to keep her as close as possible.

"You've signed all of your contracts and secrecy agreements," the major said after a moment. "So, I can finally let you in on some things we've learned." She cocked her head toward the Obelisk.

"For example, we've conclusively proven that thing is not from this planet."

Alex nodded. It had been a theory going back to the day of Dee's collapse. As outlandish as she once thought that idea, no other possible explanation had ever presented itself in anything even resembling a plausible fashion. "You're sure?"

"Whatever it's made of doesn't exist anywhere on Earth." Ribeiro crossed her arms. "The team examining it for the past six years doesn't even have names for the materials used to build it. They've gone over every inch of it with X-rays, penetrating radar, spectrographs, spectroscopes, spectro-whatever the hell you call them. If it could be used to take a reading or measurement, they threw it at this thing. The best we've been able to come up with is, it's not radioactive and it's somehow generating its own energy. Our instruments can pick up that much, but not a source. For all we know, there could be anything from a nuclear reactor to a hamster wheel inside that thing."

Alex said, "So, they still haven't found a way to cut into it?"

"Not a damned thing." Ribeiro sighed. "Diamond bit drills, lasers, you name it, they've tried it, including a few things I'm still not allowed to tell you about. Nothing's even made the first scratch. All that's left is to try blowing it up, but that won't happen for obvious reasons. Oh, I'm sure some moron's considered it, but I've got the president on my side."

"The energy readings," Alex said. "They're not constant, right?" Recalling the initial failed attempts to examine the Obelisk, she added, "There were detectable variations even back at the beginning."

Ribeiro replied, "There are definite upticks, several times a day." She gestured to Dee. "They correspond to spikes in his brain activity. It's doing something that affects him in some manner, but don't ask me what."

"Any luck deciphering the markings?"

The major blew out her breath. "We brought in some of the pre-eminent linguistic experts on the planet. We're talking people who study languages that died out thousands of years ago. They've got theories on what might constitute an alphabet of sorts, but there's no way to test their ideas. Nobody speaks Martian. Or Klingon. Whatever."

"I can introduce you to people who speak Klingon," Alex quipped.

"At this point, I'll try anything."

Moving away from Dee's bed, Ribeiro stepped closer to the window separating them from the Obelisk. "So, we've got an artificially created object not of this world, which looks to have been purposely buried in solid rock. We can't carbon date it, but we tested the surrounding stone from the quarry. It's been there for at least five thousand years, but don't ask me who put it there." She cast a grim, humorless smile over her shoulder as she looked at Alex. "As you can see, you're here at just the right time."

NOW

It was the same as it had been that first day. The slight, almost electrical sensation playing across her skin… The hum filling her ears… A blue glow emanating from deep within the Obelisk's core…

"Oh, my god," Ribeiro said, moving to stand next to Alex. "It hasn't done that in years."

"This is the fourth time, right?" Following Dee's collapse and the colonel's team taking charge of his care along with custody of the object, Alex knew of three other occasions when the Obelisk reacted in this manner. They occurred without warning and with irregular and unpredictable frequency.

"Right," Ribeiro said. "The last one was four years ago."

Both women flinched at the abrupt chorus of beeps and pings that began sounding off from the equipment around Dee's bed. Alex moved closer to study the readings. The first thing she noted was a spike in his brain activity. Then his breathing grew stronger and his pulse rate quickened.

"Are these…?" Alex began.

"Higher than anything we've monitored since day one," Ribeiro said. She pulled a mobile phone from her pocket and pressed a single icon before holding it up in front of her. "This is Ribeiro. Code blue. I repeat: Code blue. I'm with Boyd and Doctor Casey. No one else in or out until further notice, and not without my direct order."

"*Copy that, Colonel,*" a stern male voice replied through the phone's speaker. "*Implementing code blue protocols.*"

Alarms sounded outside Dee's room, and Alex heard a metallic click as the door's automatic lock engaged. From this point on and until or unless the colonel ordered otherwise, she and Ribeiro were stuck here with Dee. Across the room, the Obelisk now cast an even brighter blue glow behind its protective barrier.

Though she anticipated it and even braced for it, Alex was still unprepared for the rush of nausea that washed over her. She stumbled, leaning heavily against Dee's bed.

"Erica?" she called out.

Then, Alex gasped as DeShawn Boyd opened his eyes.

"Holy shit!" That was all she could say before her voice caught in her throat.

His eyes.

The light brown eyes that had once looked at her with love and affection were gone, replaced by stark white orbs devoid of even the slightest hint of pupils or irises. He did not blink or look disoriented. Dee simply sat up in his bed. The sheets resting on his chest fell into his lap, revealing bare skin and the various electrodes and other equipment leads connecting him to the monitoring machines. He briefly examined his surroundings before bringing his gaze back to her.

"Alex."

It was not a question uttered in confusion. Dee talked to her with clarity and confidence as though fully aware of who she was despite the passage of time. His voice was deeper than the last time she heard him speak.

"Dee?" Alex heard her voice crack as she said his name. "Is it... are you...?"

"It's good to see you." He turned his head to his left, and Alex realized he was looking past her to Ribeiro. "Colonel Ribeiro."

Moving to stand next to Alex, Ribeiro asked. "You know who I am?"

Dee nodded. "I do. Thank you for looking after me. I know you and Alex and so many others have numerous questions. I'll do my best to answer them."

"You've been in a coma for *twenty-five* years," Alex said. "Are you saying you were aware? The whole time?"

A small smile teased the corners of his mouth, which along with his eyes made his expression more than a bit unsettling. "I was aware, but I could not communicate. I tried, that first day, but then everything...changed. While you cared for my body, my mind remained quite occupied. I guess I've...been away, in a manner of speaking."

Alex exchanged looks with Ribeiro before returning her attention to Dee. "Away?"

"Where did you go?" the colonel asked.

Dee replied, "A voyage of discovery. A journey of understanding."

He reached for her hand and Alex let him take it. His touch was warm, and she felt his gentle reassurance.

"I've learned so much. It's incredible. That's why they took me, Alex; so I could learn. So I could be ready. So I could be here, to help us all."

"Help us?" Alex frowned. "With what?"

His smile widening, Dee squeezed her hand.

"With what comes next."

ESCAPE VELOCITY

Aaron Rosenberg

CONTROL," TARYN WU CALLED, SPEAKING SOFTLY THROUGH THE INSIDE of his helmet. The word seemed to reverberate. "Are you seeing this?" He swiveled his head slowly to make sure the built-in cameras could get a proper view.

"Roger that, Taryn," Marissa Shraeder replied from the mission desk back at Launch Complex 1. "Images coming through nice and clear." Her tone, as no-nonsense as always, told Taryn that she might be looking but she wasn't actually seeing the same thing he was. Not really.

Then, over the helmet's speakers, he picked up a second voice, fainter than hers: "Oh. My. God!" It sounded like Alex Polonov, Marissa's assistant. "That's insane!"

"What?" Taryn could hear the annoyance in her voice. "Get it together, Alex!"

"Look!" he insisted instead. "Stop studying the readings and really look!"

She must have complied because now Taryn heard her sharp intake of breath, followed by a whispered curse. Yes, now she saw what he was looking at—a room, perfectly domed, its walls glimmering like quicksilver in the light from his suit, its floor perfectly smooth, utterly unadorned and completely empty except for the slender pedestal placed at its center.

A room under the surface of the chunk of rock labeled X-39, deep within the extensive system of caves scans had indicated were there and Tam had confirmed when his spacecraft landed on the asteroid's surprisingly level surface.

A room that was clearly crafted, in a place where humans had never set foot before. Over three hundred million kilometers from Earth.

This is it, Taryn couldn't help thinking as he took a slow, careful step forward, his heavy boot clomping loudly as its sole came to rest on the floor of the chamber. *This is the proof we've all been looking for. This shows that we're not alone in the universe. That we never were.*

He advanced across the floor, moving slowly both because he felt cumbersome half-floating in his suit and because he wanted to make sure he did not damage or overlook anything. Back at Launch Complex 1 everyone stared at the screen, following his progress with their eyes.

Not everyone remained idle, however.

In the back of the room, a man pulled out his phone and tapped the single button displayed on its screen. "Are you seeing the feeds?" he asked as soon as the woman on the other end picked up.

"Yes," came the reply. "It's glorious. Everything I'd hoped and more."

"What do you want me to do?" the man—Reggie Chambreau— asked.

"You know what to do," was the answer, curt and clear. "Exactly as discussed."

"Are you sure?" Even as his hand gripped the phone, his eyes followed Taryn's steps onscreen.

But the line had already gone dead. With a sigh, Reggie lowered the phone and slipped it back inside his jacket pocket. He'd hoped for a change of heart, but, of course, he should have known better. His employer had always made it abundantly clear that her wants and needs were her top priority—and therefore his as well.

"I hope you're getting all this, Control," Taryn stated. He had reached the pedestal and stopped before it, gloved hands still at his sides even as his eyes drank it in. It appeared to be made of the same silvery material as the walls—hematite, perhaps? Or something similar? —and rose to his chest, its stand a graceful curve blossoming into a disc roughly the size of his head, like a stylized flower.

Resting upon that disc was a cylinder perhaps eight inches long and two in diameter. It rested perfectly in place despite the almost complete lack of gravity here, held either by its own weight or by some force or mechanism he could not see. It looked to be carved from some sort of stone, a pale, milky rose in hue. Incisions and engravings dotted its side. He couldn't make them out properly. But there was no doubt it had been carefully shaped by an intelligent mind with precise tools.

"What do you want me to do here, Control?" Taryn asked. He itched to pick up the cylinder, but part of him screamed to exercise caution, not to touch it. What if it was booby-trapped somehow? What if it was radioactive? What if it was some strange otherworldly poison? "Do I leave it here—or collect it and bring it back for study?"

Back at Mission Control, Marissa glanced over to where Reggie watched. He nodded, and her eyes narrowed, her lips thinning in disgust or disdain, he couldn't tell, but eventually she turned back to the monitors. "Bring it back, Taryn," she instructed, her voice not betraying whatever her own thoughts and feelings might be on the subject. "But be careful. Treat it like a biohazard."

"Confirmed," the astronaut agreed. Was that relief in his voice—or regret? Through the helmet and the intervening miles, it was difficult to tell. But he obediently moved away, retracing his steps back to the chamber's entrance and then back through the tunnels, to where his Rover waited. From the all-terrain vehicle, he retrieved his specimen collection kit, which he then carried back down.

Reggie had half-expected—and maybe even slightly hoped—that the chamber would have disappeared by the time Taryn returned to its location, but no such luck. The astronaut crossed the room again, and, setting the kit down beside the pedestal's base, used a set of insulated forceps to clasp the cylinder and lift it from its resting place. He then placed the foreign object in a sterile bag, which was sealed tight and then returned to the kit.

When Taryn Wu left that chamber for the second time, he carried the cylinder with him, safely stowed away in his kit. It was completely out of sight, but there was no question that it was on the mind of everyone in the room. Which made Reggie doubt the effectiveness of his own instructions, but he knew he had little choice but to carry them out nonetheless. Regardless of the consequences.

Even with the first-time-in-the-field neutrino drives, the flight from Asteroid X-39 back to Earth took fifteen days. Taryn Wu spent the time exercising, meditating, monitoring the science experiments he was running, and performing routine checks and maintenance. Despite the careful regimen of exercise, diet, supplements, and sleep, by the time his ship had re-entered the atmosphere and settled back onto its launch pad he felt as if he had run an endurance marathon, his entire body jittery with nerves and lack of sleep; every muscle ached, his senses were raw, and his head throbbed. Nonetheless, he held his head high as he stepped out onto the ramp and marched back down to solid ground. He wore his pack on his back but clutched the specimen kit protectively against his chest.

The entire crew was gathered behind the blast walls. They hurried into the launch room once the engines had shut off and the heat and exhaust had been vented, though they still kept to a safe distance. A cheer rose as Taryn stepped into view. He smiled, acknowledging the waves and cheers and applause. Marissa and Alex waited for him just past the end of the ramp, along with a tall African-American man Taryn vaguely recalled seeing at some of the initial planning sessions.

"Welcome back, Taryn," Marissa told him, offering her hand. They shook, and Taryn did his best not to flinch from the burst of light as several cameras captured the moment. He was, after all, the first astronaut to travel as far as the asteroid belt, and still one of only a handful of astronauts to have successfully completed a privately funded space mission.

"Thank you. It's good to be back."

Alex was next, and more effusive, hugging Taryn despite the kit sandwiched between them. "Welcome back, man!" he cheered, pounding Taryn on the back. "Awesome job!" His enthusiasm made Taryn smile.

Then it was the stranger's turn. "Mr. Wu, congratulations," he said. His handshake was firm and cool. "We're all very pleased with your success." His eyes dropped to the kit. "Is that it?"

"Yes, sir." There was no need to ask what the man meant, and even though he hadn't given his name or position the fact that he was here with Marissa meant he must hold some level of authority over this project.

"Excellent." The man held out his hand. "I'll take care of it if you don't mind." It wasn't really a request.

Taryn opened his mouth, ready to object, but Marissa beat him to it. "I'm sorry, sir," she interrupted smoothly, her voice cool and crisp and completely business, though Taryn was surprised to see a spark of glee in her eyes. "As a foreign object, there are certain protocols we must observe before it can be cleared. You understand."

His frown said that he did not care much for such formalities. "I'm sure it's been made clear to you . . ." he started, but again the mission controller cut him off, her small stature in no way diminishing her ability to stop someone in their tracks.

"I am well aware of the mission parameters, and of the final disposition of its findings," she assured him sharply. "However, I am also aware of the protocols agreed upon by every space agency, as established by the CDC, DARPA, and others. To violate those procedures would not only result in heavy fines, it would also result in this entire program being shut down, most likely permanently, with every scrap of related equipment *and* material confiscated." The grin she offered him was razor-sharp. "Or you can wait while we follow the correct procedure, and then claim the object without any difficulty or repercussion."

For a second, the still-unnamed stranger stared down at her, leaving Taryn feeling like he was trapped in an Old West showdown between two gunslingers, his body tense as if any second their conflict of wills might spill over into gunfire. Then the man sighed and took a step back, raising his hands in mock-surrender.

"Very well," he agreed. "Please keep me informed of its progress, and I will remind you that any findings must be kept confidential." His gaze strayed to Taryn. "That includes any discussion of the mission in general," the man reminded him. "Your contract requires it."

Taryn nodded. He knew only too well what the contract stated. Until details were cleared for public release, he was not even allowed to say what he did for a living, only that he was a test pilot for experimental craft.

He had never thought that restriction would weigh on him as much as it did now, as he handed the kit over to the scientists who rushed forward to collect it and realized that these people around now him might well be the only people who would ever know where he had been and what he had seen.

"We've hit a slight snag," Reggie reported over his phone. "The object has to go through testing before it can be cleared for release. International guidelines."

There was a pause. "Fine," came the reply at last, the single clipped syllable clearly relaying the speaker's impatience. "Make sure any test results are for our eyes alone. And I absolutely do not want any word of this leaking out."

"Of course," he promised. Nor did he expect that to prove too difficult, all the way out here at the tip of New Zealand's North Island. No, he expected the secret was nearly as safe here as it had been up on X-39.

Maybe even safer.

"Hey hey, the wanderer returns!" Old Kai called out as Taryn stepped into the Rocket Café, the door banging shut behind him. The other occupants all turned to look; a few raised their hands in greeting. Taryn smiled and waved back, exchanging hellos as he made his way across the small room. The café was the only restaurant of any sort in this part of Mahia, making it the closest place one could get to from base if one wanted a drink beyond huddling with some of the other crew and passing around a bottle. And right now, Taryn felt he really needed to be off-base.

"Just get back?" Kai asked. Taryn nodded, claiming one of the stools before the bar. The café wasn't exactly fancy, but it wasn't like it had any competition. Besides, Kai was a decent sort and a welcoming host, and the food here was solid and appealing. Taryn made a point of driving over at least once a week. That made him something of a fixture here which had won over the locals who also frequented the small restaurant.

"Yeah, yesterday," Taryn admitted. He'd had to go through the usual barrage of tests before they'd clear him to leave base, though.

"Where was it this time?" the proprietor inquired, filling a pint and setting it before Taryn without his asking. One of the advantages of coming here regularly. "Mars? The Moon? Saturn, maybe?"

Taryn smiled, wrapping his hands around the glass. The condensation tingled against his skin. "Farther," he admitted. He figured there wasn't much harm in saying that. Everyone here knew what Launch Complex 1 was, anyway.

"Truth? Get out!" Kai slapped his hand on the bar and laughed. "Nice!" He eyed his customer with a practiced eye. "Stew?" he asked. "Bread's fresh, too." There was almost always stew going—most of the time it was seafood, though occasionally it was game bird instead. All local catches, of course.

Taryn nodded, finally raising the glass to take a long gulp. The beer was good and cold and crisp, and he took another swallow before setting the pint back down, now half empty. He was starting to relax a little and didn't start when someone slid onto the stool beside him.

"Farther than Saturn, really?" It was Izzy, another regular, though she was a local, born and bred. She'd always been friendly, and to be honest, Taryn found her very appealing, with her red curls almost bleached by the sun, her freckles all but hidden beneath her constant tan, and most of all her smile. "That's a long way to go for a sandwich." She laughed, and he and Kai and the others listening all laughed with her.

"Well, perhaps not as far as Saturn," Taryn replied after a second. "But farther than Mars."

He didn't expect any of them to know what that meant, but shouldn't have been that surprised when a fisherman he knew only as Ari chimed in, "So, that'd be Jupiter or the Asteroid Belt, yeah? And Jupiter there's no way you could land, so I'd say the belt for sure." *That was what I get for underestimating people,* Taryn scolded himself.

He couldn't actually confirm their guess, of course. Still, these were his friends, so he raised his glass in salute. If they took that as acknowledgment, who was he to say?

Izzy leaned an elbow on the bar, regarding him with bright green eyes. "Find anything worth the trip?" she asked, her voice husky.

Taryn smiled. "You know I'm not allowed to talk about it," he said and took another drink to keep from letting anything else slip. His audience all nodded knowingly. They understood, and he hoped that meant they wouldn't push him on it. As it was, he hadn't really told them anything they couldn't have figured out for themselves, so he considered himself still well within the confidentiality clause.

Having settled that in his head, he focused instead on the piping-hot stew Kai set before him, the hunk of fresh-baked bread that came with it, and chatting more with him, with Izzy, and with the others. After over a month locked in that tin can all on his own, his only communication the updates back to Marissa and the rest of Control, it felt good to just unwind and be around other people once more. People who talked about the weather, the fishing, the gossip from the nearby school, and other topics that had nothing to do with space or the oddities one could find out there.

"It's not allendeite," Raquel declared, studying the results on her monitor. "Not exactly. Some similarities to carmeltazite, but not a precise match there, either."

Devon slid his chair over to her desk to see. "Hm, that's a bit like Hypatia, isn't it?" he asked, pointing at one row of details. "Lots of nickel, aluminum, moissanite."

"Sure, but there's no silver iodine phosphide, and no phosphorus," she countered. "And check out the density. It's nearly off the charts! 5.87 g/cm^3! Carmeltazite's only 4.12!"

"That's...insane!" Devon burst out. "That's almost twice diamond's!" They looked at each other. "Are we even sure the scans are accurate? The machines aren't rated to penetrate something like that—nothing is!"

She frowned, tugging a pink-dyed curl down from her right temple as she thought. "I think it should be all right," she answered slowly, "but I can't swear it." Then she brightened. "You know who'd know, though? Professor Hidayo!" He had been their instructor back at CalTech and was considered the world's foremost authority on analyzing crystalline structures.

"Well, yeah," her partner agreed, scratching at his chin. "But it's not like we can tell him! NDA and all."

Raquel was already pulling out her phone, and calling up her email. "We won't tell him what we're studying," she promised. "Just the gist of it. He can help us check the calibrations, that's all."

Now it was Devon's turn to frown, but he didn't argue as she typed in the question. After all, better to be sure they were doing this right. And as long as they didn't tell their former teacher exactly what they were studying—or where it had come from—they should be fine.

"You know what it reminds me of, don't you?" Hu muttered, adjusting his glasses where they had once again slipped down his nose.

Beside him, his partner Manny rolled his eyes. "If I say yes, will that stop you from telling me?" he asked, but he patted Hu on the shoulder to reassure him that it was merely a joke. "Go ahead and tell me, I'd hate for you to pop something," he added.

Hu smiled, but it was an absent expression, his gaze still transfixed by the images slowly cycling across the screen. "Look at the patterns," he said softly, raising one hand to trace one carving as it angled down, then back up, then down again. There was something soothing in the regular rhythm of that motion, and Manny thought he could almost hear Hu's finger dipping and soaring like a conductor before an orchestra—

"It's a record!" he shouted, causing Hu to stumble in surprise. "Like one of the old phonograph cylinders!"

This time his partner's smile was warm and alive. "Yes," he agreed. "I believe so. These are almost certainly sounds." He frowned. "But there's more to it than that. I think there's a second layer of meaning here, beyond what could be played back audibly. I'm not sure what, though . . ." he trailed off as he typed a quick query into the computer, scanning the results that popped up and clicking on one. "There. She might know."

Manny read the information scrolling down the new page. "You think so?" He looked back at Hu. "I mean, maybe, but even if she did, it's not like you can tell her about it."

"No no, of course not," Hu agreed, gently hip-checking Manny out of the way and slipping into the chair there, tugging the keyboard toward him even as he clicked open his mail program. "But a quick, random question from an old classmate, that's nothing to be remarked upon, is it? Nothing specific, just a general question about certain shapes and patterns. Utterly innocuous."

Manny sighed but shifted behind Hu and began rubbing his shoulders as he typed. "I suppose that's okay," he admitted, but he wasn't convinced. Still, it couldn't hurt, right?

"There is some radioactivity," Dom stated, reading the gauges and dials. They still preferred their equipment old-school, which amused Hanover to no end. "Nothing dangerous, though. Less than a moon rock, more than regular old granite."

"Those wavelengths are odd, though, aren't they?" Hanover pointed out, tapping one gauge in particular. "Non-ionizing, to be sure, but they're so even. Almost perfectly uniform." He glanced at the other readings, then at his screen, which displayed the same information but in what he considered a vastly superior format. "Look, it's actually broadcasting that same intensity across the entire spectrum!"

"That's . . . not possible," his friend muttered. "The only way that could work is if—"

"—it's black-body radiation!" Hanover shouted, grabbing Dom by the shoulders and whirling them around in a circle. "An actual black-body! Right here in our lab!"

Normally, Dom was so cool as to be considered aloof, but right now, spinning with Hanover, their slim features were stretched into a wide, almost childlike grin. "Incredible!" they agreed happily, laughing with delight. "We have to document this!"

"Oh, hell, yes!" Hanover sang. But then, as their revolutions slowed and they both gasped for breath, he returned to reality. "But we can't publish it, can we?"

To his surprise, Dom waved away his objection. "We'll fudge some of the details about its origin, our location, and so on," they replied. "And we'll post it anonymously—for now. That should satisfy those ridiculous waivers we signed."

Hanover hesitated. He was not used to being the cautious one of their team, but something about that statement worried him. Still, there was no way they could not document their find—no one had ever so much as seen a real black-body before! And if Dom thought it would be all right, and they were normally so careful—well, it must be okay, then, right?

Even inside its bag, and that wrapped within an outer casing, Reggie handled the object as carefully as he would an active hornet's nest, holding it as far from his body as he could manage without overbalancing himself. Yes, he'd seen the reports, but he didn't exactly understand them—the eggheads who'd studied it for radioactivity had assured him it was not dangerous, but they'd started babbling something about full spectrums and idealized frequencies and maximum intensities and so he was keeping as much distance between himself and the object as possible because he liked his hair and not having his eyes film over or his skin slough off or whatever else it was that radiation did to you.

There was a car and driver waiting at the edge of the facility. It took Reggie and his precious cargo out of the complex and deeper into the island until finally it deposited him at a small private airstrip. A plane waited for him there, engines idling. As soon as he was onboard and in his seat they took off, carrying him swiftly from the island and anyone else who knew about the recent mission or what it had brought back. Several uneventful hours later, the plane landed at Haneda Airport, in Tokyo. Another car whisked him away, cutting through the city until it reached Minato Ward. The car pulled into the garage of Motoazabu Hills, the most exclusive building in the high-priced neighborhood, not to mention the tallest. The guards had clearly been apprised of Reggie's arrival, and helped him out of the car, leading the way to the elevator and pressing the button for the twenty-ninth and top floor, then typing in the access code.

The elevator opened directly onto the penthouse apartment. Reggie's employer occupied the entire floor, which made sense, seeing as how she owned the whole building.

She was waiting for him in the foyer, and her eyes lit with anticipation when they fell upon the case in his arms. "Is that it?" she asked, her voice filled with more eagerness than he had ever heard from her before.

"It is," he acknowledged, handing it over. Though only five feet tall and slight, she took the heavy case without difficulty, turning away and carrying it over to a nearby table. There she slit open the packaging and, after wrestling it apart, finally reached in and extracted the alien cylinder.

"It's beautiful," she whispered, holding it up in both hands so its surface reflected the sunlight streaming in from the end-to-end glass ceiling. Its rosy surface almost seemed to glow, making it look as if she were somehow cradling a living sunrise. "And you're sure no one knows anything about it?" On a beautifully carved teak table up against one wall there sat a handsome base of pure black basalt. She set the cylinder upon it almost reverently.

"No one," Reggie confirmed. "Just the staff and they know better than to say anything."

"Good." His employer nodded, but her eyes were still fastened upon her new acquisition. "See that it stays that way."

Reggie wanted to ask why such secrecy was necessary, but he did not. Truth be told, in the years he'd worked for her, he'd learned a bit about what she liked, what she valued. Many collectors delighted in showing off their possessions, watching the envy crawl across the faces of their audience. Others were the opposite, wishing to wholly possess their things so that even the knowledge of their treasures resided with them alone. His employer was one of the latter. For her, it was not about others admiring her collection. All of these items were for her and her alone, and she was happiest when no one had ever heard of them, much less that she owned them.

In this case, that had been far easier than usual, given that there were literally only a few people in the world who were even aware of the cylinder.

As he took his leave and exited the apartment and then the building, slipping back into the car that would take him back to the airport, Reggie congratulated himself on a job well done.

Still, he couldn't help but feel a small pang at the thought of what he'd just deprived the world of. Actual proof of intelligent life among the stars and no one would ever know it even existed.

A week later, an anonymous scholarly article appeared in a physics magazine, talking about black-body radiation—and citing a very familiar, if supposedly hypothetical, shape.

A few days after that, a professor blogged about a cylinder that could contain both a phonograph recording and a visual seal, and how combining the two would stretch the bounds of current science.

Around the same time, a professor elsewhere released a paper hypothesizing a new mineral compound, one that could never have originated on Earth.

Then the wires picked up a local New Zealand story about a trip to the asteroid belt—and how the person making that trip had not come back empty-handed.

Each story exploded onto the Internet, spreading across the globe in days—hours, even. And with each new facet, a fresh wave of conversation and speculation burst forth, faster and faster, as another piece of the puzzle slotted into place.

In a very exclusive apartment in Tokyo, a certain object remained, scrupulously locked away from prying eyes. But its image, its composition, its components, its very existence had already escaped those bonds, flying far and wide.

Now they belonged to the world. And they could never be locked away again.

DAWNS A NEW DAY

Danielle Ackley-McPhail

> "I get knocked down, but I get up again.
> You're never gonna keep me down."
>
> – Chumbawamba

CHARLIE DIDN'T KNOW WHERE THEY CAME FROM. WHAT THEY WERE. ALL that mattered was that her momma had held them dear. There were so many memories of her raising her hands mere inches from the plastic-wrapped mounds of boxes, her expression filled with awe and fear and longing in equal measure. Beneath those, the barest flicker of hope, all but extinguished.

These were remnants from a past Charlie had never seen. Never touched. No one had touched them. That was the point. The thing that made them so precious.

Part of her longed for these things. To open and explore those boxes and all they contained, driven by an insatiable curiosity. Part of her remained indifferent, not understanding the significance of those untouched objects. How could she? Charlie had never been a part of that world, the one that existed before *it* was found.

From the journal of
Amelia Gates,
Forensic Technologist,
Circa 1 N.A.

The artifact was discovered in a pile of cooling rock at the edge of
a new fissure vent on Mount Vesuvius. Markings covered the

*sleek tooled-metal sides, vaguely familiar, as if we <u>should</u> know
them, but unlike any identifiable form of writing ever studied
since the beginning of recorded history. Smooth and ageless. A
timeless work of art. Clearly manufactured but by no means
anyone recognized, of materials that defied identification. The
object evoked a sense of wonder in all who saw it, followed by
the overwhelming desire to discover its secrets. Some said it
glowed faintly green outside of direct light. They craved to
touch it. Others couldn't get away quick enough. To the media,
it was pure gold…even though it wasn't.*

They lived in a library. At a college where Momma had sometimes
taught in the before time. Not out in the open, where anyone could see
them through the plate-glass windows, but in a back room—Momma
called it a break room—with no windows at all. But at night… from a
young age, Charlie had roamed the stacks by moonlight devouring
any book she could reach. The words on the page fascinated her
nearly as much as Momma's boxes. Agriculture. Science. Modern
Dance. Computer Programming. Cooking. Herblore. Mathematics. Any
and all knowledge drew her interest.

She explored her little world, imagining what it was like full of
people doing and working on things she'd only read about. She sat
at the computers and pretended they were still full of light and life
and knowledge. But never when Momma might catch her.

Sometimes for hours she would sit there and turn them on and off
just to watch the screen glow to life, powered by the solar panels they'd
installed on the roof.

*From the journal of
Amelia Gates,
Forensic Technologist,
Circa 2.3 N.A.*

*They didn't bomb us into the Stone Age – whoever <u>they</u> are…
or were – but they did set us on our collective technological
asses. It took us a little while to figure out what was going on.
The virus spread over time, slow but steady. Unrealized and*

insidious. We don't even understand how it happened. How it <u>could</u> happen. The damage already irreparable before we even figured out what was going on. Like any social disease, by the time someone determined how it spread the damage was done. In less than six months one hundred years of computer development began to unravel.

You would have thought the first systems affected would be those in direct contact with the artifact, but they weren't. The world had begun to deteriorate even before the object hit the testing phase. We were doomed the moment it was found. The moment the kid who fell over it picked it up in awe to marvel at his find. No one bothered with quarantine procedures. It was a thing brought up from the earth, purified by fire. Who would have thought we needed to?

At first innocuous things — like ATMs and health trackers and home PCs — glitched, then seemed to be fine. Until they weren't. Driving any car built after 1968 carried an element of risk in proportion to the number of computer chips that went into its design and their respective functions. People fell back on the old ways. Thrift stores and consignment shops and junkyards became the new places to shop. Anywhere people could find old tech. The type anyone could repair. Things that didn't need a computer degree to operate.

The attack was multipronged, we determined that much.

Things couldn't fail all at once. That would be self-limiting. Our dependency had to persist for the contagion to spread. Anything mankind touched became a carrier until every computerized system melted away like so much broken code.

Not all of our tech failed. Just anything with roots set in Silicon Valley. Like a person with dementia, the hardware worked just fine; the software…that shredded like books torn page from page. Anything networked followed. Corporate. Government. Military. International. It didn't matter. No system was safe. Not even those beyond Earth's sphere. We didn't learn that until satellites started falling from the sky. And who knows what happened to the ISS.

Our technological base crumbled as exponentially as it had grown. No one knew how to cope, knocked back into a strictly mechanical world.

Charlie had always been told never to touch the things in Momma's prohibited stash, but they called to her. Captured her attention and would not let go. They were smooth and bright and looked cool to the touch. She resisted the call for a while, but couldn't manage forever.

Once, when Momma was away finding food, Charlie crept close and pulled one of the objects from its cocoon. It was flat, like one of the handheld chalkboards she'd learned her words on, but when she touched a depression on the side bright light came from beneath the center glass. A mere touch called up pictures that moved, colorful and cute, like it was meant for a child. She was lost in the glow and the movement, hardly noticing Momma's return.

She had looked up from the tablet to see a look of horror on her mother's face. Charlie quickly dropped her gaze and thrust the forbidden object away from her. She watched Momma through her lashes as Momma snatched it up and the shock turned to awe as she swiped a finger across the screen. Within ten minutes the pictures had stuttered and gone dark, but Charlie would never forget the awe in Momma's expression or how the ever-present flicker of hope had fanned higher.

Momma had dropped the dead tablet and scooped Charlie up in a tight hug, murmuring, "Could it be that simple?" Charlie hadn't known what she meant. Then.

She remembered growing tenser as the seconds passed, her nerves on overload until she had stiffly jerked away, avoiding her mother's fleeting look of hurt as she bobbed back and forth until the stress bled away.

"Don't worry, my special child," Momma had murmured. "I understand."

Momma has been gone a while now, the life gone out of her, just like the computers out in the library. Only there was no way to turn her on and off again. All Charlie had left of her was her journal, the pages soft and creased and worn with rereading, still echoing with Momma's voice.

Charlie used the knowledge she'd gained from it to carry on.

From the journal of
Amelia Gates,
Forensic Technologist,
Circa 4 N.A.

We tried to rebuild and that is when the truth came out. It wasn't just the computer systems that had been scrambled. The virus messed with our minds, rewrote our DNA and jumbled our thought processes until anything related to computer tech read like ancient Greek.

Going off the grid was no longer a matter of choice. The preppers had a field day being right. Everyone else clambered to catch up. Alternate energy sources kept the lights on, so to speak. Factories reworked their high-tech processes and dusted off mothballed machines from a bygone age. Craftsmen of any type were once more shown respect. It wasn't enough to save us.

As a society we became brutal. Grabbing for whatever we needed. Grabbing for what we could keep. Instead of working together to rebuild, most of us went to ground, afraid of the ensuing chaos. Some helped their fellow man...as much as they were able...but the new normal terrified us.

Individually, we are capable of being noble. But humanity as a whole is horrifying when it's afraid. We could have sustained society quite well on low-tech, as we had for most of our existence, if not for our fear. Unwittingly, we destroyed technology. Knowingly, we destroyed ourselves.

It was time to remove the plastic. Time to open the boxes. It was time to honor the legacy Momma had left her because without that legacy, there was no way to rebuild. For a fleeting moment,

Charlie bobbed in agitation. The stricture against touching these things firmly ingrained. But the inner conflict could not stand against her overwhelming desire to discover the mysteries those boxes held.

First, she moved everything from the room in which she had lived for fifteen years, all but Momma's stash, the large, battered linoleum table, and a single chair. Then she cleaned the space until not even a speck of dust remained, then cleaned it again. The linoleum was well beyond shining, but it did gleam.

And then she stared at Momma's legacy. Large boxes and small, the word "Gateway" emblazoned along the sides. Fitting, even if Charlie had no idea why that word was chosen. With meticulous care, she opened each one, drew out its hidden treasure, and set the box aside, careful to group the contents with the papers for each component. Monitors. Keyboards. Towers. Mice. Laptops. Tablets. Five of each, except the tablets. All untouched until now. All uninfected. Once destined to teach the next generation. Now destined to save it.

A small foundation upon which to rebuild the world.

Challenge accepted.

Without even unwrapping the manuals, Charlie set up her empire. Wires neat and orderly, components correctly and precisely placed, power source engaged. She reached for the power button, then slowly drew her hand away. Momma's written words came back to her: *the hardware worked just fine; the software...that shredded like books torn page from page.*

Alone in this back room, touched only by her hand, these computers were fine. But no matter what she did here, it would never be enough. She had to rebuild. She had to reconnect. The infrastructure was out there, blank and void and waiting, but she never could dare touch it running on the old code. She needed to rewrite the language...she needed an anti-virus.

Pushing away from the table, she went for a walk, her mind working furiously on the problem. For days, then weeks Charlie went on many walks…

From the journal of
Amelia Gates,
Forensic Technologist,
Circa 5 N.A.

–The final entry–

> *Society shattered like a finely balanced glass globe knocked*
> *from its plinth. Have the past five years been our crucible? Will*
> *the shards of society be reformed better or worse than what we*
> *had been? Right now all I see is a dark time, but I have*
> *begun to expect not everyone has been affected by the virus.*
> *That those on the spectrum, like my Charlie, are wired different*
> *enough to remain unaffected.*
>
> *Is this our light in the darkness? I look at my daughter and*
> *wonder...*

Charlie sat back hard on her heels and tracing the webbing of scars across the back of her hand to restore order to her own mind. Agitated, she resisted the urge to flutter that hand just as much as she resisted the urge to reach out and run her fingers through the pile of shards before her, looking for order in the chaos, her mind already fast at work on putting that meaningless puzzle together, no matter how pointless it might seem.

She watched the play of light and shadow on the dusty fragments, hinting at their former brilliance. The refraction of the images captured in the larger fragments. Her gaze narrowed and her hands twitched, her head going completely still as her mind dove into the enigma, followed by her hands, sorting bits of glass with short, sharp motions, heedless of the specks of blood left behind on them. Her hands sorted glass, but her mind sorted facts. So many facts stored away over what had to be over a decade of reading the scholarly treasure trove that filled her home. She was almost there this time. Nearly broken through...

Abruptly, she drew her hands back, her motions rigidly controlled as she rose to her feet and hurried to her hidden warren, seeking out the blank pages at the back of Amelia Gates' journal.

Back to the pristine monitor and tower she'd dared not touch, unwrapped from its plastic and patiently waiting for the dawning of a new day. The dawning of a new way.

It was here. She had it. The start of a new way of thinking. A way out of the darkness. A way back up to the stars. And Momma so help her, when she got there, she was going to make the race responsible pay.

BUILDING BLOCKS

Jody Lynn Nye

I SAY THEY'RE ARTIFICIAL," DR. BRAN CAMPBELL SAID, LOOKING BACK OVER his shoulder as he led Dr. Anyess Chopard down the battered, gray metal corridor. The two of them bounced at every step in the ultra-low gravity of the elderly exploration ship. Anyess enjoyed the rare sensation of weightlessness. It took the pain out of her arthritic knees and back better than a physiotherapist's pool. "No one believes me. They think these rocks are a natural formation like the basalt pillars off the west coast of Ireland. That's why I called you in. You saw the video of where we found them. I know once you examine them, you'll agree with me. I've read all of your papers and watched all your videos."

Excitement and hope in the young geologist's earnest freckled face made it glow. Ayness gave him an indulgent smile. Though humankind had spread far beyond the confines of the Sol system decades ago, it had yet to find any other species than those that existed on Earth. All the speculation about extinct settlements on Venus, Mars, the moons of Jupiter or Saturn, or even Neptune, had all come to nothing. So had the hopes of finding Vulcan, or Tatooine, or Gallifrey, or Pern, or one of the other fictional worlds that had helped make the vast universe feel less empty. Humanity didn't like shouting into the void and hearing its voice disappear into the parsecs. For all that it considered itself to be tremendously special, it did not want to be *unique*. So far, though, Fermi's paradox seemed to be distressingly accurate. The absence of fellow spacegoing beings became ever more inescapable the farther humanity traveled out into the galaxy.

Most people believed that aliens had to be somewhere. Anyess herself held secret hopes that one day they would come across beings that humans could befriend. She refused to believe in monsters or heartless conquerors. If they did find such a species, well, she'd deal with it then, once she got over the wonder of finding fellow beings.

Her summons to the space station in the middle of the asteroid belt in between Cancri 3c and 3d was the twelfth call-out from her quiet university office in four years. She had been shown to the objects that the hopeful miners or settlers or prospectors had discovered. While they had watched, she measured, tested, and assayed the items. With the most generous will in the world, she scrutinized scratches that the discoverers hoped was a written language; but in the end, been forced to see that hope melt away. She chuckled, a little ruefully. Those pioneers had to settle for a viable planet, fantastic discoveries, or valuable metals instead of company in the galaxy. *No matter how much you have, you always want more*, she thought. But in this case, she dearly hoped that this time, she might find evidence that would stand up to scrutiny. This trip was her last chance to make that fantastic discovery. After a distinguished academic career spanning nearly eight decades, she would be retiring by the end of the year. The university had sponsored this tour as a farewell gift to their soon-to-be professor emeritus.

Campbell bounced to a halt a few meters from the end of the corridor in front of a huge blast door with warning notices in nine languages etched into its surface. A chip of enamel flaked away from the frame and floated past Anyess's nose. The young man looked embarrassed.

"Our mission is low priority," he said, "so they assigned us the oldest ship in the fleet. Everything still works!" he added, in haste to reassure her.

"I've stayed on worse," she said, giving him a kind smile.

He flipped open a hatch beside the door and handed her a pressure suit.

"The cargo bay is open to vacuum," he said. "We hardly ever have anything valuable or breakable in it. Until now."

Anyess slipped her narrow frame easily into the floppy jumpsuit, bundled her long silver hair into the helmet, then attached the gloves. Standard operating procedure. A thumbnail image of Campbell with his name and credentials appeared on a heads-up display above her eye line.

As soon as her lights went green, the young scientist cycled them through the airlock.

Like on any interstellar mining ship, the cargo area stretched away into the distance. Once they started building craft in space, size—and configuration—was limited only by the shipwrights' imagination and budget. So at least a couple of *Starship Enterprises* plied the spaceways, along with at least one *Millennium Falcon*, and a host of others culled from books and videos. Working ships, however, generally had only the basics; in this case, life support in the cabins, sturdy drives, and a hold large enough to bring home enough goods to make the journey out worthwhile.

The trip had obviously already paid off. Gigantic gray nets filled most of the available space. Anyess saw streaks of metal here and there on the massive rocks the crew had captured. Clear cases containing crystals, transuranics, and rare earths were clamped to the bulkheads in an enormous filing cabinet of treasure.

Dangling like a uvula from the top of the cargo bay, the bright red net containing some of the putative artifacts drew her eye at once. Campbell signed to her to take one of the hand-held thrusters from a bracket on the wall and follow him. They wove in between the regular cargo, past cargobots and the occasional crewmember who threw dirty looks at the young officer.

"You're wasting space with that junk," a gravelly man's voice said in Anyess's ear.

"Maybe not, Moretti," Campbell said, cheerfully. Anyess recognized the bravado and smiled. He had put his reputation on the line, and maybe more, to bring her there. A true believer. She was one herself.

The net proved to be far larger than it had appeared from the distant portal, almost fifty meters in diameter. Campbell turned off the thruster and hooked it to his belt. Anyess did the same. They clung to the cargo net and peered between its strands. Within it floated a sampling of the objects she had seen in the three-dimensional video. Immense flat oblong plinths of gray stone with the sheen of river rocks tumbled in zero gee, occasionally bumping into one another then rebounding in opposite directions, like people in a crowd accidentally touching and retreating from contact. In vacuum, she couldn't hear them clack, but she imagined the sound. She had seen millions of rocks and shards in her career, but she had to agree with Campbell that these were different. Except for the cataloging numerals in red paint on each, they were almost impossible to tell apart. Anyess held her breath.

"You see?" he said, his energy causing the net to bell out as he pointed to one stone after another. "Look at them! Regular as though they came off an assembly line. They're virtually identical in every way. You can't tell me that those are natural. These are the building blocks of countless structures!"

Anyess had the data that Campbell had sent her, but she needed readings of her own. She aimed her handheld scanner out and collected psychometric data. The stones, of a granite-like material embedded with tiny crystals, measured, within tolerances of plus or minus two percent, approximately ten meters in length, five wide, and two deep. The density reading indicated that they were solid right through. Apart from some impact fractures and chipped edges, they had no other markings.

"Where did you find them?" she asked.

"In sector eight of the asteroid belt," he said. "Clusters of them are floating together. *Immense* clusters. You don't know about this belt, but it's an irregular smear in orbit around Cancri 3. Our xenogeologists posit that this was once a planet circling the star. Some disaster blew it up, and the remains have drifted ever since. I counted millions of these stones, all in the same area where I took these samples. I think they were once buildings in a major city!"

"Crap," said the gravelly voice. Its owner now jetted toward them. Through his clear mask, the expression of disapproval on Moretti's broad, tan face was its most distinctive characteristic. "They're rocks. Lots of them. Whatever formed them just kept on making them. Now they're floating in space. The shape doesn't mean anything special."

Campbell appealed to Anyess. "He's wrong, I know he is! An alien culture made these. Tell him. You're the xenoarchaeologist."

Anyess shook her head. "You know the chances are very slight, doctor. Billions-to-one against. I've spent my entire career looking for proof of alien life."

"A chance is a chance!" Campbell wrung his gloved hands. "Please check."

Ayness felt a pang of sympathy for him. She had been disappointed so often, but it wasn't fair to bring down his dreams. Reality would do that soon enough.

With the help of floating minerbots, Anyess wrangled one of the flat boulders out of the net and into the open. The bots kept it steady while she all but crawled from one end to the other, measuring and recording as she went. Her initial readings remained unchanged. From her kit, she took a microlab, an analyst in a box the size of her palm, and set it over a decorative streak of quartz crystals she found five meters from the painted end. In a short while, she heard a beep in her earbud and checked her recording computer. Granite, so close to that found in the Sol system as made no difference. Campbell and Moretti watched her, Campbell anxious and Moretti skeptical. Over time, a number of others thrustered over to join them. Anyess did a second full check, just to make certain. When she finished, she beckoned to the crew, and projected a hologram on the stone's surface large enough for all of them to see.

"I'm sorry," she said to Campbell. "I've checked this stone for marks of tools, or casting. The stone isn't homogenous enough to have been manufactured. It wasn't formed by anyone. It's not artificial. These are natural stone, a metamorphic rock like granite, tumbled into this size in vast watercourses, I would estimate, then part of a gneiss formation at the bottom of a primeval sea, which smoothed them flat over eons. It's pure chance that they're all so close to the same size."

"Hah!" Moretti said, waving his hand in the younger scientist's face. "I told you, Campbell! You called this woman all the way from Sol for no reason and cost the company hundreds of thousands!"

Campbell cringed.

"But," Anyess said, raising a finger, "It's almost that unlikely to be chance that they were in the same place, in your sector eight, in such huge quantities. They almost certainly had to have been *selected*."

"Selected? For what?" a fine-boned, dark-skinned woman asked. The hovering image in Anyess's helmet identified her as Dr. Christina Kwome.

"Building," Anyess said. "Have you ever seen a dry stone wall? Those are composed of individual pebbles and rocks that fit together perfectly without mortar."

"Are you sure that's what these were?" Kwome asked.

"It's a guess," Anyess said, her palms upturned, but the remote possibility set a quiver through her stomach. "We archaeologists guess a lot, but they're educated guesses, based on our observations of other cultures and lifestyles. It's too unlikely that millions of identical pebbles would appear together for no reason—without millions of other size stones mixed in."

Excitement dawned on most of the scientists' faces. Like Campbell, many of them wanted to believe in aliens. Kwome peered back at the cargo net.

"What did they build out of these things? What did these buildings look like?"

"I have no idea," Anyess said. "Without mortar, or chisel marks, or paint, it's going to be difficult to estimate how they were arranged, and how many of them were used where. Archaeologists of the past have been able to reconstruct ancient buildings out of fallen blocks and stones, but those were *in situ*. It would be better if we knew what kind of people lived on this planet—because now we can begin to think that some did. Then we could begin to speculate about the shape of their domiciles and other structures."

"You're pulling this out of your ear, doctor," Moretti said, dryly. "Without organic remains, this still could be a naturally occurring cluster on a planet that blew up. One scenario is just as likely as the other. This isn't a find. It's just a bunch of rocks, identical or not. Sorry to have wasted your time. You can have dinner with us, then Campbell will take you back to your ship."

Moretti's harsh voice sucked all the excitement out of the atmosphere. What he said was true: Anyess had no *real* evidence of an ancient culture. She was unlikely to be able to get funding to explore further. Grant sponsors didn't get excited about rocks, no matter how regular in shape. If it had once been an inhabited planet, anything organic was long gone. No find, no aliens, therefore no money. Humans were still alone. She was going home empty-handed, and would retire without ever achieving her dream. The realization dragged her shoulders down with gloom.

Despite her disappointment, Anyess did her best to be an entertaining guest in the refectory. The dining room cum entertainment center cum assembly hall was as battered and elderly as the rest of the ship, with overhead lights that flickered and occasionally went out, but the food was good. She said so, and Kwome and another female scientist, Dr. Aya Arishi, looked pleased. Dr. Mike Lippert, the team's chemist, had brewed beer to go with it.

"How long ago did this planet shatter?" she asked, scooping up a spoonful of a savory bean dish with a scrap of soft, bubbly injera bread, and following it with the last sip from a bubble container of the delicious homebrew.

"By our estimation on the radioactive half-life," Moretti said. As long as they were talking about scientific fact, he could be expansive, even charming. He handed her another bubble container of beer. "Two point three million years."

"Any idea what caused it?"

The senior officer shrugged. "Don't really care. The mineral wealth in the asteroid belt here will give us all a healthy payout. We'll get paid for the ore we bring back, and we get a finder's fee for steering the mining companies to this spot. The rocks Campbell brought back are junk, but the core of the planet's a jackpot."

He looked pleased with the prospect, but Campbell, Kwome, and at least two of the other crewmembers, had really been hoping for more. Anyess felt sorry for them.

"Well," she said, "don't space those rocks. Load a few on my ship. For further study. Dr. Moretti, I'd like to ask a favor."

Moretti's broad face split in a brilliant smile. "Sure. Name it."

Anyess leaned forward and put a thin, veined hand on his. "I've only watched three-dee videos of the location. Could one of your crew take me out to the site? Even if it's unlikely, I'd like to take images and see if I can get any ideas from the ruins." She gave him a sad smile. "I have come a long way, after all."

Moretti groaned. "Burning fuel hours for a snark hunt? Oh, what the hell. Sure. We'd be happy to oblige. Campbell can take you in one of the scout craft."

"See, this is the area of the video I sent you," Campbell said, his distorted voice in her earbud. "I mean, what you said about there being too many to have come here by chance. Look at them!"

Anyess peered through the transparent shield. Like the three-dimensional video she had studied, millions, perhaps billions, of identical rectangular stones hung in a frozen spray like a photograph of surf hitting rocks, lit from below by the huge white sun. Behind them and lapping up around the array were massive, city-sized chunks of sedimentary rock, some of it fused to clusters of the oblongs. Ayness recorded every kilometer she could. If nothing else, perhaps she could create a computer simulation that put this section of the doomed planet back together, and see if this could have been the remains of a town or city. Her imagination went wild trying to decide what the buildings might have looked like. How did this long-lost people power their city, if they did use artificial power? If they had space travel, did they escape the cataclysm of their world? "We shape our buildings, and thereafter they shape us," the philosopher Winston Churchill had said a couple of centuries ago. What shape were these people?

In the midst of the ruins, something caught her eye. Another rock, but there was something different about it. It was exactly the same shape, but smaller than the others. *Smaller.* Her instincts pinged like alarm bells.

"Dr. Campbell, do you see that?" she asked, aiming a laser pointer at the floating stone.

The young scientist's eyes followed the red dot, and his mouth dropped open.

"Yes!"

"I have to see that. Can you get it for me?"

"Gladly!"

Moretti surveyed the oblong through the plexiglass of the vacuum chamber. Anyess held it gently in the giant waldoes the scientists used for examining large mineral specimens.

"It's just another stone," Moretti said, dismissively. "The same shape, but small. Like I said, nothing special about it."

"It's very special," Anyess said. "Look at the scans on the scope. This one is hollow. It's a box."

"A *box?*" the research chief looked more than dubious.

"Yes. See the seam?" Anyess turned it in one glove and pointed at it with the other. A fine line, narrower than a human hair, ran around the perimeter. "It was split, then put back together."

Moretti shook his head. "We've seen that kind of split in naturally-occurring formations. It could have a crack in it. Ma'am, I can show you stones the size of a city with divisions like that. This could be a geode. All you'll find in it is crystals."

"I think you'll find," Anyess said, her voice catching in her throat with the excitement that threatened to choke her, "that there is a recess inside it, but not a product of nature. I don't know how large, but I will stake my reputation on it. Indeed, I would stake my life!"

The scientist gave her a wry smile. "You don't have to go that far. If it's a box, then open it already. What are you waiting for?"

"I have to document everything with the greatest care," Anyess said. She had to force her racing mind to calm down. Could this be what she had waited for all her professional life? It had to be. "Notepad, bring up the checklist. Record all angles, temperature, chemical composition—everything."

"Yes, Dr. Chopard," the mechanical voice said.

The rest of the crew huddled behind Moretti, watching Anyess document everything she could about the stone. Unlike its millions of gigantic colleagues, this one measured only two and a half meters across by one high and one deep, of the same material and the same origin, but it had been changed, by unknown hands, an unknown eon ago.

"We only have one chance at this," she said. She surrounded the stone and the mechanical gauntlets with an impermeable plastic bag then pulled at each of the halves.

All of them held their breath as the stone opened. A visible wisp of gas, less than a ninth of a cubic meter and tinted faintly yellow, lifted from the center. Immediately, a tube sucked it in and sealed it in an analysis bubble. Anyess prayed that it hadn't missed any. It was the last remaining trace of an atmosphere preserved for millions of years.

"High oxygen content," she said, reading the scopes. "Also high methane. Mostly nitrogen, with sulfur compounds, traces of helium and hydrogen."

"This place would have stunk," Kwome said, her voice hoarse. The others tittered.

"That atmosphere might be the most precious thing about this artifact," Anyess said. No one disputed her use of the latter word. How could they?

It was, as Anyess had predicted, a box. Behind the puff of air, objects tumbled out of it, a riot of color that shocked the eye after the plain surface of the stone. Some were irregular in shape, but the rest were a cloud of oblong blocks of stone, just like the polished rocks that floated in their millions in section eight, except they were colored oxblood red and ochre yellow. Far from being natural extrusions, these could not be anything but manufactured items. Artificial items. Artifacts of *non-human* origin. She knew it, and all the others knew it, including Moretti.

At last.

Anyess let out a breath she didn't realize she had been holding.

"This is a moment in history," she murmured, wishing she had thought of something profound to say should the opportunity ever arise, like Neil Armstrong's "One small step." "Oh, my God, this came from an alien civilization!"

Immediately, all the others grabbed for their personal devices and took images, chattering with excitement.

"This is going to look amazing on my site!" Arishi exclaimed, cradling her mobile phone. "I'll get a billion likes!"

"Take a picture of me with it!" Kwome said, handing her glass bar to Campbell. "Then I'll do one of you!"

"Put those away!" Moretti snapped, turning a baleful eye on his staff. "*No one* posts even a hint of this until I say so! You want to cause a riot across the galaxy? Get a clue! We don't put up anything until we know what we've found! Anyone who disagrees with me can go out the airlock. *Now!*" Grumbling, the others lowered their screens. "Dr. Chopard?" he said, with the first hint of respect he had shown her since she came on board. "What are these?"

Anyess's hands trembled. She scanned each of the objects and recorded their shapes and mass into her recorder. *Why are you so nervous?* she chided herself. Wasn't this why she had studied archaeology, gone for advanced degrees, seconded on every spaceship that would take her out to the far reaches of the galaxy? This was everything that she and myriad others like her had hoped for: proof that humankind was not the only intelligent species out there.

"Who did this belong to? What did they look like? What happened to them?" the others asked, voicing all the questions in Anyess's own mind.

"We'll be debating this for centuries," Anyess said. "But let's take a look at what we have here." She reached for a dark blue device over a meter long that looked as though it would fit into a hand, though not a human one. It had a hole at one end and a squeeze mechanism at the other. Another dark blue object with an obvious barrel was mounted on a flat platform that had two rows of three spheres that would allow it to roll on a surface.

"Those look like weapons," Dr. Lippert said. "I wonder if they still work."

Anyess shook her head. "They're some kind of solid polymer, doctor. No moving parts or power supply that I can see."

"They're probably ritual items of some kind," Dr. Campbell speculated. " — Or training weapons. And there's their target!" He pointed to a red object that tumbled over and over. Anyess reached for it. "It looks like Godzilla!"

"No, it doesn't!" Kwome said, scornfully.

"Well, it kind of does," Campbell said, with a sheepish grin. Anyess had to agree with him. The upright but squat red figure had spines down its back, extending onto a heavy caudal feature like a massive tail. Like the weapons, it had been constructed of a very strong, slightly flexible material. "These aliens look like dinosaurs. Our first alien life forms are dinosaurs!"

"I bet this is their enemy," Moretti said, watching her display it from several angles.

"Why do you say that?" Arishi asked.

He pointed. "Look, it's been hacked with some kind of sharp object. Several sharp objects. Its head is gouged all over."

"Was this its head, or another body part?" Kwome asked, skeptically.

"No, it's the head," Moretti argued. "Look, it has features! It's got eyes, and that's got to be a mouth."

"Those could be simple decoration or important symbols."

Anyess cleared her throat, trying to bring them back from wild speculation.

"So, you all agree that these are artifacts. An artificial object, made by someone."

They all turned to stare at her. "Yes!" Moretti said, then reverted to his native pragmatism. "No. I don't know. But... but, it's *something*. How do we deserve to be the ones who made this discovery?"

"Campbell made it," Kwome pointed out. "You told him it was junk."

Moretti held up his hands. "Okay! So it's not junk. But what were all these used for?"

"You've got a future in xenoarchaeology," Anyess said to the young man. "Tell me a story. What do you think they are?"

"I bet they are ritual items," Campbell said, his face dreamy. "This had to belong to a high priest of some kind. I bet the stones were for casting runes, determining the future of their endeavors."

"You've been reading too many epic fantasies." Lippert laughed. "What is all this really, Dr. Chopard?"

Anyess manipulated the figure, turning it over and over. Yes, this part was clearly meant to sit on a surface. In gravity. As she examined them, she realized that so were most of the others, but a couple were not. She reached for a rainbow-striped cone. As soon as the glove flicked it, it came alive and spun in midair, casting incandescent light in patterns on the wall. The others threw up their hands against the light, but Anyess stared, a smile beginning on her face.

She made a guess, an educated guess, but her gut instinct came to an inescapable conclusion. She saw a picture in her mind as clearly as if the scene unfolded in front of her. Like her own children or grandchildren sitting on the floor of the family home, these objects had been used in the very same way.

"It's a toy box." Anyess held up the red dinosaur-like figure. "This is a doll."

"A doll? What about the damage?" Moretti asked.

"Perfectly natural, if you ever had children, doctor. The child who owned it chewed on its head and loved it almost to destruction. It's damaged, yes, but look! The child considered it too precious to throw away, even when it grew older and had more sophisticated toys. There's plenty of room in this box for little treasures."

"Little?" Dr. Kwome exclaimed. "It's three meters across! That… dinosaur is a meter and a half tall! It chewed on it! With sharp teeth—sharp enough to leave gouges. These people were monsters!"

Anyess shook her head. "Not to its parents. The owner of this box was a child of its kind. Other than far larger than human beings I can't tell you what it looked like, but," Anyess said, as certain as she was of her own name, "it was a child. Not a priest, not a warrior."

"Wouldn't it look the same as that thing?" Moretti asked, his nose almost against the glass.

"Not necessarily," Anyess said, smiling, "any more than you look like the teddy bear you slept with when you were a baby."

"I had a bunny." As soon as the words were out of his mouth, Moretti looked embarrassed. Campbell's face was bright red with the laughter he held in. Anyess smiled at both of them.

"My point stands. We don't know *now*, but we can begin to investigate. We have absolute proof right here of their existence, but who they were we won't know for certain until we cross paths with their many-times descendants, somewhere out there. Which I hope they are."

"You think they still exist?" Dr. Arishi asked. Her eyes were wide with wonder.

Anyess shook her head. "I have no idea what our long-lost friends looked like, or if they knew about the coming destruction of their planet. This may be all that is left of them. I sincerely hope not. But here we have the building blocks for our understanding of their life and culture. I hope we can find more and learn about them. I like what we have found so far. Don't you? I can't wait to share this with the rest of our people. We're not alone. This is our new beginning, and all thanks to this big little child." An honorable retirement for her, and perhaps a new career for the clever young man who had seen possibilities where no one else had. She smiled at Campbell, who blushed.

In her imagination, she pictured a little whoever, hiding her or his or its cherished belongings in its secret chest, meaning to come back to it, but never getting to do so. She hoped it had gone on to a long and happy life somewhere else.

Thank you for your treasures, little one, Anyess thought fondly, spinning the chewed-on lizard statue around and around in her waldoes. *I promise I'll take good care of them.*

THE STUFF THAT DREAMS ARE MADE OF

Christopher L. Bennett

T STARTED WITH A PIRACY ALERT FROM A SHIP THAT COULD NOT POSSIBLY BE under attack. *Chapungu* was a research vessel returning from a Kuiper Belt survey, still in open space outside the Main Belt, with no other drive emissions visible anywhere near it. Since no Strider would be so irresponsible as to fake a piracy alarm, and since invisible ships were a thermodynamic impossibility, Yukio Villareal found the mystery too enticing to pass by. Even with *Seikoku*'s speed and maneuverability, it would take days to rendezvous with *Chapungu*, but his ship would be the first one that could — unless invisible pirates were a thing after all, in which case the situation would definitely call for a Troubleshooter.

Over the following days, further transmissions made it clear that the alleged piracy came from within. The research ship had a combined crew from the Cerean States and Vesta's New Zimbabwe habitat — a rare thing in these divided times. In the seven years since winning independence from Earth, the fiercely autonomous Strider communities of the asteroids had fallen into internecine conflict over resources, territory, and ideology. *Chapungu*'s ambitious Kuiper Belt expedition had been a show of solidarity amid the Troubles, an attempt to stem the dissolution of the wartime Belt Consortium by showing the benefits of continued cooperation. Yet now the Cerean and Vestan segments of the crew were battling for control of the ship, each trying to divert it toward its own home port to take possession of... whatever it was the ship had discovered out beyond Neptune. Both the CS and New Zim had launched military squadrons to intercept *Chapungu*. Other Vesta-orbiting states like Rapyuta and Vestalia had also launched ships toward it, as had several more distant habitats. Even Mars was sending ships. Whatever was on that research vessel, it was about to escalate the Troubles into a full-fledged Solar war.

"And yet you're still racing into the middle of it," Sally Knox told Villareal as he strove to get a bit more thrust out of *Seikoku's* plasma drive. "You really think you can head off a war? One lone Troubleshooter?"

Villareal spread his hands and gave a dashing grin. "There's only one war."

Sally, as always, remained stonily unimpressed by his confident charm. That was why he cherished her so—along with the exceptional administrative skills and pragmatism that anchored his flamboyant heroics. The fact that her meter-twenty frame added only 40 kilos to his ship's mass was helpful too at times like these.

Of course, she had a point. Villareal and the few dozen others like him—Striders who had chosen to use their transhuman modifications or special expertise to protect the innocent in these lawless times—could only accomplish so much acting alone. He had tried to convince the other Troubleshooters that they needed to work as a coordinated, self-regulated group if they wished to make a real dent in the chaos. But people like them—like him—were rugged individualists even by Strider standards, and so far only one other Troubleshooter had agreed even in principle.

As Villareal's sleek, speedy scout ship closed on *Chapungu*, he hailed the vessel, gave his name, and asked to speak to both sides. *"Villareal?"* came the answer from whichever side currently controlled the radio. *"The Troubleshooter? The one they call Shashu? The Archer?"*

"Since you know who I am, friend, let me get right to the point: I'm here to help you resolve this dispute before it becomes a shooting war."

"Yes! Yes! If anyone can, Shashu… But I don't know if the Cereans will agree."

"Well, you're the ones in a position to ask them."

It only took a few minutes before both sides of the ship's crew agreed to a truce, allowing Villareal to board and discuss the situation. "There, you see?" he said to Sally. "Only one Troubleshooter. A symbol is more powerful than a person."

She gave him a sour look. "Which is why it's a difficult thing for a person to live up to. Don't get cocky, and don't get killed."

As the ship docked, Villareal donned his full Shashu armor and made sure his glossy black hair and prematurely graying mustache were well-groomed. Image was vital to his work. As the Troubles had worsened, those transhuman champions who had risked and sometimes given their lives to fight for peace had been mythologized as virtual superheroes, and Villareal had chosen to embrace that inspirational image in full, the better to win the Striders' trust. As Shashu, he wore lightweight, green-and-gold body armor whose stylings suggested a samurai Robin Hood and even included a waist-length, hooded cape. He didn't carry a bow, but his infallible aim with his stylized stun-dart gun—interfaced with the laser targeting of his bionic left eye—added to his reputation as the Archer of the Asteroids.

It was Villareal's hope as he boarded *Chapungu* that his armor would be needed only for show. His reputation as a peacemaker had been enough to achieve a truce; he hoped he could reason, charm, and cajole the crew into making it permanent. He had encouraged the spread of the "Troubleshooter" nickname because it suggested an itinerant problem-solver rather than a warrior. His bionics gave him superhuman combat skills when he needed them, but it was combat that had cost him so much of his original anatomy in the first place. He never wished to inflict that agony on anyone else if he could avoid it.

Villareal was met at the airlock by two women, one strong-featured and brown-skinned with closely shorn hair, the other pale-skinned and plump with pure white hair. "Welcome aboard, Troubleshooter Shashu," said the former. "I'm Captain Veronica Moyo, and this is Doctor Eszter Belasz of New Zimbabwe University." She blinked. "Is it Shashu? Or Villareal-*san*? Or..."

He gave her a charming smile. "Whatever you're most comfortable with, Captain. We're still inventing the etiquette." He furrowed his brow. "It's a pleasure to meet you both, but I'd expected to meet representatives from Ceres as well."

Moyo's expression darkened. "We've isolated them in one side of the habitat module, away from the control room and the labs. They've agreed to grant you safe passage to meet with them. First, though, you need to know what it is we're fighting over—and why there's no way I'll risk letting it fall back into Cerean hands."

The object in the quarantine box was nothing much to look at: an irregular, slightly curved slab of glossy black material the size of a loaf of bread, moderately pitted on its faces and worn and rounded on the edges. It looked like it had been drifting in space for millennia, its original gloss partially worn away by dust strikes. But it was unquestionably a technological artifact.

"You... found this? In the Kuiper Belt?" Villareal asked. His bionic eye seemed to resist focusing on it. He felt a growing sensation of awe and anxiety, as if he were gazing upon something numinous. If the Vestans were telling the truth about its nature, maybe he was.

"In orbit of a small comet," Doctor Belasz answered. "We were drawn there by anomalous magnetic and spectroscopic readings, and we found this, circling it like a tiny moon." The aging scientist sighed. "It's clearly just a fragment of a larger artifact. But we searched the comet exhaustively, scanned back along its orbit, and found no trace of any other pieces."

"'Artifact,'" Villareal breathed. "You've found proof our system was visited by aliens!"

"Extremely long ago," Captain Moyo clarified. "We estimate at least ninety million years."

He stared. "It's not nearly eroded enough for that."

Moyo nodded at it. "Go ahead. Try to touch it."

Villareal approached the workbench atop which the quarantine box was secured. As he moved closer, his sense of anxiety intensified. He realized that the artifact hovered slightly above the bottom of the box, even though the ship was under low thrust, decelerating toward Vesta. He shivered, his shoulders tensing as if some ghostly presence were breathing down his neck.

Let me get right to the point, he thought, using his catchphrase as a focusing mantra. He slipped his hands into the gloves built into the box's side and reached for the artifact. Some invisible force resisted him, growing stronger the closer his fingers came. Even with all his bionic strength, Villareal could not touch the alien object.

"The glove box is just for protocol, and convenience," Belasz said. "Easier to move the thing once we got the box around it. The field prevents any direct contact, although sufficiently fast micrometeoroids can break through to the surface. We don't have anything on the ship powerful enough to get a sample—we've had to rely on non-invasive scans, and even most of those don't work. We think it's surrounded by vacuum-energy fluctuations that are disruptive to many types of detection devices."

"Including bionic eyes," Villareal said.

"And if we *could* touch it, I'm not sure we could cut a piece off. It's incredibly dense, yet relatively light, perhaps porous on the interior. Or maybe it just cancels its own mass."

Villareal stared sharply. His concentration broken, he reflexively jerked his hands free and stepped back, compelled by the aura of anxiety that seemed to surround the item. "You think it could do that?"

"We don't know *what* it can do. But even broken apart and drifting for millions of years, it's still active. That anxiety you feel? It gives off a strong magnetic field that induces that response in many human brains. Hallucinations as well. Ironically, similar magnetic phenomena were known to cause delusions of UFOs and alien encounters back on Earth."

"Ah." That explained the presence he'd imagined.

"The field is strong enough at close range to have a diamagnetic effect," Moyo said, "repelling even organic tissue. It's gotten stronger since we brought it aboard—it absorbs ambient heat, light, even sonic energy as a power source."

Villareal crossed his arms, considering the artifact. "So. We know it's alien, incredibly advanced, and powerful. But we can't touch it, scan it, or sample it, and we have no idea what it does, beyond giving people the heebie-jeebies. Is that about right?"

"It doesn't have to *do* anything," Belasz insisted, a fervent light in her eyes. "Just sitting there, it points us toward multiple scientific revolutions. I suspect it may be some kind of smart matter, engineered at the quark level so that every atom is part of a superpowerful computer. That's the only thing we can hypothesize to account for the vacuum fluctuations."

"Not to mention the way it gathers and harnesses energy," Moyo added. "It could give us more powerful, efficient ships, shielded against impacts or weapons."

"You think too small, Veronica. The data that might be stored in its atoms could reveal the secrets of the universe!"

"I think I see," Villareal said, "why you and the Cereans broke your alliance."

"This was our expedition," Moyo said proudly. "Our chance to show New Zimbabwe's advancement, our prosperity, our commitment to a unified Strider future. We thought the Cerean States shared that commitment when we reached out to them for funding and support. But as soon as our Cerean crew realized what the artifact was, they demanded we bring it to Ceres, insisted they were better qualified to handle and study it. When I reminded them that this was a New Zim ship, they mutinied, tried to force us to divert course. Their distress signal claiming we were the pirates was a sick joke, the classic entitlement of the powerful who see the sharing of power as an assault.

"Which is why you must help us protect the artifact from them, Shashu. The CS is the largest state in the Belt, the most like Earth. Look how quick they are to try to dominate the rest of us. Give them this power and they will try to replace Earth as our masters."

"Please, Shashu, you have to help us liberate the artifact from the Vestans!"

The plea came from Ezequiel Zhang, the gray-haired lead scientist of the Ceres contingent, almost as soon as Villareal had been granted entry into the Cerean-controlled side of the ship. "You know the corruption that's rampant there, the mob violence," Zhang went on. "Oh, Moyo and the others are as honest as Vestans can get, I'll grant that, but there's no way their university administration is free from mob influence. Even if they don't hand it over to the Yohannes syndicate or the *yakuza* voluntarily, it's only a matter of time before it's stolen to adorn some crime lord's trophy room."

"There's far more at stake than that," said Samorn Mendelssohn, the lean, bionic-legged Cerean security officer who'd led what she described as a defense of Chapungu against the attempt of the New Zimbabweans to hijack it from its originally agreed-upon course to Ceres. "The artifact is no mere museum piece. You've been near it, right?" she asked Villareal. He nodded. "Then you've felt it. The presence of God. You've heard Their voice in your head."

"I experienced some sensory effects," he replied with care. Mendelssohn spoke with conviction and wonder, but she appeared rational. "I was told —"

"That it was just a magnetic field inducing hallucinations." She shook her black-braided head. "That's the mechanism, not the meaning. The field just unlocks the part of the brain that lets us commune with the divine. Is it so hard to believe that aliens able to cross the stars and create a device like that would have found a way to come closer to God?"

"If that's so," Villareal said to her, "then shouldn't that opportunity be available to everyone?"

"Yes, then you agree!" Zhang cried, grinning and nodding. "Only the States are strong and unified enough to ensure that. Only we can protect it from the chaos of the rest of the Belt. No offense to you and your fellow Troubleshooters," he added. "You've saved many lives, and of course, we're forever grateful for your role in negotiating the Great Compromise. But I needn't remind you that it was the Vestans who launched that 'stroid at Earth in the first place. You stopped their escalation then, Shashu, and turned that victory into a peace we could all live with. Now you can do it again, by making sure the artifact is in safe, responsible hands."

Back on Seikoku, Sally Knox asked, "So what do you think the artifact is?"

Villareal affected a drawl. "The, uh... shtuff that dreamsh are made of."

The stern features framed by her short, curly blonde hair grew even sterner. "Are you suffering neurological aftereffects from your exposure?"

"Oh, Sally, you have got to let me show you *The Maltese Falcon*. Or a Hitchcock marathon. That alien dingus is a classic MacGuffin."

"A *what??*"

"A MacGuffin. Hitch's term for an object of priceless importance to the characters, but essentially irrelevant to the audience. The secret plans in *North by Northwest*. The uranium ore in *Notorious*. The film barely bothers to explain it, because its nature doesn't matter to the viewer—only the fact that the characters desire it desperately and will do anything to possess it. It doesn't even have to be of real value—it can be a glorified paperweight, so long as the characters *believe* it's worth fighting and dying for. Making it a blank slate lets the audience project their own dreams and desires onto it and identify with the characters' cravings."

Sally nodded. "I see. Since we know nothing about the alien artifact—since it even resists our ability to learn more about it—that gives people an excuse to read whatever nonsense they want into it, to convince themselves it reinforces their prejudices."

"I wouldn't have put it quite so harshly, but you're right. By revealing nothing, it becomes anything and everything. This cosmic MacGuffin is a magnifying mirror for the desires, beliefs, and fears of whoever perceives it. And that makes it incredibly dangerous — even if it doesn't actually do a damned thing."

Over the next few hours, as Villareal contacted the other approaching ships and tried to convince them to stand down, he only received more evidence to support his MacGuffin theory. Their governments or corporate owners had learned of the alien artifact through their spies on Ceres and New Zimbabwe, and all saw different potentials or dangers. The Vestalians wanted to put it on public display as the most priceless extraplanetary gem ever discovered — and to get a head start on prospecting the Kuiper Belt for more like it. The Rapyutajin believed it would let them connect the Striders on a spiritual level and restore balance to the Belt. The ship from Olbersstadt was a known asset of the Yohannes syndicate and was no doubt coming to take it by force. The Martian ships were divided between those who wanted to use the unknowable powers of the MacGuffin in service of their own fights for independence and the corporate-state loyalists who wanted to keep it from them.

And the crew from Bhaskara, an older Inner Belt habitat, simply wanted it destroyed. *"You see how it's already tearing apart what little peace remains,"* the Bhaskaran captain told Villareal. *"Please, Shashu — destroy it for us, so we don't have to take it by force. Stop this war, as you stopped the last one."*

After the captain's face faded from the monitor, Villareal leaned back and brooded. "This is impossible. They should be rejoicing over the confirmation of alien intelligence, but all they want to do is fight to control it. None of them will ever agree to entrust that kind of power to any other nation. They're all too afraid of what it might turn out to be, or too convinced it's exactly what they need."

"Well, there's one thing they all agree on," Sally told him. "They all want *you* to fix the problem for them. The savior of us all, the architect of the Great bloody Compromise, ooh." She waved her stout-fingered hands in the air.

"I just diverted the asteroid, and I had plenty of help on both sides. It was the people we brought to the table after that who worked out the Compromise." He sighed. "Forget my boasting — one lone Troubleshooter isn't enough. And my reputation can only last me so long. We need to work together, to build something with real influence and staying power. We need an agency, a corps."

"It's the other Troubleshooters you need to convince, not me. Maybe what you need is a MacGuffin of your own."

Villareal's eyes widened. He beamed at her. "Oh, my sweet Sally, you've done it again! I'd kiss you if you wouldn't punch me for it."

"Keep dreaming, Yukio—you know I'm way out of your league."

"Don't worry, my friend." His grin grew devious. "My sights are set on a more attainable prize."

It took all of Villareal's charm to convince Moyo and Zhang to meet for peace talks aboard the neutral ground of *Seikoku*—not because they were unwilling, but because precise terms had to be negotiated to guarantee Zhang's safe passage from the Ceres-controlled side of the ship to the main airlock on the New Zim side. Villareal was keenly aware that with every hour's delay, *Chapungu* drew closer to the fleets converging on it.

Once the two factions' leaders had arrived, he greeted them briefly and entrusted them to Sally's care while he bowed out, nominally to finish preparing a special meal for their benefit. In reality, he sealed his Shashu armor, deployed the inflatable emergency helmet in his hood, donned a thruster pack, and exited through the backup airlock. The ships were coasting at the moment, and Sally had hacked *Chapungu*'s external cameras and security system so he could cross to it unseen and enter through its drone bay hatch. The bay was adjacent to the science labs, which should allow him to reach the MacGuffin (as the artifact was now indelibly named in his mind) without encountering any of the crew.

Or so he had thought. No sooner did he exit the inner lock into the drone control room than he was confronted by an armed guard. He had underestimated Moyo; no doubt she'd placed the guard there in case the Cereans tried to enter this way. But from the surprise on the young man's face, he hadn't expected a Troubleshooter. The momentary opening allowed Villareal to quick-draw and fire his tangleweb gun. The sticky fibers immobilized the guard's limbs, adhering him to the adjacent wall. The guard managed to get off a shout for help before Shashu could gag him. That was the tradeoff for not wanting to hurt anyone. His shockdarts were as nonlethal as they could get, but that didn't make them harmless.

Still, Sally's hacks let him seal the lab doors to keep the other guards out for a while. He stopped briefly at the equipment lockers, rummaging through the emergency gear and lab supplies until he found what he needed. Bringing it with him into the main lab, he faced the quarantine box on its central workbench and shot out its lock. Struggling to ignore the crawling of his skin and the hallucinatory aliens whispering in his ear, he worked a mineral sample bag from the lockers around the MacGuffin and its eldritch repulsive field. The bag bulged as if inflated, but at least it was something he could grab and carry.

He barely had time to finish up at the box before the lab doors opposite him slid open. He looked across the workbench to see Moyo and Zhang entering side by side. The captain had a lethal Gauss pistol pointed at his head. "Don't do it, Shashu," she said. "You have no right."

"Do you? Does Zhang? Does anyone?"

"We discovered it! We organized this whole expedition!"

Zhang glared at her. "Which you never could've done without us!"

"That doesn't give you the right to steal it for yourselves!"

"We are the best equipped to study it, to protect it from theft."

"Which one of us has the gun on the thief?" Moyo countered.

"If I may make an observation," Villareal said. "You're both just proving why Solsys can't trust either of you with the MacGuffin."

They stared at him. "What's a MacGuffin?" they said in unison.

Villareal rolled his eyes. *Cinema is dead.*

"Remember who it is you're facing, Captain Moyo," he said, hefting the puffed-out sample bag in his arms. "Do you really think you can stop me?"

"I doubt anyone could be as impressive as your reputation. And I also fought in the war." She gestured with the gun. "My aim may not be bionic, but it's good enough at this range. And I know I can't hurt the artifact."

"Would you really kill to control it? Would you kill *me*? What will history think of you? Of New Zimbabwe?"

"What will history think of you, Archer? How will the Striders trust any of your precious Troubleshooters to keep the peace if you do this?"

"Keeping the peace is exactly what I plan to do. In a more literal sense than you realize."

"You can't destroy it," Zhang said. "Jettison it into space and a dozen ships will track its course."

He looked them over. "Give me an alternative. Show me you can share this discovery for the good of all humanity, like you meant to do when you started this expedition. When you spent months working side by side as partners, as colleagues. When you trusted each other with your lives."

Moyo and Zhang stared at each other. "You did initiate this," Zhang admitted. "I can see a way clear to letting NZU keep the artifact."

"And that is?" the captain asked.

"Relocate your habitat. Join us in Ceres orbit."

Moyo was shocked. "And be overshadowed by you? Colonized by you? You're no better than Earth!"

"You'd rather stay at the mercy of Vesta's crime lords?"

"Better thugs in the shadows than in the government!" She turned back to Villareal, correcting the drift in her aim. "And you! No more distractions. No more silver tongue. Just hand it over!"

"To which one of you?" he asked.

"Me!" they both shouted.

He shrugged. "So be it."

Villareal tossed them the sample bag he held and watched them both grab at it. Moyo let the gun drift, and the two leaders began wrestling over the bag. By the time they pulled it open and discovered the spare inflatable emergency helmet inside, Villareal had already ducked into the drone bay and sealed the door behind him, with the other sample bag containing the real MacGuffin still gripped between his legs.

"Attention, citizens of Sol System," Villareal broadcast from *Seikoku*'s cockpit. "This is Yukio Villareal—Troubleshooter Shashu, as you have come to know me. Let me get right to the point. Many of your leaders are already aware of what I am about to reveal. It is the reason so many nations' fleets are converging on Vesta, ready to go to war. You all deserve to know why they have deemed it necessary to take this action."

He went on to show the ancient alien artifact to the entire system, explaining its origins and nature and transmitting all the scientific data that Chapungu's crew had gathered. It was classified information, but Moyo had not required him to sign a non-disclosure agreement, for she had expected him to side with her voluntarily — just as everyone else had, for they were all (except the Olbersstadt gangsters, presumably) convinced that he would see they were in the right. What he had to do now was get all of them to agree that he was in the right.

"This discovery is too large, too important, to be monopolized by any one state or corporation," he went on. "Any such attempt, as we have already seen, will only breed resentment and conflict. Thus, I have reached an agreement with the discoverers of this remarkable artifact — which, for ease of reference, will henceforth be known as the MacGuffin."

Sally sighed and rolled her eyes.

"From now on," Villareal announced, "the MacGuffin artifact shall be the joint possession of all humanity. To ensure that it is shared freely and available to all, my organization — the Troubleshooter Corps — has agreed to administer it." Sally's disdain gave way to open shock, a far more satisfying reaction.

"As you know, the Troubleshooters are non-governmental special operatives dedicated to preserving peace and protecting human lives. We may appear to act autonomously, but we are united by this common purpose. I and my fellow Troubleshooters come from all across the Belt and serve no state, no corporation, no ideology, no master — only the cause of peace and justice. We have the skill and ability to defend ourselves against all threats, and to cope with unique challenges no other group can handle. Thus, the TC — ah, the TSC — is the entity best suited to watch over this extraordinary discovery." *Should've picked the acronym beforehand,* he thought, annoyed at his fumble. *This* has *to be convincing.*

"The Troubleshooter Corps will make the MacGuffin freely available for any legitimate study by scientists and scholars, either in facilities we will arrange, or at their laboratories under Troubleshooter escort. The rest of the time, we shall protect it from theft by any party and hold it in trust for the good of all.

"It is my fervent hope that, in this way, we can allow this remarkable new insight into the cosmos to unite our species in peace, rather than become an excuse for renewed conflict and division. Let us all move into the future, my friends… together."

The hours that followed made the outcome clear. Neither the Cerean States, New Zimbabwe, nor any other competing nation was happy with Villareal's ultimatum. But the chorus of public opinion was a different matter. Whether they were excited by the potential for new discovery or alarmed by the imagined dangers of the MacGuffin, the masses of Solsys agreed that they would rather entrust the extraordinary artifact to a system-wide corps of superheroes than to any more conventional authority. The governments had little choice but to bow to that consensus and accept the Troubleshooters' guardianship of the artifact. Even the gangsters retreated rather than face an entire corps of heroes.

"Only one problem," Sally said as Villareal accelerated *Seikoku* away from *Chapungu* at last. "There *is* no Troubleshooter Corps."

"There is now — in the people's minds. As with the MacGuffin, it's how the Troubleshooters are perceived that gives us power. Now, with the help of our aloof cosmic paperweight, the Troubleshooters will be seen as a legitimate, unified bloc with a voice in Strider affairs, rather than a bunch of lone wolves with fancy costumes."

"So you're no different from the rest. You're using the MacGuffin to mirror your own agenda."

"At least I'm honest with myself about it."

"If not with anyone else. How do you think the others will react to being involuntarily recruited into your Corps?" So far, the other Troubleshooters had been silent, perhaps out of shock.

"The others understand the value of reputation as well as I do. The perception of unity will make it easier for us to do our work. They'll see they have to make that perception into reality if they want to retain its benefits."

He chuckled. "Besides, none of them will be able to resist getting a look at our marvelous MacGuffin. Whatever that hunk of junk was ninety million years ago, it's an inspiration generator now. And it'll make a fine Excalibur about which to build our Round Table."

Sally remained reassuringly unimpressed. "The stuff your dream will be made of. Well, bully for you. Meanwhile, as always, it'll be up to me to figure out where we're going to *keep* the bloody thing…"

THE BLACK BOX

James Chambers

ENSIGN RANDOLPHA SANCHEZ STARED AT SATURN, THE PLANET INDIFFER-ent and spectral through Titan's immutable atmospheric haze, and fought back tears. Titan Colony Ohio's observation platform afforded a clear view of the Utica Dome wreckage, but she forced herself not to look, fixating instead on the mother planet that filled one-third of the sky. All the colonists accepted the risks when they left Earth but hoped against reason they would beat the odds. Utica reminded them how swiftly Titan's environment could claim their lives. Across Sanchez's view streaked a plume of ice crystals from the dome's ruptured oxygen banks, the frozen tears of a colony spilling from an open wound.

They had lived nearly three years Earth Standard Time without so serious an accident. Now thirty-seven dead, the microbial lab destroyed, and Saturn still hung above them unchanging, uncaring. Its rings appeared utterly still, though Randolpha knew they rotated with an orbital velocity range from the inner rings to the outer of…

She couldn't remember.

Landis would've known. He loved their new home so much, he always knew the things she forgot. She ached to hear his voice and feel his hand on her shoulder, their faces so close their breath mingled as he whispered the answer in her ear.

The new life they meant to live together on this new world, over before it really started.

She lowered her gaze and dared to look.

Bits of Utica's wreckage close to the blown tanks still glowed with fading orange heat fueled by escaping oxygen that froze a moment later. A six-person recovery crew flitted around the debris, protected from temperatures far below zero by winged hot suits.

Thermal insulation and micro-nuclear power cores sustained internal heat at 58 degrees Fahrenheit while powering breathing gear that mixed oxygen with nitrogen from the atmosphere. The outfits' glide sleeve wings allowed the workers to leap and fly thanks to Titan's low gravity and dense atmosphere. As they dipped and swooped, gathering parts and equipment into a surface carrier, the dome resembled a broken toy to Sanchez. It helped her to think of it that way, to visualize it abstractly and keep it at arm's length. But only for a moment. Then the truth of her loss — of everyone's loss — avalanched over her until she wished she were down there with Landis, dead to the pain of her grief.

She shuddered and fresh tears came.

In a few hours, she would leave Titan's surface for the first time since colonial planetfall.

She took comfort in her anticipation.

MISSION ANALYSIS, COLONIAL XENO COUNCIL,
FEBRUARY 28, EARTH STANDARD TIME

On February 6, 23 —, Earth ST, Governor Petrie authorized the launch of the scout ship, *Seeker 2*, from Titan Colony Ohio to investigate the so-called Black Box discovered orbiting Saturn by TCO's chief astronomer and lead intrasolar cosmographer, Dr. Wendy Armitage, who located it via orbital anomalies in the rings. Scheduled to depart on February 7 EST, the mission delayed its launch until February 10 EST following the Utica Dome accident that day and the loss of expedition volunteer, Mission Specialist Landis Kozinski (Xenobiology). In hope of rallying the colonists from their tragedy and providing a productive distraction, Governor Petrie issued a call for a replacement volunteer and pushed the launch back only three days. On February 10 EST, a crew of four — Captain Nick Holbrook, Mission Specialist Lee Okahara (Intrasolar Astronomy), Mission Specialist Piotr Atwatunde (Xenogeology), and Dr. Kozinski's replacement Ensign Randolpha Sanchez (Engineering) — departed Titan Colony Ohio's spaceport at approximately 17:23 EST and slightly over five days later reached their objective at approximately 19:54 EST. They established orbit in tandem with the Black Box above the central plane of Saturn's middle rings. Initial spectral analysis and visual observation confirmed Dr. Armitage's assessment of the manufactured nature of the object but revealed nothing of its purpose or origin. At 04:37 the next day, Governor Petrie authorized contact.

The crew of Seeker 2 prepared for and executed a difficult space-walk, avoiding contact with nearby objects. Forty-three minutes later two of the crew touched down on the Black Box.

The sight of the Black Box fulfilled a lifelong desire of Piotr Atwatunde.

No longer need he wonder if humanity alone occupied the universe for here before his eyes floated an object singular in all of human history and proof of sentient life superior to that found on Earth. Seen firsthand, it defied Dr. Armitage's description as a "black box." Though its cubic dimensions suggested the shape, its skin appeared light deflective rather than black. Seen in the close, direct glare of their helmet-mounted lamps it displayed a dull, shimmering magenta hue. Piotr set down on the surface, and Sanchez arrived a few meters away. Their magnetic boot pads found sufficient iron content to hold them firm. They waited while their sensors scanned the object and delivered initial telemetry to *Seeker 2*.

Piotr took the first step along the surface. He and Sanchez had landed roughly centered on one side and the edges lay half a kilometer in every direction. Holbrook activated the exterior lights on *Seeker 2*, hanging above them, transforming the murky, smooth surface into a patchwork of magenta tiles, lines, and depressions, all comprised of squares of varying size. Every line Piotr followed formed part of a square, every square part of a larger square. They spied no openings or windows nor any means of propulsion.

"You seeing all this with us?" Piotr said.

"Roger," Holbrook radioed back from *Seeker 2*. "Transmission is clear and relaying to TCO Council HQ."

"It's astounding," Okahara said from the ship. "Fantastic. Truly extraterrestrial."

"Indeed," Piotr said. "It must have been here for thousands of years, maybe more. Where did it come from? Who built it? What does it do? How did it come to be here?"

"Whoa, slow down, Piotr," Okahara said. "We're all wondering the same things. Let's go one step at a time."

"Whatever, Lee," Piotr said. "I left Earth because I believed something better *must* exist. A world and a race without genocide, hate, and war, without rape and corruption, and that only such a unified and consciously moral and compassionate race could muster the will and resource to travel among the stars. This proves me right, no? How does it feel to find proof we're part of an inferior, cockroach species, confined to our own solar system by our ineptitude, too busy killing and devouring one another to ever achieve greatness? It stings, no? But now you can all accept what I already know."

"Stow it, Dr. Atwatunde," Holbrook said. "For all we know this is a suitcase that bounced off some alien's luggage rack. Get off your soap-box. Focus on the work at hand. Worry about what it all means later."

"Yes, yes, fine," Atwatunde said. "Sanchez and I are moving to the next side."

"Moving with you," Holbrook said.

Seeker 2's navigation rockets burned for seconds and the ship's lights painted another side of the Black Box, casting Atwatunde's and Sanchez's long shadows across the structure. The pair crossed the square and continued. Servo-cameras on their shoulders recorded everything around them, 360 degrees. Everywhere, they saw only squares within squares. They crested the next edge and explored a new side. More squares appeared in *Seeker 2*'s lights.

"Do you think it's hollow?" Okahara asked. "Our scans for density are inconclusive."

"How would I know, Lee?" Atwatunde said. "Maybe a couple of aliens will pop out and invite us in for tea and show us around."

"Sanchez, you've been awfully quiet. What do you see?" Holbrook said.

"Squares, sir. Everywhere I look I see squares," Sanchez said.

"Investigate one more side and then return to the ship," Holbrook said. "You're almost at your life support midpoints."

"Wait! Look there."

Sanchez angled her lights along an array of tiny, equal squares comprising a rectangular patch, a large break in the pattern of the object's skin.

"What is it?" Atwatunde said.

"The only non-square we've seen so far. The material looks differ-ent. More ceramic than metal. Or perhaps metal coated with powdered ceramic." Sanchez crouched. "Whoa! Did you see that?"

"What? Where are you looking?" Atwatunde said.

"Watch this."

Sanchez passed her gloved hand over the uniform, square tiles as if testing the heat of its surface. In response, the tiles wavered. Their substance shimmered and drifted along the trail of her fingers. She lowered her hand, and they bowed inward as if pushed down by an invisible ball between her palm and the tiles. She withdrew, and they flattened.

"Astounding," Atwatunde said. "Let me try."

He knelt beside Sanchez and played the trick himself, watching the ripples within the tiles and then flexing their aggregate surface up and down.

"What if I do this?"

He reached down until the flexing tiles parted, exposing a black opening.

Lowering his hand farther widened the opening until his lights exposed a compartment beyond it. Sanchez leaned over and added her lights to his, revealing a magenta room with walls formed of more small tiles.

"It's some kind of door," Atwatunde said.

"Okay, good work," Holbrook said. "Bring yourselves back to *Seeker 2* so we can make sense of this and confer with the Colonial Council about next steps."

"Roger, Captain, but, ah…," Atwatunde said, "…whatever field controls these tiles seems to have locked on my hand. I can't pull loose."

"Sanchez, help him," Holbrook said.

Sanchez gripped Atwatunde's arm and lent him her strength. "Pull, Piotr!"

"I am pulling. Do you think I am not pulling? Of course, I am pulling! Something's pulling me the other way. What is…?"

Atwatunde pitched forward, dragging Sanchez with him. The tiles curved into a funnel. Atwatunde vanished inside it, and then the tiles sealed themselves tight after him, clamping tight against Sanchez's waist. The tiles crushed her. A crystalline stream of air jetted from her suit. Her scream filled the comms. The tiles reopened, and she sank into the Box, the aperture resealing itself after her.

MISSION ANALYSIS OVERVIEW, COLONIAL XENO COUNCIL,
FEBRUARY 28, EARTH STANDARD TIME

Atwatunde reported a force pulling him and Sanchez into a square room with walls made of the same miniature tiles they encountered on the Black Box surface. Radio contact continued for a time but telemetry failed immediately as did all exterior sensors on the pair's spacesuits. The tiles had seriously injured Sanchez and compromised her suit. She sealed her suit breach but could not move her legs. Advised by Holbrook and Okahara from the Seeker 2, Atwatunde attempted to exit the Box. The interior tiles, though, did not respond to his touch. Within the uniform walls, he soon lost his sense of which of the six surrounding panels had admitted them. Sanchez's damaged suit quickly bled out its remaining life support resources. By the time Atwatunde's systems hit critical he had made no progress toward freeing himself and remained unsure of the environment within the compartment due to sensor failure.

Holbrook and Okahara attempted a rescue, sending Okahara to the Black Box to activate the opening from the exterior in hopes of freeing her crewmates. Tethered to the Seeker 2, she traveled to the object's surface. All communication from Atwatunde and Sanchez ceased at that time, indicating the prospect that Okahara might only recover rather than rescue her crewmates. She found the surface as described: magenta in close light and comprised of an infinite variety of squares. The tiles of the rectangular access point reacted to her presence, but her lights revealed only more tiles on the other side, no sign of her crewmates.

Reviews of Okahara's suit cam recording (files attached) confirm her report.

Seeking her crewmates, Okahara lowered herself into the opening. The tiles closed after her, leaving a gap around the tether line. Inside, Okahara discovered Atwatunde's and Sanchez's spacesuits, floating discarded in the chamber, no other sign of their occupants. She, too, failed to manipulate the inner walls, even when pressing her fingers into the gap around her tether to pull them open. She then requested Holbrook remove her by withdrawing the tether. The force within the Black Box intensified, though, until its opposition to the Seeker 2 risked impact between the ship and the Box. Captain Holbrook's quick disconnection of Okahara's tether and firing all nav engines at full power kept the ship from colliding with the Black Box.

He briefly resumed radio contact with Okahara, who acknowledged his correct decision to protect the ship. He then lost contact. Checking her last logged suit telemetry, Holbrook saw Okahara's life support nearly exhausted.

Okahara found the life support resources in Atwatunde's and Sanchez's suits run down to null and Sanchez's irreparably damaged as she examined them.

Nervous, she checked her own reserves and discovered them draining at an alarming rate.

Even if she escaped the Black Box, she lacked the air and power to return to the *Seeker 2*.

Her calls to Holbrook remained unanswered, as if the Box had cut her off.

She prodded the impassive walls, poked around in every corner. If she couldn't leave she wanted to explore, but the tiles imprisoned her. Everywhere she looked, she saw neat, identical, squares, each one built of many smaller squares, which in turn held still smaller squares. She wondered what a microscope would reveal.

Her air grew stale. Alert lights flashed in her helmet.

She gasped for breath. Soon her vision grayed and cold crept into her.

Her life support had drained impossibly fast, and external sensors failed.

She controlled her breathing and hung on as long as she could.

When pain filled her empty lungs, and her chest ached, she said, "The hell with it," and released her helmet to float along with the other discarded gear, surrendering to the instinct to breathe. Instead of the freezing blast she anticipated, soft warmth tickled her face. She gasped and inhaled sweet air. The ache in her chest subsided. Her breathing calmed. Her sight cleared. A sinking feeling gripped her stomach as artificial gravity activated. She dropped alongside the discarded equipment onto a panel of the room. She no longer knew which one in relation to the entrance.

The next moment fire ignited in her skin, and she screamed, batting at herself.

No, not fire, she realized, calming.

Itching.

Every inch of her flesh itched as if a cloud of mosquitoes had fed on her.

She scurried out of her suit, driven by the unbearable irritation of it against her skin, pausing to rub her flesh raw as each piece came off until she stood in her underwear, gear piled around her. The itching subsided. Aside from streaks of red where she'd clawed herself, her skin appeared fine. The sugary taste of the air lingered on her tongue.

She stowed her gear with Atwatunde's and Sanchez's in a corner then leaned against a wall and closed her eyes.

A screech of static startled her. It pierced her ears for nearly a minute, rising and falling in modulation, a pattern she couldn't decode. When it ended, she shut her eyes once more and fell back against the wall.

The tiles gave way under her weight.

Okahara fell through into an adjoining chamber formed of yet more squares.

The wall closed behind her.

She climbed to her feet. Square buttons, meters, and oscillators blinked and jumped on the walls of this new space.

A gluey wetness tickled Okahara's bare feet. The square beneath them exuded an oily, amber fluid that rose to her ankles. More sugary air whooshed into the room. A series of deep thuds above her preceded a square panel opening to permit the descent of a shimmering cube formed of the same oil, held in shape by an invisible force. The oil at her feet cemented her in place as the cube—large enough to contain her—lowered, running down her face like warm shampoo. She held her breath as long as she could. When she finally gave out, the syrupy fluid flooded her throat.

The cube completed its descent.

Underfoot, the floor panel opened. The gelid prison descended into the Black Box, taking Okahara with it.

Mission Analysis Overview, Colonial Xeno Council, February 28, Earth Standard Time

Holbrook attempted for three hours to reestablish communication with Atwatunde, Okahara, and Sanchez. He observed and recorded the Black Box, which showed no outward signs of activity during that time, and maintained steady communications with Council HQ, who advised him to maintain orbit and wait. What occurred in the subsequent hours remains uncertain. Holbrook suffered a memory loss from approximately 16:13 to 19:22 hours. He watched the Black Box from *Seeker 2* up until 16:13 — when consciousness returned, he found himself piloting *Seeker 2* back to Titan with Okahara and Sanchez on board. Holbrook has no recollection of how they returned to the ship. His memory resumes with his hands at the *Seeker 2*'s controls, the Black Box already a hundred thousand kilometers distant.

Okahara and Sanchez declined to discuss with him their experiences inside the Box or what had happened to Atwatunde. Sanchez refused to remove Atwatunde's space suit, which she had taken for her return. Holbrook reports they spoke only in whispers to each other for the trip home, isolating him. He felt threatened by the uncertainty and exclusion, by "sidelong glances" in his direction, and a sense of condescension as if they no longer viewed him as their mission leader but as a hired pilot. Okahara seemed most like herself. Sanchez shirked all her duties and spent her time reading and rereading reports from the Utica Dome accident investigation.

Debriefings of Okahara and Sanchez agree they saw no signs of extraterrestrial life on board. The ship appeared to work automatically, fueled by an unidentified power source.

Okahara posited the Box as an "automatic alien ambulance" that allows injured or sick beings to "fall" inside the "airlock" but contains them until it heals their illness or injury. As a function of the treatment process, the Box interferes with life support, draining it, and forcing entrants from their spacesuits before infusing their bodies with nanite-laden air that reports their biology and health status to the Box's operating system. The burning/itching sensation Okahara experienced, a side effect of the nanites, motivates the patient to remove any gear that could hamper treatment. How the Box might treat incapacitated patients remains unknown.

Okahara suggested the Box's light-absorbent exterior camouflages it at a distance and that the Box may even have caused Holbrook's blackout to conceal its location.

Two members of this council believe Okahara withheld information observed or received inside the Box, although she has cooperated more fully than Sanchez, who has refused to remove Atwatunde's spacesuit since returning to TCO, and, during the Council's entire investigation, has single-mindedly demanded access to Utica Dome, which the Council has refused.

Sanchez confirmed, however, that, consistent with Okahara's experience, both she and Atwatunde "fell" from the airlock into adjoining chambers where cubes formed of an unknown, highly viscous substance contained them and proceeded to "heal" them. She noted that the pain of her injuries vanished the moment the cube made contact with her.

In her debriefing, Okahara described this experience as follows (full transcript attached):

> OKAHARA: Light. Warmth. Flavors—weird, I know, but there they were, salty, sweet, and acidic, like it was cycling through for the one I liked best. It settled on strawberries. Not real ones. The kind used to flavor candy. Artificial strawberry. I've always loved that taste. Light refracted in the fluid and created shimmers, especially bright to my peripheral vision. Inside the cube was peaceful, like watching a fireworks show too far off to hear the shells burst. The fluid massaged me. It took tissue samples and drew blood right through my skin. First, it studied me to... well, I think to determine what sort of being I am. Has it ever met a human before? Is our DNA in its memory? It couldn't have been, right? Whoever made the Box would've stocked their own DNA and that of other species they knew, not humans—although we're there now. Considering what it did to Sanchez, I'd say it recognizes multiple forms of life and attempts to find genetic analogs when it encounters a new one. Missing a leg or your skin's burned down to bone? It replaces it with the closest match in its data and improves it if it can. That's what it did to Sanchez, but it repairs everything it identifies as damage, physical and psychological. It not only heals your wounds, it fulfills your needs. To put soldiers right back in battle, better and stronger, more resilient to whatever injured them, readier to focus on their objectives. It heals and enhances.

In later sessions, Okahara divulged that she and Sanchez encountered Atwatunde after the Box released them. It had fully healed

Sanchez by this time. The three came together in yet another square chamber where their gear awaited them. She saw no physical alteration in Atwatunde but knew the Box had enhanced him in response to its "diagnosis," because Atwatunde refused to leave. "You know Piotr is so damn cynical," she stated. "The Box gave him what he wanted most, and what he most wanted was to be proven right." As she and Sanchez donned spacesuits, fully recharged by the Box in an unknown manner, their suit cams recorded Atwatunde (videos attached) gesticulating and yelling. The following excerpt represents his state of mind:

> ATWATUNDE: I'm better now. You understand? Better than you, better than anyone else. Yes, yes, I was always better than you all, but the cube made me even more so. You're not fit to lick my shoes now! I must be patient with you, like a parent with a feebleminded child. I'm superior to you all. I never belonged on a planet as primitive as Earth, much less that toxic wasteland, Titan. I belong in the stars, out there, with them, on other worlds, better worlds humans will never reach. I've always known the truth in my heart, but I suppressed it out of fear humanity would reject or ostracize and condemn me. I was never meant to be part of you! I only need to prove it to the Healers and then the Box will take me to the better life I was born to live! I'm never going back to living on that cloud-choked hell of a world. The only good thing ever about Titan was that it wasn't Earth! I'm going to prove myself by healing the colony, healing Earth, healing all of you!

Dr. Armitage's recent observations of the Black Box place Atwatunde's words in an alarming context. She has tracked several changes in the Box's orbit, culminating in steady motion on a trajectory predicted to intersect with Titan within two days as of this writing. This morning, Sanchez removed her spacesuit.

In the ensuing chaos, she injured two council members and several security personnel.

Sanchez slammed her fists against the small table top in her quarters.

The council investigators seated across from her jumped.

"Please calm down, Ensign," Council Member Isadore Bartlett said.

Beside her, Council Member Takeshi Verde offered a sympathetic expression. "If you'd only talk to us. We want to help you. We want to understand."

"Let me leave. That's all you need to understand," Sanchez said.

"Remove your suit, and we'll do what we can to persuade the council to approve your request," Verde said. "Surely you understand their reluctance since you've told us so little of your experience inside the Box, while Dr. Okahara has been most cooperative."

"Don't trust, Okahara."

"Why not?" Bartlett said.

"Let me out!" Sanchez said.

Verde shook his head. "Remove your suit. Let us see how the Box affected you."

Tension filled the room for long seconds before Sanchez stood and raised her hands to her helmet. "You know what? Fine. There's no time left for this. I tried. I really did try to do this the right way."

She disengaged her helmet and raised it.

The atmosphere in the room changed as gasses bled from within her suit and mixed with those outside it. Sanchez gasped, struggling to breathe the air with human lungs reduced in size to accommodate new ones the Box had grafted into her. The council members coughed as the filtration system kicked in to correct the shifting nitrogen-oxygen balance.

Sanchez's spacesuit fell away. She stepped out of it and stretched, raising her arms. The fleshy pink membranes spanning from her wrists to ribcage snapped taut. Her coarse, thickened skin scraped and rustled with every move. Five magenta squares, each made of smaller squares, hung from her waist on a belt of square links.

"I'm going to Utica Dome now, to heal them. Please don't try to stop me," she said.

Her voice, much deeper than it once had been, resounded in the small room.

Bartlett and Verde recoiled. Sanchez sensed their instinctive disgust at the shock of her transformation. She saw to the equal fascination in their eyes, the slow return of control as they formulated questions she had no will to answer. She hated the way they looked at her, hated their repulsion, their curiosity — their excitement at her altered body. She needed the one who would understand it best. She would hold him again and make him like her.

Together they would put things right; they would fix the broken toy.

Sanchez flipped the table at the council members, knocking them both to the floor.

Bartlett screamed for the guards posted outside.

Three burst through the doorway and froze at the sight of Sanchez.

She used their surprise to her advantage, pushing the upended table at them, crushing all of them aside then fleeing.

Her new shape and metabolism slowed her down, made her awkward, but no one tried to stop her. They stood rooted to the ground and gaped as she passed them, the squares bouncing at her hips. She made for the nearest airlock and relaxed only once the inner doors sealed behind her, and the vents switched on. External air blew in, surrounding her in a haze. She looked at her altered shape, shadowy in the yellowish light, thankful for the mist, grateful it hid her from the peering eyes at the porthole window, that it hid her from herself.

The outer doors opened.

She inhaled deeply, her old lungs closing, her new lungs rejoicing.

The cold barely penetrated her new, tough flesh.

She stepped out, spread her arms, leapt—and flew.

Mission Analysis Overview, Colonial Xeno Council, February 28, Earth Standard Time

This investigation can offer no substantive explanation for Sanchez's altered physiognomy. The attached videos show her active and surviving on Titan's surface without an environmental suit. She flies in the same manner as our winged hot suits, relying on Titan's low gravity and gliding through the dense atmosphere. A security team has monitored her since she exited the colony, keeping a distance to avoid sparking another violent outburst. In the hours since, she has unearthed 28 of 37 corpses from the Utica Dome wreckage and gathered them at the far edge of the ruins. Sub-freezing temperatures appear to have greatly slowed their decomposition, although several of the bodies show signs of grievous injury, limb loss, and decapitation. After completing her efforts, Sanchez placed a cube from those strapped to her waist upon each body. As she depleted her supply, the leftover cubes reconfigured themselves into two smaller cubes at her waist. The dispensed cubes soon enlarged by an unknown means until each one fully contained a single corpse. The magenta sheen of the cubes then faded to amber.

At this time, Dr. Armitage alerted the council to an abrupt increase in the speed of the Black Box, reducing its estimated arrival time from 48 hours to 12.

From the observation deck, the full council watched the shocking occurrences in what remained of Utica Dome. After eleven hours "incubation time," the amber cubes thinned, grew translucent and allowed all to see movement inside. Though no one wished to accept it, no other explanation seemed plausible but that the cubes had miraculously reanimated the dead colonists. Over the next hour, the cubes dissipated into Titan's haze, exposing 28 healed colonists, limbs restored, bodies altered in a manner similar to Ensign Sanchez's. Thick-skinned and deformed, they walked in Titan's open atmosphere. They jumped and glided. For a while they simply moved, testing and adjusting to their transformed bodies.

They later gathered around Sanchez, who singled out one among them, recognizable as Mission Specialist Landis Kozinski. The two embraced. The others encircled them, reverent in their presence until they parted, and the group then set to salvaging debris, creating makeshift shelters.

At the council's order, the security team approached.

Sanchez, Kozinski, and three others quickly turned them back.

They promised they meant no harm to anyone and would allow them to inspect Utica Dome once they prepared it sufficiently, citing a lack of time before an important event would occur. At this time, the Black Box appeared to the naked eye in Titan's sky, beating out all of Dr. Armitage's estimates. Okahara, who had remained in quarters during these events advised the Colonial Council to prepare for conflict.

> Okahara: That will be Piotr. He's here to destroy us all. I told you the Box healed and enhanced. It rebuilt the wounded to better prepare them to meet their goal. Imagine soldiers focused on a single objective, falling into the box, then emerging better equipped to concentrate and deal with the ever-changing conditions of combat. Your enemy has a secret weapon? One survivor returns to the

Box and updates the programming to make all those healed later resistant. Your enemy is physically superior? Not so after the Box fixes you. Your adversary holds an intellectual or psychological advantage? The Box corrects for that as well. It did no less for each of us. But ask yourselves this: What did each of us perceive as our objective or opponent? Because the Box only sees things in terms of conflict. It didn't reveal who made it or how it came here, but that much was very clear. Sanchez wanted to make her life on Titan. Piotr wanted freedom from the limits of his humanity. He overlooked the irony that he received it from a war machine. And, yes, I see your question. What about me? I love humanity, and I love Titan. When Piotr lands, I'm going to take the Box from him and use it to heal everyone and set all humankind free.

The Council ordered a security team to take Okahara into custody. As they approached her, she emitted an unknown form of energy that killed the entire team instantly. Okahara stated their deaths meant nothing because they would be healed and restored once she seized the Box from Atwatunde. She then killed most of the Council to stop them from interfering with her. She did the same to any who opposed her. Only three members of the Council escaped. We complete and transmit our report to Earth in hopes of warning you. The power contained within the Box relates purely to conflict. It heals only to better destroy. We cannot explain its origins or how it came to orbit Saturn. We cannot guess how the conflict about to begin here on Titan will end. Whatever the outcome, Earth must prepare.

Standing atop a shattered wall at Utica Dome, Sanchez watched the Black Box descend through Titan's clouds. Landis joined her, taking her hand in his. Behind them, others of their new kind gathered. Sanchez unleashed an ardent cry that carried deeply through the air.

The Black Box touched down, swirling the yellow haze.

Sanchez leapt and spread her wings. Landis launched at her side.

The others like them followed, each one echoing her defiant call.

THE PUZZLE

Keith R.A. DeCandido

"OKAY PEOPLE, HERE'S THE STORY."

Michaela Kralnova spoke to all the assorted engineers and technicians in her employ, assembled in the meeting room.

"LES has finally cleared the Spire after the meteor strike yesterday, so the repair crews can go in. That means us."

Sitting between an engineer and a technician, Engineer-in-Training Consuela de la Vega clutched a mug of the terrible coffee that Michaela provided for staff meetings. Normally, these meetings were held a few hours later, but time was of the essence. And with the Spire out, nobody's fone was working, so Afeo Akingola, one of the engineers, had come to Connie's bunk to fetch her physically rather than calling her in. She in turn had been asked to do the same for four other employees until they were all together.

"Tsukuyomi has assigned us to fix the antenna," Michaela said, referring to the company that owned the Spire, as well as the dome in which they all lived and worked. "I have to say, this is a coup for us. That's the most important part of the Spire, and *we* get to fix it instead of Khonsu or one of the other companies. I'm putting Engineer Akingola in charge of the specific repair schedule and assignments, but every single one of you will be working. Trust me, the job is big enough to warrant it."

"The *antenna's* big enough," the technician next to Connie muttered.

Connie hadn't actually been asleep when Afeo came to get her, as she'd been working on her homework. Michaela was paying for her long-overdue certifications to be an engineer instead of a technician. She had the ability, but not the paperwork—that cost money—but Michaela was willing to cover the cost as long as she committed to continue working for Kralnova Fine Repairs.

The problem was that she was still working for Kralnova, and they'd all been working overtime thanks to all the meteor strikes.

The one on the Spire was the worst, though. It had severely curtailed lunar communications and completely cut off all communications traffic off the moon. They had no means to send a message to Earth or the asteroid belt or the Mars base, or to any ships or satellites, and no means to receive anything sent from any of them. But repairs couldn't even be started until Lunar Emergency Services gave word that all the personnel in the Spire were evacuated and being treated and that it was structurally sound enough for the repair teams to go and do their jobs.

"The good news," Michaela continued, "is that our internal links are working again thanks to Engineer Bresci and Technician Hsu, so check your pads for your assignments."

Connie set her coffee down on the floor by her feet and pulled her pad out of her pocket. It had crashed, so she had to wait for the startup sequence to run before seeing that Akingola had assigned her to assist Allison Stein with repairing the lower junctions.

"Let's get moving, people," Michaela said, clapping her hands, and everyone got up. "There's a shuttle that will take us to the Spire, so follow me out."

As everyone filed toward the exit, Connie went to Afeo. "Why did you team me up with Allison? I can do those repairs, or she can—it doesn't need two of us."

"You're an engineer *in training*," Afeo said, "and this is too important for us to screw up. As far as I'm concerned, you're a tech for this job."

Connie swallowed her objections—she'd spent her entire time at Kralnova being told that she was "just a tech," and shouldn't try to do the engineers' jobs. That she was an engineer trainee due to her great skill had done nothing to slow that down. But she also knew better than to object to someone who still outranked her in the corporate structure.

Afeo went on: "Also it *does* need two people just for speed—there's seventy-four lower junctions and they *all* need to be checked, repaired, and tested."

"Okay," Connie said with a sigh. She couldn't deny that particular truth. The moon was completely cut off from outside contact and had its inside contact compromised. Speed was more important than anything right now.

The nice thing was that Allison didn't share Afeo's bias against Connie's abilities. The lower junctions were all in a circle around the base of the antenna, and once they arrived at that spot, Allison said, "Look, this is gonna take forever as it is. I'll start here and work my way clockwise, you go counter-clockwise, and we'll be done when we meet back up."

Connie nodded, relieved.

"Figure we can cover this in three hours?"

Shrugging, Connie said, "Maybe? I mean, we haven't seen the damage yet, so it's hard to tell."

They divided up the bag of replacement parts and started on the repairs.

The first two junctions simply had parts that were damaged by the meteor strike and needed to be replaced. Connie did that, and tested them. The third was all clear, but the fourth had not just damaged parts, but also frayed wiring. That wasn't from the meteor strike, that was just maintenance that needed doing, but Connie couldn't just let it go. She stripped the frayed wires and replaced them with new insulation.

As she went, she kept finding tiny objects. At first, she thought they were just debris, but after the fifth one, she realized that they were all faceted. After the tenth one, she looked more closely to see that they were all octagonal.

By the time she was through twenty-one of the roughly thirty-seven junctions she was responsible for repairing, she'd collected twenty of the tiny octagons. Since she was getting thirsty, and she was ahead of schedule—it had only been an hour, and she was more than halfway done—she took a break for some water and a quick snack.

After choking down a Zwaren Bar—it tasted like sawdust, but it fit in a pocket of her jumpsuit, was dirt cheap, *and* contained a full meal's worth of nutrients—she washed it down with water from her canteen.

Then, on a whim, she picked up one of the octagons, held it in her palm, and poured a bit of water onto it, just to remove the dust and dirt.

As the liquid cascaded down onto her palm, the gunk of space sluiced off, revealing that each of the eight sides was a different color. One was red, one pink, one orange, one maroon, one purple, one blue, one turquoise, and one teal.

Pocketing the clean octagon with all the still-dirty ones, she got back to work.

By the time she linked back up with Allison, she had completed repairs on forty-two junctions.

"Nice work," Allison said as she finished off her thirty-second. "I had three that needed complete replacement, that's why it took so long."

Connie swallowed. She decided not to tell Allison that she had five such junctions, and still got more done in the time than Allison did.

Instead, she asked, "Hey, did you find anything like this?" She pulled a couple octagons out of her pocket.

"Yeah, a ton. I tossed them into the waste bag. You kept them?" Allison chuckled.

Shrugging, embarrassed, Connie said, "I think they're nice."

"Whatever. Sorry I didn't save them for you."

"It's okay."

After they finished their work, they climbed down the scaffolding to the base of the Spire and reported to Michaela—in person, as their fones still weren't working.

"Good work, you two," Michaela said, consulting her pad. "Allison, they need another engineer at the top level. That's it, though, everyone else is going along nicely. Connie, you can go home and get some rest. We'll get back to our usual routine tomorrow."

Connie frowned, recalling her original schedule for today before the meteor strike on the Spire sent everything into chaos. "If you don't need me here, I can go do the Sunnasdottir job."

Michaela blinked. "Um—" She shook her head. "Honestly, we told all our clients that everything's on hold until the Spire's fixed, but we're on schedule so…" She smiled. "Yeah, sure. Thank you, Connie, that's very thoughtful. You sure you don't want more sleep?"

"I'm fine." She was still running on adrenaline from all the work, and she wouldn't be ready to sleep for several more hours. And the Sunnasdottir job was a simple repair of a cooling unit.

"Okay, get over there, then."

Connie finished the Sunnasdottir job in an hour. This pleased Olga and Markus Sunnasdottir no end, as they had expected their storage facility to remain sweltering for another day after the Spire was damaged. They even tipped her for her time, something she had rarely experienced.

Once that was done, she went back to her bunk.

All Connie could afford was a spot in QuikBunk, a facility that held five hundred bunks, two meters long by one meter high by one meter wide. She used the same bathroom that twenty-five other units used.

The bunk itself was private, if small, and also comfortable, as long as you didn't sit up too fast. She crashed as soon as she got back from Sunnasdottir, the all-nighter combined with doing two jobs exhausting her.

When she awakened, she pulled the octagons out of her pockets. The one clean one was dusty again thanks to sharing a pocket with the others, and she decided to head to the communal bathroom and wash them all.

As she clambered out of her bunk and climbed down the ladder to the floor, she frowned. Something seemed off.

Once she jumped down the last meter to the floor, she examined the semi-clean octagon again.

The colors were the same, but they were in a different sequence. She could swear that the red one was surrounded by the maroon, orange, pink, and purple, yet now the four sides adjoining the red side were turquoise, teal, blue, and orange.

Instinctively, Connie thought, *I must have misremembered.*

As she went to the large communal bathroom at the end of the hall, she reconsidered that reflexive belief—honed over most of her short lifetime—that she was likely mistaken. It was getting away from that mindset that brought her to the moon in the first place, and it was being beaten down by that mindset that kept her an overqualified tech for so long.

She was an engineer-in-training, dammit, and the colors *had* changed.

Upon arriving in the bathroom, she nodded to those going out, and the one person by the sink.

As Connie rinsed the octagons, a voice came from behind her.

"Hey, Connie, shouldn't you be out fixing the Spire?"

It was Raisa Slavasevitch, who had the bunk beneath Connie's, and who was stepping out of the shower. A janitor at the Lunar Academy, she'd been working nights lately, so she was probably just getting ready to start her shift.

As Raisa toweled herself off, Connie said, "We got our part of it done, so Michaela let me come home."

"Okay." Raisa wrapped the towel around her chest and came over to peer at what Connie was doing. "What the heck are they?"

"Some objects I found in the Spire. Probably from the meteor."

Raisa watched as Connie patted the octagons dry. They all had a similar color pattern to the first, though the colors themselves varied from octagon to octagon. Some were brighter, some duller, some darker, some lighter. But no two were alike.

"Damn, now I wish I had asked Allison to dig hers out of the trash."

Smiling, Raisa said, "You can put them on your mantelpiece — if you ever get a mantelpiece."

"Once I get my certs." Connie smiled right back. She had promised Raisa that, once she got her certification as an engineer, and the concomitant pay raise that would come with her promotion from trainee, they would get an apartment together.

That next day, after Connie came home from work — which involved a certain amount of overtime, as all the old jobs they'd put off because of the Spire repair now had to be done, along with all the new jobs that had come in — she noticed something odd.

The octagons all had different color patterns.

Some were subtle, some were obvious, but all of them had different patterns.

Even as she noticed the changes, she started to doubt them. *They can't have changed. They're just rocks, just debris. I'm probably imagining it.*

And again she forced that thought away. She wasn't stupid.

But she was tired. Even with Michaela sending her home early yesterday, she'd been working her ass off the past few days with all the emergency jobs thanks to the meteor strikes, of which the Spire was just the worst, piled on top of the usual gigs and her homework.

So fine, let's experiment.

First, she arranged the octagons into groups. Seven on one end of the bunk, seven on the other end, and the remaining six in the middle. The fones were all back online with the Spire working again, so she held up a fist so the ring could take a picture. She got images of each of the three sets.

She left them there and went to work.

That night, all twenty octagons were right where she left them, but the color patterns once again changed. Some were just in a different order, like the first one she'd noticed yesterday, while others had a totally different color set.

Digging into her toolkit, she found her Abdallah EM-17 Scanner and ran it over the octagons.

The Abdallah's display informed her that they were crystalline rock. No electronic parts, no unnatural elements, just stuff you expected to find in a piece of a rock that flew through space.

Connie could hear Raisa opening the privacy door in the bunk beneath hers—probably heading out to shower before her night shift. Connie slid open her own door and said, "Hey!"

Raisa was, in fact, wearing a bathrobe and carrying her towel and toiletries. "Hey yourself."

"What's the name of that geology professor that's always nice to you?"

"You mean Professor Usonga?"

"Yeah. You think you can get me a meeting with him?"

Professor Kimani Usonga agreed to meet with Connie the following evening. He had a late lecture and met her at his office afterward, when Connie was off work.

"So," he said as he ran his hand over his bald pate, "you say these are items you found in a meteor?"

"Not exactly. I work for Kralnova Fine Repairs. We were working on fixing the Spire after the meteor hit it."

"So there's no proof," he said, "that these are from the meteor at all."

"I—I guess. I just know that they aren't part of the Spire and I found them—"

"The important part of science," Usonga said as he started to walk back and forth in front of his desk, "is not to guess. We are rigorous in our desire to learn facts, not make suppositions."

Connie sighed. "I know that, Professor, that's why I tested my assumptions." She showed him the before-and-after pictures from her fone. "These pictures were taken in my bunk, ten hours apart."

Usonga stared at the two pictures that hovered over Connie's ring, and then let out a hissing sound between his teeth. "This is not scientific rigor, Ms. de la Vega. Someone could have entered your bunk and rearranged the octagons."

Connie tried very hard not to roll her eyes at the professor. There were all of three people on the entire moon who knew — or cared — where she lived: Raisa, Michaela, and Afeo. Plus, the privacy door had a BioLock that could only be unsealed by Connie herself.

However, Usonga had more to say, which he did while continuing to rub the top of his head. "It's also possible that the rocks reflect light differently. Or that you imagined it, and your fone is subject to variations in light sources. Or that they are not just meteor debris, but devices that were created by someone to be colorful."

"It's not, I scanned it."

"With what?"

"An Abdallah — an EM-17."

Again Usonga ran his hand over his pate. "A decent tool. Still, there are simply too many variables for this to be remarkable."

"Then why did you agree to see me?" Connie tried very hard not to sound defensive as she asked that.

Shrugging, Usonga said, "I like Ms. Slavasevitch. The support staff is often under-appreciated, and I like to *over*-appreciate the hard work they do. She said you were her friend, and out of respect for her, I was willing to see you. Now out of that respect, I will take a few of these samples and perform some tests when the opportunity presents itself."

With a sigh, Connie gave over five of the octagons. She sure as hell wasn't going to give him all of them, especially since she expected that he was going to toss them in a drawer and ignore them.

She went back home to her bunk, and looked at the fifteen she had left, spreading them out on the bed.

On a whim, she arranged them in a circle on one end of the bunk, and then used her fone to take another image.

Then she went to sleep.

The octagons were in the same circle when her fone woke her up the next morning.

But the colors were different.

Leaving them there, she reported to work, where things had begun to return to normal. It was the easiest day she'd had in a while. In the morning, she worked alone, repairing a pair of Vandenberg Lunar Scooters. Vandenbergs were temperamental, but they were easy to fix, and they were workhorses, the best for navigating the rough surface of the moon outside the dome. Then after that was done, and she had lunch, Michaela paired her again with Allison, and another tech, to fix a Melendez A-12 generator that had suffered a catastrophic failure.

When she got back to her bunk after they got the Melendez up and running, the colors of the octagons had changed *again*.

Sure enough, the next morning when she woke up, they were, again different.

Now she had four different images of the octagons with different color patterns, She called each on up to display over her ring next to each other.

Staring at it for several seconds, she started to see the beginnings of several different patterns — but none of them were complete. Either they didn't apply to one of the circles, or they were unfinished somehow.

I'm probably trying to find something that isn't there.

Pulling out her pad, she saw that there had been a deposit to her account from Kralnova Fine Repairs. Attached to the deposit was a note: "Here's your share of the bonus we received from Tsukuyomi."

Connie went to work in a good mood that morning. With this bonus, she could actually buy food other than InstaMeals and Zwaren Bars. Maybe even something that had flavor...

She called Raisa as she sat on the tram that took her to the office. "Hey, you're off tonight, right?"

"Yeah, why? Wanna get together?"

"Let's go out to Fontanarossa's."

"We can't afford that."

"I can." She told Raisa about the bonus.

"Hot damn!" Raisa let out a whoop. "About time you got one of those."

After hanging up, she looked at the pay note again and saw that there was a label attached to the payment: TECHNICIAN'S BONUS.

She sighed. Even though she was a trainee engineer, even though the work she did on the Spire was engineers' work — and, in fact, she did it better and faster than the engineer she was paired with — she still got paid like a tech.

Nevertheless, they had a luxurious meal at Fontanarossa's, a fantastic Italian-Cuban restaurant located on the east end of the dome. Besides excellent food, the place also had a picture window with a view of Mare Vaporum.

"So how'd it go with Professor Usonga?"

Connie sighed. "Not great. He didn't think there was anything to it."

Raisa frowned. "I'm sorry. He seems so nice."

"Oh, he was nice. But dismissive." She shrugged. "I'm used to it. And there isn't that much to go on anyhow."

Belly full of Mofongo Parmigiana, Connie crawled into her bunk after dinner to see that the octagons had yet another color scheme.

Wait a minute.

There *was* a pattern, she was sure of it.

She took a picture with her fone and then put all five side by side.

Then she got rid of the first one she took.

That's it!

She called Usonga and got his mailbox.

"Professor, this is Connie de la Vega—Raisa's friend? I finally figured out the pattern to the colors. Once they're arranged in a particular way and aren't moved, they start to change colors based on the visible spectrum. The sides of the octagon facing outward are all in sequence based on how they're arranged, going from red to violet. And they keep shifting each time they're observed. I think it might be a form of communication. I'm appending the images I've taken so you can see."

The message sent, she went to sleep.

She awakened the next morning to her fone alerting her to a message from Usonga.

"Thank you for your call, Ms. de la Vega, but I truly believe that you are wasting your time—and mine. I appreciate your enthusiasm, but your efforts would be better spent on your studies and your work, not a fruitless attempt to find patterns that are not present."

Connie sighed. She really thought this pattern was for real.

Maybe I am just looking for something that isn't there.

Usonga also had a point about her studies. She'd been letting her engineering certification classes slide the last couple of days, as what little spare time she'd had had been spent either working or having an extravagant dinner with Raisa.

She needed to focus on what was important, which was getting her certification so she could get paid an engineer's rate for the work she'd been doing all along.

One week later, Connie was sitting outside Fontanarossa's. Raisa had gotten a raise, and she offered to take Connie out to dinner in return for the meal Connie had bought seven days previous.

A holo was showing the Lunar News Service.

"In other news, has the Lunar Academy found evidence of life on other planets? We go now to Christopher Tseng at the Academy."

The image switched from a news reader standing in the middle of the street to a short man standing next to Professor Usonga.

Oh hell no.

Angry, she sat up and watched the holo.

"I'm here with Professor Kimani Usonga of the Lunar Academy Geology Department, and he has an amazing discovery. Professor?"

"Thank you, Mr. Tseng. Yes, we have made an amazing breakthrough. The meteors that have struck our fair moon lo this recent week have revealed items that we are now sure came from an alien intelligence."

Then he held up one of Connie's octagons.

"This is one of dozens of crystalline rocks that have been discovered in meteor debris. Most were thrown away by careless engineers and repair technicians, though a few were able to scrape together the wherewithal to save them — and thank heavens they did! The samples have all shown color patterns that are clear mathematical progressions based on the visible color spectrum. This cannot *be a natural phenomenon. There has to be an intelligence behind it, and all that is required now is that we figure out where it came from. I have already spoken with the personnel in StarCore V and at Arecibo on Earth to try to determine where the meteors that have struck the moon have come from. We will* find *out what is behind this, and where this intelligence lies."*

"This is an amazing find, Professor. I assume you'll be at the vanguard of the exploration of this find?"

Usonga chuckled and ran his hand over his head. *"Let us not get ahead of ourselves. For now, let us see where this discovery of mine leads us."*

"That bastard."

Connie looked over to see Raisa approaching. "Yeah, well."

"No, not 'yeah, well.' He's taking credit for *your* discovery!"

"He's also got the resources to actually figure out what it is — which is why I wanted to talk to him in the first place." She sighed. "Would've been nice if he wasn't a complete jerk about it…"

"I'm telling you right now, I'm forgetting to throw out his trash. And I'm making sure his floor gets cleaned *before* I change out the filter."

Connie smiled. "Thanks, Raisa."

"I'm sorry I introduced you to him."

"I'm not." She shrugged. "I'm just a trainee engineer who lives in a two-meter bunk. He's a geology professor at a prestigious university. Of course he's the one who's gonna actually figure it out and get to be on the news. It's the way it works."

"It's stupid," Raisa said.

"Forget it," Connie said. "Let's eat."

THE CARDAVY LETTER

CAPTAIN JANEL ISENSTADT EYED THE COSMOS THROUGH THE SHIP'S viewscreen. She shook her head, exasperated. "Rashid," she said to the *Maspeth*'s Chief Science Officer. "We've been out here for weeks. Anything we can use?"

The *Maspeth*, an older but efficient starship in NaMerica's Exploratory fleet, was sent to study the Ushanabe Quadrant, an uncharted region along the outer rim of the Milky Way galaxy.

"The computer's been running everything it has on file, as well as some new code I uploaded as a workaround," Sadiq al Rashid said. "There's a lot of interference. It's going to take time. The *Ulysses* might be able to cut through a lot faster" — Rashid rolled his eyes — "if they're willing to help."

Isenstadt leaned her ebony hands on the console. She'd been staring at an agglomeration of stars, wondering if the unidentified radiation pulsing throughout the quadrant was just another in a long line of prickly jokes the Universe had plotted at her expense.

Loriobu, the closest celestial body, was at least ten days out at maximum speed. But the various spatial distortions and electromagnetic pockets the *Maspeth* had been encountering forced them to adjust course and reduce propulsion more than they anticipated, such that the distant planet might as well have been in a different galaxy altogether.

Isenstadt had told Andre Granger, captain of the *Ulysses* — the most advanced ship in the NaMerica fleet — that she could track the quadrant as effectively as he could. The *Maspeth* might not have been the newest, shiniest ship on the lists, but she was a good one. A damned good one. They'd traveled the Milky Way together, and then some.

"No," Isenstadt said, straightening up with a groan. Her back hurt more than it used to. Especially since her horrendous stay in MedLab at the end of the Great War, when mankind nearly met its end. "We're already here. Let's not give up before we—"

Tanya Li interrupted. "Captain," the Security Chief said with a laser-locked stare. "We have an incoming message. It's weak, but..." — Li pressed her earpiece tighter—"I can't decipher it. I don't recognize the code."

Rashid manipulated the instrument panel. "I can widen the scope. Try again."

"Raise the audio," Isenstadt acknowledged. "Let me hear."

The *Maspeth*'s overriding mission may have been to scout the unknown, searching for sentient life beyond Earth, but that didn't mean she liked surprises.

Rashid filtered out most of the interference. The signal was clearer now, stronger, but still unrecognizable. "I don't... I've never heard anything like it before." He shook his head. "I can't translate it, but... it's on a loop. Yes. It's repeating."

I don't like it," Li said. "Suggest Yellow Alert."

"Or maybe," Isenstadt said, "we need to take the message at face value."

Deceptively fierce given his outwardly genial nature, Rashid looked up from the console. "How so?"

Isenstadt felt like a family of mice were scurrying inside her heart, their tiny feet plucking at the strands of that wounded muscle. The infected bodies she'd found on the Galapagos Islands, the result of biological warfare during the Great War, taught her that man was unworthy of its place in the universe, and as a species, had gotten what it deserved. At the very least, she had, given the choices she'd made.

"Because rushing to judgment can lead us the wrong way."

"Captain!" Li said. "Look. On screen. There."

An unknown object drifted in and out of the scattered radiation pockets, like a moon behind a cloud.

"Magnify and scan," Isenstadt said.

Rashid did as instructed. "No life forms detected, Captain. Is that... one of ours?"

"No," Isenstadt said, pondering the object. "It's not."

Whereas the Maspeth was shaped like a flattened salamander, the satellite resembled an enlarged atom, four cylinders of equal proportions connected at the center. The cylinders rotated around their connection point. The satellite's beacon light flashed a pulsing blue.

"Raising shields," Li said.

Isenstadt let it stand.

"Each protrusion registers nine point six four meters in length," Rashid said. "Two point two three meters in width. But I can't identify its point of origin or power source. I've never seen a design like that. Do you think this is—?"

"Weapons?"

"Negative," said Li, a former Olympic mixed-martial-arts medalist who always gunned for a fight, even when there was no quarrel to be had. "Not that I can detect. But I don't trust anything we find out here."

Isenstadt didn't either.

"Noted," Isenstadt said, wondering if they had in fact discovered proof that life existed beyond their own, or what that life would think of humans, if they thought anything at all. "Rashid... try to establish contact."

"Aye, Captain." Then through the headset, "This is the starship *Maspeth*, a science vessel in NaMerica's Exploratory fleet. Please identify yourself." They waited. "Nothing, Captain. It's the same code, on a loop. I've been running an analysis. The satellite's configuration and design are considerably more advanced than ours. And based on a quick-scan carbon dating, the satellite is at least seventy years old."

Isenstadt's instincts were to protect the ship and crew, and to fire upon the satellite if necessary. But not yet. There was too much to learn.

"Ask if they're damaged or if they need assistance."

Again, no response.

"All right. Let's get a closer look at the—"

"Incoming!" Rashid said. "The Aussies."

"Red Alert," Isenstadt said. "Open a channel."

Designed like pterodactyls with upturned wings, the Australian warships were prone to attacking unsuspecting vessels without provocation. She'd encountered them once before. Many lives were lost.

Other than a handful of minor territories scattered across the globe, the only factions to survive the Great War were NaMerica— the northeast corridor from Maine to Delaware, of what had been the continental United States— Alaska, and Australia.

"Aussie vessel. I am Captain Janel Isenstadt of the starship *Maspeth*. Please identify yourself."

The Australians appeared on screen.

"We do not identify," growled its captain, a small mountain of a man with a bald pate, and tattoos covering most of his massive arms and neck. "We claim, we pilfer, we leave." The captain grazed a button on the arm of its high-backed chair. "And if we are displeased… we destroy."

"I'm well aware," Isenstadt said. "Just as I'm aware that our weapons are locked on your engines." A smile from Li. "And if you don't identify yourself within the next five seconds, I will be displeased. Test me if you wish… but I wouldn't."

The Aussie captain narrowed his eyes, then grunted at his crew. "My ship is the *Velcroy*. You… will call *me*... Darnash."

"Darnash. Fine. What's your business here?"

"You don't question the Aussies!" Darnash said, and eyed his crew.

"Captain!" Li said. "They're firing cannons!"

Four blasts rocketed from the *Velcroy*. The green-fissured pulses missed the *Maspeth* by fifty meters. A warning shot.

"Anything in the outback of space is ours. We take. We pilfer, we—"

"Yeah yeah, you leave. Which is a tremendous idea. We're analyzing the satellite and will—"

"Captain!" Li repeated. "Another vessel, hard to port!"

"We're being hailed," Rashid said.

It had been almost three years since Isenstadt last saw combat, not since her disastrous run on the Galapagos. After her return to health, she completed the mandatory retraining and was cleared to command a weaponized vessel again.

She knew, however, that simulations were no substitute for engaging a hostile enemy in deep space. Her heart thundered.

"On screen."

"I am Captain Elginoo," the third captain said, an Alaskan, an Inuit, her long, black hair coiled into a long braid. Elginoo and Darnash were visible via split screen. "My ship is the *Ashta*."

Standing on a platform while holding an elaborately carved staff, Elginoo was short and round-faced, with brown skin, thick eyebrows, and a wide, depressed nose. She was adorned with a black vest made of animal fur atop a spiked metal chest plate.

"We have not encountered NaMerica since the Great War. But no matter. Our mission is sacred. We have come to honor the satellite. To listen and learn. But whatever its intentions, it is only for Inuit. We are the chosen, the survivors, warriors of the new age. Stand down... and be on your way."

Before Isenstadt could respond, the *Velcroy* fired multiple shots upon the *Ashta*, a tank built for space. As before, the green-fissured energy pulses passed within fifty meters—more warning shots.

Li nearly snarled. "Captain. All weapons charged."

"Wait," Isenstadt said, resisting the urge to let her open fire. "Just wait." If any faction left on Earth deserved a good vaporizing, the Aussies topped the list. "Rather than blast each another into dust, I suggest another course of action."

"Bollocks!" Darnash snarled. "We take!"

"Or perhaps," Isenstadt said with barely contained contempt, "we could talk."

On a secondary view screen, the satellite continued to orbit the sector, repeating its message. Li muted the audio, speaking offline.

"Captain! You can't talk sense with them. The Aussies are savages, with no moral code. They forage through the dumpsters of space and claw your eyes out in the process."

"I'm counting on it," Isenstadt said. "Rashid. Re-open a channel to both ships. And run a deeper diagnostic on the message. We need to translate it before they do."

"Aye, Captain. Nothing from the computer. I've never come across an algorithm like this. I'll keep at it."

The satellite disappeared into one of the spatial distortions, then re-emerged.

"Captain Elginoo," Isenstadt began, intentionally addressing the Alaskan first, implying the Australian's subordinate position. "Captain Darnash. There's little point in battle. We were all drawn to the satellite. Wherever it comes from, it means there is life beyond Earth. For us... the dawn of a new age. Each of us has an existential yearning to understand its call, and our place among the cosmos. We all have an equal claim on the satellite."

"Of course, there's life beyond our cesspool of a planet," Darnash said. "Didja really think we're alone? That us dirty stinkin' humans are the best the stars can do? We ain't superior to Jack. Hell, we're barely even people. Just slimy, seething maggots with slightly better tech." He laughed incredulously. "We battled to control the planet. Now we battle for the stars. And that satellite," he said, pointing into space, "has power we ain't seen before. And if there's power like that to be had, it's ours to possess. And if need be, to destroy. So no talk! Go!"

"The satellite is elusive," Captain Elginoo said calmly, ignoring Darnash's threats. "We are Inuit, not Eskimos. We have been searching for the Creator's voice, out here among the stars. The satellite drifts within the quadrant, into the pockets… then emerges as it does. It speaks to us. We listen."

"No speak! No listen! No—!"

Elginoo stroked the ridge of her left cheek, then laid the tip of her long black braid across the spikes on her chest plate.

"Only children make demands that will never be fulfilled," she scolded Darnash. "Our ships are of comparable fortitude, speed, and weaponry. We have scanned one another, assessed strengths and weaknesses. There is little point in combat… for you. Out of necessity, Inuit have become the great warrior race. Our tactics superior, our bravery unmatched. Make no threats upon us lest you desire a test of will."

Darnash snarled at the rebuttal then disengaged from screen, leaving only Elginoo to deal with.

"I appreciate your diplomacy," Isenstadt said, hopeful she had brought Elginoo closer to reason. "We are not looking for conflict. We will engage if we have to, but all things being equal, I'd prefer a peaceful solution."

Pudgy and round-shouldered, Elginoo comported herself with a weathered confidence borne out of a brutal existence and extensive combat.

"We encountered this satellite four years ago," Elginoo said. "Its possession was within my grasp. An unexpected power failure disabled my ship. It rendered pursuit impossible. It has taken me this long to rediscover its signal. Now that I have found it, I will not relent. Inuit alone will hear the message."

Isenstadt knew about lost time. And the obsession that comes with reclaiming what you believe is rightfully yours.

Against Granger's fierce objections, during the Great War she had taken a rescue ship to the Galapagos Islands, her last decision as Captain of her previous ship, the Abacus. Her intent had been to transport as many survivors out of the contaminated zone as possible.

But because of her, fourteen of her crew died from the rapidly spreading virus that wound up eradicating half the life on Earth.

Granger pulled her out before it destroyed her, too. There were many nights she wished he hadn't.

"I understand," Isenstadt said to Elginoo. "I'll confer with my crew."

She then nodded in agreement before Rashid took them off-screen.

"Captain," Li said. "If they've been chasing the satellite for as long as they claim… don't they know more about it than they're saying? If there's other life in the universe, if this satellite is proof we're not alone, do you really think they're searching for their Maker? Do you really believe it's the origin of their people? Or by that logic… ours?"

"My guts are screaming to fear the satellite," Isenstadt said, "to consider it a threat. But we're not the only dog in this fight." She instinctively grazed her right hip with her fingers. The doctors had fused metal plates along her spine, enabling her to walk without a cane. Feeling intensely vulnerable, she turned to Rashid. "They haven't attacked us… or the Australians. Which tells us what?"

"They're afraid the satellite will be destroyed in the process," Li said. "Since when do warrior races waste time with politics?"

Rashid ran yet another analytic program in an effort to decipher the satellite's code. "When they have more to lose than they want to admit."

"Or," Isenstadt realized, "they want someone to do the dirty work for them… then steal the find for themselves. No. Elginoo's smart, but she tipped her hand. The search-and-retrieve mission was sanctioned by her people, knowing there'd be others on the hunt. Or… she's gone rogue."

Li looked up from her control panel. "Or they're more afraid us, or the Aussies, than she's letting on."

"Either way," Isenstadt said, "we better stay sharp. Run another scan on their ships. Maybe we missed something."

"I think you're right," Li said. "Look!" The *Velcroy* vanished, then reappeared twelve hundred kilometers starboard and above.

"A jump drive," Isenstadt said. "Damn."

"It's engaged a tractor beam on the satellite!"

"Do the same."

The two ships, the *Maspeth* and *Velcroy*, were in a tug of war. Not to be outdone, the *Ashta* activated its own tractor beam. The satellite hovered in place, pulled in three different directions.

"This is trouble," Isenstadt said. "Hail all parties. On screen. And" — as much as she despised doing it, it needed to be done — "send Granger an encrypted subspace message. There could be other enemy ships out there. We need reinforcements."

Rashid shook his head. "I'm sorry, Captain. Radiation pockets have blocked all subspace communications. We'd have to leave the sector to get a message through. As long as we stay here… we're on our own."

Held in place by the competing tractor beams, the satellite's flashing blue beacon light continued to broadcast its signal.

"Darnash," she said. "I suspect the radiation pockets are interfering with your tech. If you could jump with the satellite, you would. If you could fire immediately after a jump, you would. But now… we know you can't."

Startled by confrontation, the Aussie captain blinked, his face like a slab of stone.

"Captain Elginoo, your journey beyond the stars is worthy of song," Isenstadt continued, appeasing the woman's ego. "The satellite you have sought these long four years is not simply an object of your desire, but the scepter of a noble quest. Your sacrifice, your commitment… only a true warrior could sustain such an endeavor."

Isenstadt offered her a subtle, yet noticeable nod — a tip of her cap.

"Yes," Elginoo said, nearly blushing as she twirled her long, black braid around her hand. "These have been… trying times."

Isenstadt nodded. "And now to be so close, only to find yourself in a stalemate, must elicit in you a myriad of emotions. It surely would in me, had I traveled your path."

"Words!" Darnash shouted. "You distract, but you don't make sense! Don't talk bollocks! Speak!"

Rashid spoke offline to the captain. "You'd better get to the point or we'll need medical to —" He looked to Li, to the viewscreen, then back to the captain. "Medical. Yes! That's it!"

"What?" Li said. "What're you thinking?"

"I have an idea." Rashid feverishly programmed new code into the computer. "Let me try this."

"Captain Isenstadt," Elginoo said. "Despite the odds, I find myself agreeing with Captain Darnash. Have you a solution? A proposal?"

"To put it in the parlance of our tattooed friend, my suggestion is this." Isenstadt looked to her crew, who likewise awaited her response. "No fight. No pilfer. No flee." She simpered. "We share."

"Share?" Darnash repeated. "What do you mean… share?"

"It means," Isenstadt said, "that the three of us—*Maspeth, Velcroy, Ashta*—all release the satellite from our tractor beams—"

"No release! There ain't no share!"

"I *propose*," Isenstadt repeated, "that we release the satellite, and fall back two thousand kilometers each. We monitor it from a neutral corner of the quadrant until one of us can decipher the code. This satellite could finally bring us together, for the first time in our history, as one people, of one Earth… rather than tearing us apart."

"Your proposal engenders risk," Elginoo said, the whites of her eyes drawing darker somehow. "From where the message comes is still a mystery, a mystery from the stars. The one who possesses that knowledge becomes the superior participant, and the Maker's holy servant. But then… the message may be harmless. Or even a distress call. Or perhaps the signal aims to scan our vessels and destroy us. One cannot know for certain."

"Yes!" Darnash growled. "Listen!"

"Your analysis is thoughtful and on point," Isenstadt said. "Access to information, including who obtains it and when, is an obvious concern."

She paused, giving Darnash and Elginoo time to calm their anxieties, and for her to better control her own. Even if Li's hands weren't hovering over the weapons console, Isenstadt understood that combat could erupt immediately and with little provocation.

After the virus she'd contracted on the Galapagos nearly paralyzed her from the neck down, leaving her helpless, immobile—unable to feed, bathe, or relieve herself without help—she swore that if she ever got out of MedLab she'd never jump into another situation again without vetting it first. She'd known it then, but let emotion get in the way.

"To ensure compliance," Isenstadt said, "I also propose we establish a triangulated relay that will *automatically and instantaneously* distribute the message across all three ships so that no one of us would have the advantage. No matter who deciphers the message first, we all have access to and possess it at *exactly the same time.* Our connection to the satellite… and to the very beings who launched it… will be one and the same." She waited for an outburst that did not come. "No one keeps the message for themselves. As I said… we share."

"Don't gimme that sharing and harmony bollocks," Darnash said. "We're all starving beasts, ferocious for our next meal. It's all about the power. My power. I'm gonna wrap my hands around that bloody satellite. And if I can't do it... I sure as hell ain't gonna let you."

"Captain," Li said offline. "We can't trust them, and they don't trust us. Like Elginoo said, there's no telling what that message contains or who it was meant for. If the Aussies decipher the message, assuming they even can, they'll never share it with us. We have to know first. It's us or them."

"We need to stall," Rashid said. "I remembered that our medical logs are written with a specific syntax and grammatical structure we use as shorthand. I applied that frequency and sequence analysis to the satellite's message to see if that would work. I think it's... I think the source language is..." —a look of awe came over him— "English."

Isenstadt saw a flash of white before her eyes. Blood pounded in her ears. "English...? How?"

"Honestly," Rashid said, "I don't know. But it's starting to come through. Let me —"

The *Maspeth* took a hit, disrupting communications.

"Li!" Isenstadt commanded. "Report!"

"The *Velcroy* fired on us, Captain. I don't see how they... incoming!"

A second missile struck the *Maspeth*'s hull, disabling the tractor beam. Sparks ricocheted throughout the bridge.

The impact tossed Isenstadt out of her Captain's chair. She landed awkwardly on her wrist, breaking it. She grimaced. "Evasive maneuvers! Return fire!"

Li fired off a half-dozen missiles and multiple energy pulses. The first wave knocked out the *Velcroy*'s tractor beam, leaving Elginoo in sole possession of the satellite.

The *Velcroy* fired back, this time at the *Ashta*, which also lost its tractor beam.

Rashid maneuvered the *Maspeth* in an evasive pattern while Li continued to fire. The second round of blasts were headed for the *Velcroy* when it teleported away.

The *Velcroy* repeated the maneuver, firing on both ships, evading, teleporting, then firing again.

"Captain!" Rashid said. "The message is nearly decoded. But we can't take much more. Shields are down to thirty-seven percent, life support fifty-one percent."

"Why did they fire on us? What are they" — Isenstadt froze as another *Velcroy* missile headed their way — "doing?"

Li returned fire, taking out the incoming missile. "They're firing seeker missiles into the radiation pockets, blocking our ability to track them. It's why we didn't see them. They're able to fly through the static discharge, away from our sensors, and re-enter normal space just as they're upon us. I don't know how it works, but they have tech we don't."

Like a life raft on the ocean, the satellite drifted away from the carnage.

"But why did they fire at us?" Isenstadt asked as she secured a stabilizing brace around her broken wrist. "We weren't the aggressors."

Rashid pushed back. "The Alaskans, the Australians. They don't compromise, share, or accept guidance from NaMericans. Like Darnash said, they take. Maybe they're not, but we have to assume they're decoding the message — and faster than we are. It's a race to the finish, Captain. And it's winner takes all."

Flushed with wounded pride — and fear of their pending mortality — Isenstadt had a different idea. "Li. How many times have they jumped? How many teleports?"

"Five so far. Why?"

"In what sequence? At which coordinates?"

Li retraced the jumps. "The first three... yes!" Her face lit up. "They're triangulating."

"And the last two?" Isenstadt inquired.

"They're... very good, Captain. Hold on. Let me calculate." Li studied the console. "Got it. Yes. I'm locked in. I'm ready."

"Good. Fire on my command."

"Fire?" Rashid said. "Fire on what?"

Isenstadt explained, drawing a nod from Rashid.

"Wait for my signal," Isenstadt said. "And prepare to get us out of here. Because things are going to get real ugly, real fast. And I'd rather not be here when they do."

The satellite drifted into another spatial pocket, leaving the three warring vessels in a shared stasis, each trying to determine their next move.

Until the *Velcroy* teleported, disappearing from sight. Just as Isenstadt predicted.

"Hold it," she said to Li as her console reading counted down. "Aaand" — Isenstadt held out her hand — "fire!"

Li launched three seeker missiles, directed toward an unoccupied point in space — on a seeming path to nowhere. But as those projectiles hurtled through the quadrant, the *Velcroy* reappeared from its teleport phase, in the exact coordinates the missiles would soon occupy.

The *Velcroy* immediately reactivated its tractor beam, intending to capture the satellite as it drifted back out of the spatial pocket and into normal space.

"Captain!" Li said. "Seeker missiles locked. Collision course with the *Velcroy*."

The *Velcroy* fired an intercept missile, which destroyed the first seeker. Another intercept missile knocked the second seeker off course.

The third missile struck the Velcroy's engines. The tractor beam released, setting the satellite free once more.

"Rashid," Isenstadt commanded. "Reactivate tractor beam and hail the *Ashta*."

"On screen."

Isenstadt addressed Elginoo. "Captain. Let's speak the truth. We're deciphering the code. I suspect you are not. But I understand your reluctance to share information. You've been after the satellite far too long and at too great expense to let anyone else have it. To do so would be an unforgivable sin. Believe me, I know how it feels." Elginoo did not respond. "But as I said before, I am willing to share the code with you. Under one condition."

Elginoo stared into the screen. "I'm listening."

"The *Velcroy* is damaged. Their jump drive disabled. But they're still dangerous. Use a stun-only energy pulse and fire on their wing. You don't need to destroy them, just take them out of action."

Elginoo assessed the suggestion. "Why would I do that? Firing on the *Velcroy* gives you an opening… to fire upon us. I'm no fool."

"No," Isenstadt said, "you're not. You're a cunning warrior and a brave soul. You know they'll never give up the satellite. Not willingly.

They want it for themselves, but more so, they know *you* want it. Which is reason enough for them to get it first. If you fire on them, too, their only choice will be to stand down… or battle us both. And we know that's a lost cause."

Muted, Elginoo discussed with her crew. She re-engaged. "Agreed. Stand by."

"Captain," Li warned. "She's pious and unwavering. There's no way she'll share. "

"I know," Isenstadt said. "But we have the one thing they don't. Right, Rashid?"

"Two more minutes. Just hold 'em off 'til then."

Isenstadt spoke with Elginoo. "Confirmed, Captain. Ready when you are."

The *Maspeth* and *Ashta* broke off, separating in the quadrant. And then the *Ashta* fired on the *Velcroy*, destroying its wing.

"The *Velcroy* is down to eighteen percent life support," Rashid said. "Engines disabled."

"Reactivate tractor beam," Isenstadt said.

"Aye, Captain. Ready for… Look!"

The Aussie ship barely holding together, Darnash threw a final, violent tantrum, launching the Velcroy's last four seeker missiles at the satellite.

"Countermeasures," Isenstadt ordered.

The *Maspeth* and *Ashta* immediately launched their own intercept missiles at the *Velcroy* seekers.

"Captain!" Rashid snapped as the Velcroy projectiles were about to strike. "There's an energy surge within the satellite. I think it's going to —"

In defense of itself, the satellite launched an EMP, a blistering pulse of white light. The magnitude and frequency of the electromagnetic pulse disabled the *Maspeth* and *Ashta*, blowing out their engines, fracturing their hulls, and setting off a series of explosions within both ships that left most of the crews injured or dead.

The *Velcroy*, in its already weakened state, exploded.

A bloody, battered Elginoo appeared on the *Maspeth*'s view screen, her crew buried beneath the wreckage on the bridge. "You fuh… fool," she groaned. "I finally found the Maker, ready to hear her voice. And now it's too late."

"I'm s-sorry," Isenstadt said as blood streamed down her head.

Struggling to maintain consciousness, she looked upon Li, slumped over the console, Rashid crushed beneath a fallen support beam. Isenstadt slid onto the floor.

During the Great War, Granger had warned her to stay away from the Galapagos, the risk of infection far too great. But her husband, an epidemiologist studying the new and deadly virus, was down there on one of those tiny islands, among the afflicted.

As a wife, she couldn't leave him. She had to get him out. At least, she had to try. But as a captain, she had violated her oath and failed her crew. She swore she'd make up for it someday, to fix her mistake.

Only as the *Maspeth's* command console shorted out, that last chance slipped away.

The bridge went silent then except for a single message, on a continuous loop, spoken by the computer's male voice. Rashid's algorithm had finally deciphered the satellite's message:

This is Nadnali Lenala of Earth's Cardavy province. After the Great War, we traveled the cosmos, in search of a fresh start, for a place without hate.

It's been seven months since I landed on Loriobu. Do not enter the quadrant. Radioactive pockets have caused irreversible seismic activity. We must leave this planet before it is too late. So I send this message now, by satellite, in hope that it finds you well.

To my wife Tesha and our baby girls Rein and Bala...

I should have been back by now. I'm sorry. But we are not alone in the great reaches of space. Oh, we are not alone! The Lorioban are a kind and generous race. Though they look nothing like us, and their language is difficult to speak, they are not so different from you and me. They lived through their civil wars and ugly strife, finally, to find peace, in unity. They are my friends. If the fates are on our side, and you are ever to meet, they will be your friends, too.

Although I am far away, you are close to my heart.

So dream of me... as I dream of you.

Do not fear the stars. They are a guiding light, for those who know which ones to follow.

THE SOUND OF DISTANT STARS

Judi Fleming

THE SCREECHING FEEDBACK THROUGH EVELYN'S COMM MADE HER instinctively cover her ears making her club the bubble of her plazglas helmet with her awkward sampling gloves. The specialized collection fingertip attachments scratched across the side of the clear plazglas adding an irritating squeal.

She toggled off the external comm on the command screen inside her helmet with a flick of an eyeball and switched to the text-only screen in frustration. This was the third time today it had done that.

"Supervisor Shelly, I'm text only on incoming comm because of the feedback for the rest of the sampling assignment."

The acknowledgment of "Noted" scrolled across the interface and she flicked an eyeball to clear the screen. Back to work.

Evelyn trudged down the slope to the coordinates at the base of the canyon close to where she had landed her survey skiff. Looked like they wanted samples of the deep red bands of rock at the base of canyons today.

This planet was old. Old and dead. Carved with millions of deep chasms, which coiled and flowed around the entire planet surface. Irregular enough to be natural, but irregularly irregular enough that it seemed constructed. Huge deep canyons ten times deeper than the Grand Canyon back on old Mother Earth. Beautiful and flowing, multicolored and multi-tiered, curving and sinuous, making the planet a work of art carved by a millennium of solar winds channeled through a weak atmosphere as wispy as gossamer. Thus, the need for the archeology crew's suits. Only twelve archeologists staffed this "dig" but no luck so far in finding any sort of artifact. Just a dead ball of rock. No ruins, no roads, and no trace of weathered foundations. Boring.

Evelyn had hypothesized that there had once been water endlessly rushing willy-nilly through the maze-like series of channels. Her fabulous work supervisor, Shelly, had told her that made no sense at all. The whole planet surface of canyons wound and twisted like a child's labyrinth puzzle, begging Evelyn to find her way to the center without getting lost in a dead end. At least she thought of it that way.

As the most junior of the team she did the endless samples, scraping different colored rock particles from all over the planet. Every day she took her little skiff out, fighting the buffeting winds as she negotiated the crevices to each new coordinate, returning exhausted at the end of each day to eat, sleep, and start over again. A year of hard work and no solid hypothesis on why this crazy planet had all these swirling canyons twisting deep into its surface. They had found nothing else like it on any of the known worlds the human race had expanded to either. And nothing out as far as they could see on even the newest, most powerful telescope arrays. And here she stood scraping bits of rock and sand into sample bags. She paused, stretching her aching back, flicking her eyes across the suit's command window to tighten the lumbar support to hold her angle for the next sample.

Lately, her assignments seemed almost as random as the curves and turns she explored. Evelyn was still miffed about not being able to see the results from all this work.

"Too incomplete for any real meaning," she'd been told.

She snorted. "Too much grunt work to be done is what you really mean," she muttered under her breath.

"What was that, Ev?" her supervisor asked in crisp white text on a smoky background on a small patch of the bottom right of her helm.

"Nothing, nothing. Faulty comm. Going to full text, no audio."

"Affirmative" flashed across the side text readout inside the plazglas bubble helmet. "Be careful out there, Ev."

She tipped forwarded and rested her head on the ledge, closing her eyes and sighing as the blush crept up her neck. Dumbass. Why was she always doing stupid things like that? Probably because she worked alone so much. Forgetting the connection to her coworkers as she flitted between the cavern-like abysses made by the curving walls soaring above her head.

She sighed and stood up straight. Stretching, she turned her head to the cathedral-like walls soaring high above. The weak sunset glinting off her helmet blinded her so she turned just enough to remove the glare.

An infinitesimal sound vibrated softly through her body. She froze. She shouldn't have any sort of feedback with the comm on full audio shutdown. Evelyn breathed shallowly, hearing her own pulse echo inside her helmet. No, the sound hadn't come from the comm unit. It came from *outside*.

She eyed the screen's command buttons and toggled the exterior audio on. Music seeped into her bones. Softly swelling and waning as the anemometer tagged the rising wind speeds and their directions as they swirled around her.

The sky faded to blue then indigo and stark black as she gazed fixedly at the sliver of the heavens far above, enjoying the music. Evelyn watched the stars spark into existence and then the winds picked up, crashing a symphony of sound around her. She gripped the rock face, glad she had stiffened the back support.

The helmet's autoclean warmed her face and she sniffled, realizing that tears had been streaming down her face as she stood transfixed. Still, she could not look away or move a muscle, afraid that the beautiful, heart-wrenching music would stop. The wind shifted again, changing and softening the sound to a pulsing, yearning rhythm that beat in time along with a particular star flashing through the thin atmosphere. She blinked. The star's pulse matched the music's beat at the same tempo. No illusion then.

A hand clutched the arm of her suit without warning and she screeched, heart racing as she whirled around to confront her attacker. Shelly stood there, hands raised in wariness to tap on her own helmet, signaling audio on. Evelyn stared dumfounded at the paragraphs of text scrolling in never-ending loops on the corner text feed on the plazglas. The red lights of her recall beacon blinked in warning, baleful dots inside the screen. And she hadn't noticed one of them. Then she noted the time. Six *hours* had passed since she looked up at that sunset.

She eye-toggled the comm audio from exterior to standard and whispered, "Sorry, I... I... I..." and fainted dead away as the music released her.

She woke in the cramped sickbay back at the main camp, body stiff, head aching, but otherwise normal... other than being very, very hungry.

A medical alert chimed. She heard rustling in the next room before the curtain around her bed slid open. Several faces peered in, but her supervisor and Commander Alexander waved them back.

Shelly sat down on the edge of Evelyn's bed, while the commander sat on the small, stainless steel stool, his bulky body made ridiculous in the space he squeezed himself into.

"Welcome back," he said gruffly. "Care to tell us where you've been?"

She blinked, puzzled. "Where I've been?"

Shelly gripped her arm saying, "Ev, you were missing for six hours. No suit signal at all and we'd drone-searched all around the skiff. How'd you get so far down the canyon beyond the sample co-ordinates?"

Evelyn blinked again. "Down the canyon?" she said stupidly. "What do you mean, down the canyon?"

The commander cleared his throat. "You were sixty kilometers from your skiff."

"Sixty..." she squeaked.

"Sixty," he said firmly. "And we ran a diagnostic on your suit. Nothing wrong except a worn-out comm unit."

She gaped at him and then at Shelly, who nodded grimly.

"The music..." she began and then stopped when she saw their puzzled looks. "You didn't hear the music the wind made through the canyon?"

Again, the puzzled looks, worry and alarm flashed across their faces.

"Seriously. I turned my comm off and thought I still heard something, so I flicked it to external. The wind blew through the canyon and then at sunset it picked up. It sounded like a symphony."

The commander sat up abruptly and fingered his comm saying, "Communications, send down the external audio from the six weather stations."

"Sorry, commander, but those data collection stations only have the standards like temp, wind stats, and a video feed. We didn't think that anyone would be standing there talking to them."

The commander swore, causing Evelyn's face to redden. She'd never heard him be anything more than polite and professional.

"Add them," he barked. "Send anyone available down now to rig the two closest at the base of a gulley. Report back to me when they are done."

He swiveled back to Shelly, ignoring Evelyn. "Who is going out next?"

Shelly blinked and said, "She is, but not before we replace her helmet."

Evelyn swung the covers off her legs and sat up next to Shelly, "I'll go do it now."

"Not before you write out your report," Shelly said, turning to the commander. "There wasn't anything different in the samples she took compared to all the others. I think it's safe to send her out again. I don't really have anyone else to spare." She shrugged a shoulder as an apology.

"Make it so."

Two weeks later things reverted back to business as usual. Tedious long-range runs out to distant canyons to collect sample bags of rock dust, return to eat, sleep, and back at it again. As if nothing had happened.

But Evelyn remembered the music. The sweet, beautiful, hauntingly delicious music. She wanted to go back to that canyon and see if she could hear it again. They had added a data collection station there. Nothing but the wind, whistling or whispering, could be heard on the newly installed audio inputs on all the data collection stations across the planet.

She trudged down the path, careful to hold onto the wall as she made the steep ascent, stopping when the cross-hairs lined up with the coordinates she'd been sent to. Plain tan rocks. She'd better collect it and get back.

Pink and purple hues along the wall heralded sunset. The night winds picked up, fueled by the heat trapped inside the strangely warped gullies. She knew that when warm air rose, the cooler air moved in to replace it, but this planet held heat oddly because of its engraved surface and heated planetary core. Almost as if it had a wind generator at its center, powering the fluctuating, whistling winds.

The particularly soft tan rock crumbled easily into the sample pouch. She trudged back to the skiff to get a warmed-up, premade meal. Hash tonight, if she remembered right.

A sparkle on the wall caught her eye further on. A tiny brilliant speck shone out of place in the rich earth tones surrounding her. She had to walk right past it, so why not stop and look?

A few steps brought her up to the spot and still the tiny light flickered under an overhanging shelf of rock. She turned on every AV input, both interior and exterior, and toggled the med feeds to shoot her with adrenaline if she stood in place for more than an hour. She had been sternly directed to do this before they allowed her to go out again.

Kneeling down, she said, "Shelly, I'm being overly cautious, but I've found something."

Shelly hesitated but answered crisply, "Whatcha got, Ev?"

"It looks like a light, not natural. Some sort of rotating crystal structure tucked under a ledge. Tiny." She swiveled her head until the built-in camera focused on the flicker.

Another pause as Shelly assessed the phenomenon. "Interesting. I'm doing a manual control zoom on my side and tagging the location. Looks like a crystal caught between some rock so perfectly that it spins in the wind."

And as if on cue, the wind picked up making the tiny crystal sparkle and the music commenced. It rose and fell like a dance partner, twirling her heart with the melodies that spun out of the wind and soared up to the stars.

"Ooooooh," Shelly breathed, not saying anything for a very long time.

Evelyn felt the jab of the microneedles along the skin of her arm, jolting her heart with a quick shot of adrenaline. She shut off the external audio feed instantly with a flick of an eye over the controls in her helm, breaking her gaze from that tiny, enticing spark.

"What? Wait..." Shelly mumbled along with what sounded like the whole staff's longing sighs.

Steeling herself, Evelyn said, "Did you get caught in the trance too?"

Bursts of comments and exclamations muffled Shelly's response.

"What was that?" Evelyn asked as she backed away, glancing up beyond the steep walls. That same star sparkled above her, pulsing in time with the tiny light just behind her now easily visible at such close range. It disappeared from view in just a few steps as she tried to slow her racing pulse and not run back to her little skiff. What the hell was going on? At least everyone else had heard it too. The music *had* been real.

Evelyn could still hear confused murmurs over the audio feed and then Shelly shushed everyone loudly, telling whoever had gathered around her to get back to their test stations.

"Ev, did you record that?" Shelly asked, voice louder and steadier.

"Yes, transmitting it now. I'm on my way back." She hesitated and then asked, "You all okay there?"

"Yeah. Uh, yes. We're fine." Her voice softened, "It *was* beautiful. Just like you said, Evelyn."

Two weeks later things weren't just back to business as usual but boring as hell. No more little sparks, no more music on the audio feeds. Evelyn ground her teeth in frustration. Were these things just little flukes that a naturally grooved planet had popped up randomly? Or had some intelligent life planted clues here?

The music haunted her. Awake or asleep, she dreamed of the music. That soaring, swelling, glorious music. Access to her full hour of her recording was highly restricted. They'd locked it down so that no one could listen to more than one ten-minute session per day. And group listening of each person's ten minutes was banned. Otherwise, no work would get done at all.

Strange that even after all that listening no one could hum or remember or reproduce the sound and texture of the music adequately. All efforts felt off-key and lacking in some way. Who knew rocks could sing.

So here she stood once again, collecting random samples, miffed at the true lack of anything useful now that she'd seen the results of her work of a year and still they sent her out. Every. Single. Day. Sure, others did the same tedious work, collecting sand, atmosphere, data on temperatures, pouring over satellite and drone imagery, but all this work yielded nothing. They would spend a max of two years here. Then on to yet another lonely planet to look for evidence to prove that some alien race had been there before mankind arrived.

Evelyn really didn't believe they could be the only intelligent life form in all the vast expanse of space and time. Even the old-timers couldn't believe it. So, they trudged on with their daily duties which bore no fruit, year after year, decade after decade, planet after planet waiting for a single morsel of hope to re-ignite their hope of finding others, like the music.

The rock sample of the day was a rich russet color. It reminded Evelyn of the chocolate caramels that had been her favorite as a kid back on Iredell 25. Her helmet chimed to signal her arrival at the correct coordinates. She pulled out the sample bag, noted the time and location in her helmet log, and scratched her gloved hand sampler across the surface.

The entire canyon rang as if she had struck a giant bell. It vibrated through her bones and clacked her teeth, the reverberations cascading softer and softer until they stopped. She stood stock still, assessing herself for damage, but found nothing unusual on the suit readouts or her biomarkers, other than slightly elevated heart and respiration rates.

Warily, she turned on full AV record and set the adrenaline alarm to just two minutes, saying, "Shelly, I got something new here."

"Ready, Ev. What do you have this time?" came the eager response.

"This time it's bells," she said and took a deep breath, bracing herself for the sound. It didn't disappoint when she scratched the surface. The rich, full sound jarred her bones with its clear, beautiful tone.

Shelly's first response to the cathedral-like sound was a low whistle. "That was pretty spectacular. I see you are just doing a normal sample collection. Anything like this ever happen before?"

"No, not at all," Evelyn said. "It's always been just a scratching sound before this."

"Stay put. I'm coming out to the GPR right now. You're not that far away. The records don't indicate anything in that area on the broad scans."

Evelyn heard heavy breathing over the audio feed as someone rushed around for a few seconds.

Shelly said, "I'd like to take a closer look since we never saw those little lights before. Now we know to be close to the ground and to look up. It'll take us about an hour to pack up and get there. Go eat while you wait. It will be dark when we arrive."

Ugh. Skiff rations. This meant the full team would accompany the supervisor. They'd all be there for a while, pacing back and forth with the Ground Penetrating Radar hover unit. They would discover the secret behind these walls.

Evelyn felt a tiny thread of excitement in her guts. Were the walls hollow and the right movement at the right time caused her to find a natural phenomenon? Or was the third time the charm and they'd actually found something *other*? Like a cave that had been occupied and artifacts or who knew what else.

She squashed that hope and walked back to her survey skiff. She climbed in and took off her helmet, rummaging through her supplies until she found the least-offensive-tasting ration bar, sucking down a water bulb to clear the foul taste. She lay back to rest in the adjustable seat, flicking screens for AV record, proximity alarms, and adrenaline feeds in case.

Well, it had been two weeks. Clearly, time for the music to return, right? So far, in each musical instance the timing and her presence were the only common denominators.

She took a deep breath and turned on the external audio. At first, Evelyn thought it was just her imagination making hope seem real. But the music whispered softly. Then it rose and dipped, like a playful weasel popping up to see who was there. She concentrated hard, trying not to be swallowed whole by the intertwining melodies as she watched the readouts of wind velocities, adding color to the skiff's sensors so she could see the music displayed as it played. That's when she noticed the stars. The tiny sparkle of light pulsed along with the music. Then she was swept away, all her thoughts melting into the music, her mind rejoicing at its patterns, its swells and eddies. *Almost like voices,* she thought distantly. Like someone trying to tell her something exciting. Important. Impossible.

The jolt of adrenaline almost broke her reverie. She ignored it and struggled back into the music, trying to understand the whispers inside the symphony. She grasped for the slippery tendrils of meaning.

Come, they said, *come follow us to distant stars. We've set the beacon. Open the door. Come.*

Evelyn blinked, heart racing. The skiff's proximity alarm clanged over top of the joyous, swelling music. She toggled the external audio off, reaching for her helmet to answer the increasingly panicked voice of her supervisor, calling for her over and over as their skiff set down next to hers.

"I'm here, Shelly. A bit groggy, but I'm here." Evelyn gathered her thoughts and slowed her breathing, saying, "I think I found an artifact," and then she fainted again.

The next several days passed in a whirlwind of data review of the skiff recording. The medic did brain scans on everyone. Massive comparisons of images. Upgrades were made on the orbiting telescope that no one had previously gotten around to. Star charts analyzed. Complex computer programs listened to the recordings of music and compared them to wind data and terrain features and planet rotations.

And they had it. The planet itself was a signpost in the road. Pointing straight to that lovely, twinkling star. Carved so perfectly, tuned so precisely that the odds of it being a natural formation marked as statistically impossible.

But why hadn't they all seen it? Brain scans revealed only the ship's commander with similar brain patterns to Evelyn's. So, two weeks to the day, they both stood next to the bell caverns which had been mapped and surveyed as a beautifully constructed rock instrument. She could see Alexander sweating and breathing heavily, the starlight glinting off the curve of his plazglas helmet.

"All set?" she asked and he nodded. Their suits had been adjusted with a two-minute auto-shutdown on the exterior audio with full AV recording on. Everyone else standing in the background had their suit audio full off.

They stood ready to dash in and recover the two of them if needed. The whole planetary team. The nerve-jittering excitement coiled ropes of ice in her guts. She reached out a hand and delicately stroked her sample glove down the rock face.

This time the bell's crescendo brought her to her knees. She glanced around wildly and saw the others steadying themselves. Commander Alexander looked stunned as the bell finished clacking their teeth and the music expanded to bounce and hop around them gleefully.

Evelyn saw the flash of comprehension wash over the commander's face. He heard it too. The sound of the distant stars called to him just as it had her. They weren't alone in the universe. They were *not* alone.

Joy suffused her, and she tried to sing along, caught the melody, lost it and then caught it again. Evelyn struggled to maintain the thread. She stepped outside of protocol, automatically bypassing all the commands she had set in her suit and stepped forward, stroking the bell, playing it as a huge instrument, in concert with the symphony to the stars. She distantly realized the others had tumbled to the ground, struggling to rise, calling to her on the comm.

And then she was alone. Somewhere else. The surface in front of her no longer the belled rockface she had been playing. Now white rock with thin black lines arched above her, high and magnificent. A message set in stone for all time to outlast the feeble years of any race.

Touch here, the music said. *And here and here and here.* And she did as they bid, joyously stepping through the doorway that opened.

GENERATIONAL SINS

A Tale from the Dark Spaces

Bryan J.L. Glass

PROLOGUE

THERE IS A SPIRIT HERE. A CONSCIOUSNESS AS REAL AS THE AIR WE BREATHE; yet our lungs inhale and exhale something that cannot be quantified. A *sentience* as tangible as the surface we walk on, though it isn't soil. I have dug up handfuls of a substance our instruments can not measure. It is with us even in our most private, intimate moments. I have known it since I was a child when its presence raised the hairs along my arms, made my belly sink into my spine, and my leg muscles spasm. Always out of sight; just around the corner; always in some shadow where if it were to reveal its true self the vision would drive me mad. At least that's what it whispered to me in my bed when it would come to visit each night. Me specifically: Abigail Whiteside. That's what made me feel so special the older I grew, that despite childhood fears, learning the terrible fate that befell my mother Marilyn, I had still been chosen. I felt it enter my room from the shadows themselves and wait there until I fell asleep.

That's when it would enter my dreams. That's where it showed me my destiny. That's where it told me its name; the name I will *not* speak aloud. I no longer believe as my father and grandfather did, that it lived here in Dark Space cohabitating with us. No. I am now convinced it *is* Dark Space itself, and it is we who have dared to live inside it.

MARILYN'S TALE

"The first find that suggested we'd discovered something extraordinary were the Olmec Temples—the ruins of them, at any rate. Over three-thousand years old, and yet better preserved than anything that's ever been excavated on Earth Prime. That was sufficient evidence to conclude we'd not actually been the first to discover Dark Space."

The gray-haired, ashen-faced professor conveyed the information as if addressing a lecture hall filled with spellbound aspirants hanging on his every word. Marilyn was puzzled as to why the grand show when he spoke just to her. She hurried to keep up as Professor Alistair Whiteside and his son, Anton, escorted her from their small transport craft through the airlock of the landing platform. The trio had just Translated down through the Greater Electromagnetic Spectrum two strata from the Prime. The platform seemed totally automated.

"But listen to me prattling on as if you could appreciate wonders you've yet to experience." Alistair's tone was light, but sounded a bit harried; and the implied self-deprecation felt like a lie. "But you're our presumed expert on the Strata, Marilyn. Why don't you share a slice of that knowledge with us." Playful, but it wasn't a request.

"I'm only the student here, Professor," Marilyn reminded him.

"And top of your class. That's why you were chosen," Alistair added. "Thus I'd like my son to hear what a Prime education sounds like." Chosen for an obscure grant from a foundation no one had ever heard of before. Marilyn was beginning to rethink the…honor.

Anton rolled his eyes. "Father, I don't need a science lesson."

"Nonsense. Our Marilyn needs something to occupy her thoughts, and I can't think of anything better than to elucidate on one's own area of expertise."

Entering the installation, Marilyn countered, "The ruins do sound fascinating. But why just pick me? You could have offered this field expedition to the entire class."

"Humor me," Alistair said, "and this endeavor will prove more pleasant for all of us."

There was an edge to this Professor Whiteside, and it had gotten sharper the further from campus they'd traveled. The opportunity had materialized as if from nowhere, but both university administration and teaching staff treated it like some prestigious corporate recruitment. It was just the abruptness of the expedition that had raised concerns, only her career counselor assured everything had checked out. The vast scale of the Strata made it practically impossible for any one stratum to know the totality of what occurred in the others.

Marilyn humored her host as they made their way down an otherwise vacant corridor. "The Strata consists of seven replicated frequencies of existence along the electromagnetic spectrum, three above and three below the Prime Stratum of humanity's origin…"

This is rudimentary, she thought. "…Only *you* contend there are sub-frequencies buffered between each strata that haven't been formally discovered; like black keys between the white on a keyboard," Marilyn said, finding it difficult not to smirk at the incredulity of the concept.

"Precisely," Alistair remarked. "Oh, we picked a quick-witted one. Like I told you, Anton—top of her class!"

A commanding voice called out behind them,. "Hold it right there!"

The trio turned to see a lone security guard leaning out from an ancillary corridor, one hand on the butt of his holstered sidearm.

Marilyn could almost swear Whiteside's expression twisted with annoyance and something close to rage, but only for the briefest instant before returning to neutral. When he turned to the guard he used his most apologetic tone, "Oh, I'm sorry. Were we supposed to check in?"

The guard didn't move his right hand from the holster, but he gestured their return with his left. "I'm going to have to see some identification."

Arms only half-raised, Alistair led them back to the guard. "There was no one to meet us on the platform when we landed. I just assumed everything was auto-cleared when we transmitted our flight plan on approach."

The guard remained cautious. "There's no record of your landing."

Alistair chuckled. "Why that's ridiculous. I'm no pilot. I just press the buttons when the onboard system tells me to. We couldn't have even landed without your platform's guidance control."

The guard extended his palm to stop their advance. "There's no flight plan or authorization on record. And your party isn't registering on any of our security cameras. I need you to state your business."

Alistair observed the man's nametag. "We're down from the Prime, um, Hendrix, is it? A bit of a family outing, showing my niece here how the dough gets made, so to speak."

At his deception, Marilyn frowned. When she opened her mouth to protest Anton abruptly silenced her with a firm but careful grasp on her shoulder. No one else seemed to notice.

Unmoved, Hendrix asked, "Your name?"

Alistair shifted just as easily to exasperation. "Alistair Whiteside. Senior Engineer. You can access my file back at your monitor. We won't bite."

Hendrix relaxed enough to lead them back to his security desk. "Hopefully it's just a formality," he said, "but if I hadn't gotten up from my station when I did and saw you crossing the corridor, I'd have never even known you were here."

"That's quite all right, young man. I'm sure such mistakes are a rarity on this shift." Alistair subtly implied guilt.

Arriving at his desk, Hendrix turned away from the trio just long enough to catch a glance at his monitor screen. "You said the name was Whiteside?"

"That's correct," Alistair said as he placed a small thimble-sized cylinder on the check-in counter above the desk. "And your first name?" His counter-questioning of the guard intrigued Marilyn as she watched him place his middle finger atop the cylinder.

"Richard," Hendrix replied out of habit. "I'm not seeing anything here on Whiteside…"

"That's unfortunate," Alistair said. As he spoke, he lifted his finger. Marilyn heard a faint click followed by a flash of light. "But it leads me to wonder what Richard Hendrix might be afraid of?"

The moment Whiteside said the words the guard locked his gaze on the monitor as if riveted. Instantly, his eyes grew wide and he began to scream.

To Marilyn it displayed static.

Alistair turned to her as if nothing had happened. "Let's be on our way." Still Hendrix screamed.

"What?" Marilyn cried. "Why are you doing this?" Anton's grip on her shoulder tightened. For the first time since father and son had escorted her from campus Marilyn felt truly afraid. Alistair remained unperturbed by the unabated screams. "Don't mind him. At this hour he's the only one on duty." Alistair glanced at his watch as he retraced their steps. "We still have a good six hours before the next shift change."

"Make him stop screaming. Please." Marilyn begged, her voice cracking as Anton propelled her after his father.

Alistair's tone dropped all illusion of charm. "I'm afraid I can't do that. Our tech linked his mind to that monitor. As for what our Mr. Hendrix is seeing — whatever nightmare has originated from the man's subconscious — those visions are of his own making."

Marilyn's eyes grew wide. "My god — you're *MysTechs*!"

This was no field trip. She trembled as she realized all of Whiteside's digital credentials would vanish as abruptly as they'd appeared. No doubt he'd done something to Marilyn's biochip as well, preventing it from emitting its location signal the moment they'd left school grounds.

Would her own records auto-delete leaving only memories of her existence to counter a bureaucracy that relied exclusively upon digital records? She knew with fearful certainty that no one would come to her rescue.

Marilyn slammed her shoulder into Anton's chest but he was ready for it. He easily wrangled her slight frame into an over-the-shoulder carry. She fought back, but no amount of struggle would dislodge his strong grip.

"The boogiemen of the Strata," Alistair exclaimed smugly. "How satisfying to learn one's legacy lives on in the next generation with such profundity."

Part of MysTech philosophy said that anything was possible; even the impossible. All that was truly required was a sufficient application of will. Deception and domination were therefore the twin foundational pillars upon which all else was built.

Alistair led the trio onward as if nothing had happened.

Five levels underground brought them to the lowest basement, and then two seldom trod sub-floors beneath that led to construction fissures and natural tunnels that seemed to serve no purpose, which Marilyn was certain made them ideal for the MysTechs' use.

One mile below the surface of this otherwise undeveloped moon there stood an alloy frame with a two-by-three-meter gap in its center like an electronic garden arch trellis.

"Secure Marilyn's harness."

Anton moved to do his father's bidding, fitting Marilyn with a belt and crisscrossing suspenders that engulfed her torso from shoulders to crotch and around her waist.

"I'm sorry," Anton whispered too softly for his father to hear. Sure he was. Marilyn wanted to spit at him but she was too afraid.

Alistair busied himself accessing the frame's control panel. "We have a network of these portals scattered throughout the darkest corners of the Strata. They're how we MysTechs go about our business relatively unnoticed."

Marilyn said nothing but her eyes soaked in every detail.

"You're probably thinking we're leeching energy from the complex above to serve as our personal Translation Engine; that such an energy drain is bound to draw attention. But no, this isn't Translation between

Strata; most certainly not, Manifestation is a different technology altogether. It's like bargaining with a higher power. Your own life aura powers your side of the deal through the harness, and *voila...*"

They stepped through the portal, from the minimally illuminated darkness of the cavern into a nearly blinding gray.

"...Dark Space itself seals the compact," Alistair announced with a staged flourish as if the trick had been his own.

Anton steadied Marilyn firmly yet not without tenderness as she wobbled and her breakfast sprayed across the ground. Bright colors, partially digested, practically glowed with their own inner light in contrast to the gray soil-like particles that served as the foundation upon which they stood. But it was far more than what passed for earth that comprised the overwhelming otherworldly blandness that was Dark Space—everything native to this realm was cast in shades of gray like a monochromatic spectrum. The air seemed like a transparent fog; though one could not see it, it felt oppressive and tangible enough that it should have been visible. But if that were truly so there would be no way to distinguish it from the solid shade of dark gray that seemed to represent the sky despite the periodic flashes of lightning that networked from one distant horizon to the other. Random and angry, they appeared more like neurons firing in the brain than any electrical discharge.

Alistair carried himself in this realm like a proud parent, as if this was his true home. Like an expectant mother, the color of his previously ashen flesh practically glowed against the gray.

Just like my vomit, Marilyn thought.

But as she raised her hands to her face she gasped, perceiving her own aura glowing like a beacon. It was beautiful. Her life was beautiful. She began to cry.

Anton's hands tensed on Marilyn's shoulders. "Here they come, Father."

"Our welcoming committee," Alistair said. "Stay sharp. And no sudden movements."

A mass of fifty or more figures had delineated themselves from the desolate background gray, apparently roving the wasteland, only now altering their course like insects drawn to the light.

Alistair grimaced. "Savages. Start walking," he scowled, the creatures' existence an obvious bane to his otherwise well-regulated world. "We have portals inside our colony complex for manifesting to the Strata, but Dark Space seems to enjoy playing this game with us whenever we return. Manifesting us back to some random location, giving these brutes a fair shot at us."

The closer the mass came, the more details emerged: arms and legs. Human. Naked. Male and female, young and old.

"They wander this landscape in the millions. We've run a few DNA tests and the closest theory we have is they're descendants of the Olmec…"

Anton added, "Interbred with every other lost civilization that found itself manifested here by choice or chance."

The mass of creatures spread out like a pack, predatory. No light of life glowing from within them despite their mobility. Their flesh and hair were as gray as their world, as if being born here, generation after generation, had simply bred the spark of life out of them.

Alistair continued, "Like us, I believe their ancestral priests bargained with Dark Space, and brought their people with them in sacrifice." He grinned bitterly. "Only they weren't worthy of the gift this place offers. Their children devolved, century after century, into these mindless things advancing on us."

The closer they drew, the more obvious it became there was no reason behind their eyes. The black stains that streaked their bodies was blood. Missing limbs and fresh gouges in their own flesh suggested something monstrous. If Marilyn had had anything left in her stomach she would have lost it at the sight of them.

"Quicken your pace. When they're not feeding on each other, they're drawn to our light," Alistair said.

Then the savages charged the trio as a ravenous horde. Anton tensed on reflex. Marilyn screamed. Alistair strode toward the pack like a 19th century colonial daring to subdue some dark continent of perceived inferiors. He raised a new device from his coat. It emitted an ear-piercing shriek that rattled Marilyn's skull and made her teeth hurt. She dropped to the ground.

"Get up," Anton barked into her ear, urgency erasing what meager tenderness he'd previously shown. He dragged her several feet forward before yanking her upright.

Alistair was equally terse. "Use your brain. It's just a noise. Show me you're worthy of this place. Not like them!"

Marilyn stumbled but stayed upright. Behind them the entire horde writhed on the ground, howling in an agony that sought to harmonize with the shrieking device.

Ten minutes into their trek, and the savages were lost from their sight to the wasteland they mirrored. Alistair deactivated the sonic emitter, and his own smug humor returned as if he reveled in the joy of demonstrating another of his self-lauding gadgets.

"They acclimate to each frequency faster than one might expect. And we learned the hard way that if we alternate the tones, those beasties literally adapt to the sequence. It's damned fascinating actually." He held out the emitter for Marilyn's inspection. "So that almost makes this toy a sort of one-and-done device," he said.

She paid him no attention.

Alistair sighed. "It'll be weeks before we can use that particular wavelength again."

They walked for another kilometer before antenna spires rose visibly on the horizon, isolated in sharp relief from the gray tones of a distant mountain range.

Alistair resumed his role as self-appointed tour guide. "Do you see those peaks on the horizon?" he asked as another cascade of lightning etched the sky. Only now did it register on Marilyn that there was no thunder. No wind. No sound at all other than what they made themselves. Another reason the sonic barrage had been so devastating.

Alistair continued, "We've never actually been able to reach them, despite countless reconnaissance efforts. It's almost as if they're nothing more than the largest painted backdrop in human history, daubed upon the boundary walls of Dark Space, yet one that recedes at the speed and distance one approaches it. I'm not ashamed to tell you I've made it my ambition to actually climb those heights at least once in my lifetime." His yearning was sincere, and almost as palpable as the totality of the impossible landscape that encompassed them.

"We've launched probes. That was back when Anton was barely out of diapers."

Anton sighed in exasperation. "I was sixteen, Father. You should remember. It wasn't long after Stratan authorities forced us into exile."

Alistair chuckled. "The boy's always been sensitive. This place hasn't helped him reconcile the distance between his head and his heart."

"About ten inches from aorta to cerebellum—anatomically speaking. Isn't that what you've always told me, Father?" Marilyn heard a faint bitter tone to his words.

Alistair ignored the rebuttal, and resumed where his lecture had cut off. "We launched probes—sixteen of them—in precise equidistant compass directions. Nuclear batteries. They could fly forever, and never stop transmitting their data back to us. Over a decade now, and they keep showing us just how astoundingly vast this single valley actually is."

Overwhelmed, Marilyn stopped listening to the particulars and fixated on the palpable tension between father and son: Anton the reluctant co-conspirator, with enough strength to constrain her yet insufficient to defy the overbearing Alistair. But she might need his empathy if she'd any hope of avoiding her inevitable fate. One didn't have to rank top of their class to thread together the available data.

The MysTech colony complex arose from the flat empty landscape like the Taj Mahal, a vast monument to humanity's stubborn determination to imprint its influence wherever it went. In a domain of desolation, the great complex of interlocking pre-fabricated domes declared mankind had come and intended to stay. A sprawling electrified fence surrounded the entire structure, frequent proof against the savage hordes. Beyond it rose an inner wall ten meters high that surely allowed the MysTechs to easily pick off any savage that got past their outer defenses.

"Ithax Base," Alistair announced proudly, puffing out his chest like a bantam rooster. "Named for a Hesychian variant of the Greek Titan Prometheus, only we're less concerned about the liver here and more consumed by the fire."

"Only not all versions of the myth agree, do they, Father?" Anton chided again.

Alistair proceeded to Ithax Base as if he'd not heard.

Within, the various MysTechs they encountered along the corridors appeared to ignore Marilyn's presence altogether. Some exchanged brief pleasantries with Alistair as they passed, acknowledging him as de facto leader of their sect.

Anton escorted Marilyn to personnel quarters and instructed her to strip and bathe herself. It was then she gleaned an inkling of her fate. This was just the next step in a terrible ritual. She realized she was not the first. She would not be the last. She wept more so for the latter than for herself.

Adorned in a white robe, Marilyn was ushered barefoot along another corridor with a gently winding slope that she felt encircled the entire colony and descended into the ground like a wide corkscrew. Anton had left her alone to rest and recover. She could have used those hours to pursue some desperate escape, but she realized there was something in the room's lighting that pacified such thoughts. Anton had clearly used the time to bath himself, now handsomely adorned in a red satin robe embroidered with arcane symbols in black thread.

Completing several loops downward, they met with Alistair once again, equally refreshed and likewise adorned in a black robe with red symbols. On his short, paunchy frame it merely looked ridiculous.

"There she is," Alistair remarked, "as beautiful as a bride."

Anton sighed. "Father… Don't make this any more difficult than it already is."

Alistair lost his smile in an instant, replacing it with a snarl of barely contained rage. "You'll not rebut, critique, or contradict me again." Anton stiffened. "You've been little more than a disappointment for most of your life, and the fact that those sheep that follow me consider you my heir apparent due to our coincident genetics *sickens me!*"

This was Alistair's true face. Marilyn realized this was her last chance to delay her fate or perhaps avoid it altogether now that she knew what they intended.

"Ruins…" she whispered.

Alistair diverted his attention to her as if he were astounded Marilyn still possessed the ability to speak. "What's that, my dear?"

Marilyn cleared her throat. "You promised to show me the Olmec ruins."

Alistair stared into space as if caught in a logic trap. Then he grinned. The grin became a laugh. A laugh so great as to suggest such humor was his natural state. Only his last joke was to be at Marilyn's expense.

"Oh, you naïve child. I am. We are. I had this complex built over top the Olmec's fallen glory."

Alistair grabbed her arm and dragged her forward with purpose, as if to force his truth over one who'd accused him of falsehood.

One more circuit, and the fabricated hallway transitioned into an ancient stonework tunnel, LED lighting panels gave way to oil-soaked torches. Ventilation was silent and unseen.

Marilyn resisted the pull as best she could but to no avail with Anton behind her blocking her escape.

At the base of the MysTech complex, serving as its ideological heart, was erected the sacrificial chamber of an ancient people; its stonework gray, as was everything built of Dark Space; the blood of millennia past stained the carved gray altar black, as in this realm nothing decayed but the souls of those who tried to claim it as their own.

Alistair pulled Marilyn onto the altar, her white robe opening to expose the breast under which her heart beat in staccato. Though she fought, Anton held her legs effortlessly, while Alistair shackled her wrists to the side of the altar.

Alistair's voice rose steadily with his passion. "Olmec priests had the spiritual purity to manifest their entire culture into Dark Space without one single iota of known technology..."

Tears streamed down the sides of Marilyn's face as Alistair pontificated. She almost — but not quite — longed for the blade, if nothing else than to be done with this pompous ass.

"Only they were mere placeholders, pioneers that showed all who followed what could be done if they only affixed the true power of their will to the goal — from le Fey to Magnus, Cagliostro to Crowley, Himmler to Parsons..."

Alistair raised an ornate sacrificial blade above his head with all the authority of a carved pagan god.

"But it took Stratan MysTechs to triumph where all those who came before failed. We, the disciples of K'Oth, are the true masters of Dark Space!"

For one brief moment, when she was certain the blade would descend, Marilyn steeled her courage enough to face her tormentor with all the defiance she could muster.

Only Alistair shifted his focus to Anton, presenting his son with the sacrificial blade. "It's time you finally earned your inheritance," he spat.

Anton took the blade and recited a mantra he'd repeated for most of his life, "The blessings of Dark Space aren't offered without a price..."

At last it appeared Alistair finally took pride in his son. Anton raised the blade. Marilyn screamed again — but not for the last time.

ANTON'S TRIAL

"Your grandfather Alistair never wanted me to succeed him. But I believe it was Dark Space itself that made the call."

Anton Whiteside sat in the driver's seat of the skimmer his hands clenched on the steering as they cruised over the gray terrain of Dark Space toward the unreachable horizon. His only daughter Abigail sat beside him, all of fourteen years old and finally ready (he thought) to receive some hard truths.

Abigail stared out the window at the endless gray waste, occasionally brightened by the crisscrossing network of lightning above. It hardly seemed she listened to him, fascinated, as always, by the silent flashes, which pulsed in tempo with the general emotional state of the colony. Like most of her generation, she'd lived her entire life in Dark Space, her experience of the Strata stemming exclusively from text-files and secondhand tales.

Anton continued, "In his final moments, I think your grandfather suspected as much and felt betrayed. Your mother and I saw it in his eyes as the life went out of them: that the creed toward which he'd devoted his entire life had actually turned on him in the end."

Abigail interrupted, "We're approaching the target, father." She had no apparent interest in whatever life her grandfather had lived, or how he'd died for that matter.

"I never wanted that to happen to you." Anton tried to convey something positive despite the heavy spirit that had plagued him of late. "So you and I are going to be the first to see whatever this thing is, eh?"

Abigail shrugged her shoulders.

Sensors usually attuned to monitor the roving migrations of the savage hordes had detected an object of unknown origin drop out of the sky exactly one hundred kilometers from Ithax Base. Anton's great-grandfather had randomly designated the direction as "southeast" over a century earlier when the MysTechs began their first tentative charting of Dark Space. Whatever had fallen emitted no discernible energy signal; more than likely it was just another piece of Strata junk that occasionally manifested into the realm by accident.

"Did I ever tell you," Anton broached, "that I wasn't much older than you when your grandfather relocated the entire colony into Dark Space?"

Abigail sighed. "The Great Manifestation was included in our Self-Study disciplines."

"The SS files are data," Anton said in exasperation. "But they can't convey what it was like to have actually…" His voice trailed off.

"If it would ease your conscious, Father," Abigail proffered with all the perfunctory empathy when granting a condemned their last meal. "Then I'm here to be enlightened."

Anton knew his daughter was only humoring him. Such was all they'd ever really managed. "You realize we're not alone here. But whatever it is that lives unseen alongside us, reached out to our ancestors in the Strata first."

Abigail immediately paid closer attention.

Anton continued, "Long before any MysTech ever actually walked this realm, prior generations had mastered communion with the spirit of this place. Embracing K'Oth as a conduit…"

"K'Oth isn't a 'what' or 'where', Father," Abigail interjected. "K'Oth's an ideology."

"But ideologies embody ideals, tangible philosophies. And whatever form this one takes…" One hand began to twitch on the steering. "…I think that's what lives here with us."

Anton's anxiety grew as the conversation seemed to spin out of his control.

"K'Oth is just a *creed*, Father. We're all taught how it's *morally ambivalent* to take from another to benefit oneself. To the individual will, one's own needs, one's own desires supersede those of any opposing need or desire. Honestly, the only thing keeping us from feeding off each other like the savages is our unity of purpose." She displayed the biggest smile of their trip. "I'm a good student, Father. Top of the class."

Anton sighed. "Like your mother." For the first time, he felt sorry for his child, and blamed himself. "Only your understanding is still in the abstract. I'm trying to convey its experience. K'Oth isn't just a creed *here*. It's a mandate, it's alive. And what you're not being taught is that one cannot exist in harmony with this place if K'Oth hasn't been nurtured in the core of one's soul."

Anton looked away at the moment of his confession. "We're no longer teaching that because we're afraid to."

"We?" Abigail asked.

"*Me*," Anton blurted. "I've been afraid to. And I feel the entire colony is paying some terrible price for my compromise."

Abigail sat forward in her seat, definitely more interested now. "Is that why you cut off manifestation to the Strata? The harmony of Dark Space compels you?" She laughed.

"I've tried striking a balance. Ever since…" he trailed off again into his own unarticulated thoughts.

Anton shook. This is what he'd run from, and thus denied his daughter her rightful heritage. Or perhaps he simply wanted to save her from his own mistakes.

"Where was I?" he snapped. It was rhetorical. "Ah, compromise. Only Dark Space doesn't negotiate."

Abigail responded bluntly. "You asked me to come with you. You've never done that."

"I want you to understand how unique you are. How difficult this is."

Anton closed his eyes and composed himself.

"You're born from a bloodline that was the very first to ever apply tech to the mastery of the mystic, and it was those ancestors who punched a hole in reality wide enough to walk through. That's our heritage. Yet those Strata plebeians considered them…*us* a cult!"

Anton felt a stirring of his father's passion and surrendered to it. He would need a bit of Alistair's rage if he were to see this through.

"Cults exist for a season. But a secret society can pass through the centuries unseen. So when humanity exploded into the Strata, that same discovery also granted the MysTechs a frontier expansive enough for the order to come out of the shadows and consolidate themselves and their findings on a single world, one accessible to every member, while still obscure enough to never be found unless one knew what they were seeking…" He chuckled at his own revelation. "An application of will. That's the 'unity of purpose' you invoked earlier."

Abigail smiled, apparently amused by the inner battle he was fighting.

Anton continued, "By congregating together, they found that communal voice they'd all experienced in their dreams *clarified*, becoming increasingly coherent the more of them were gathered together. As a group they no longer had to individually interpret the message, to grasp at straws as to its meaning. They finally understood that it wasn't they who had discovered Dark Space. Dark Space had chosen them!"

The skimmer continued on its course across the desolation, straight and true as if its occupants had an appointment with destiny. For the first time, Anton felt himself bonding with Abigail, as they never had before.

He continued, "Golganath. That's where I was born. The lowest stratum's equivalent of the Prime's Pluto. Where the MysTechs had been gathering over the span of a hundred years, from every stratum, every world, every field of scientific discipline, to finally pursue their own research and rituals unhindered by the lesser minds that governed the masses. It was from Golganath that they finally breached Dark Space, established an outpost from which to begin the metaphysical conquest of another realm, one that had opened its gates and invited its chosen people inside."

Abigail appeared impressed with his assessment of their history.

Yet Anton still flailed about in the telling. "But you also have to understand how it's an ingrained human trait for the masses to fear what they don't understand — that very ignorance exploited by those in authority to maintain their power. That's why, for centuries, MysTechs had to cover their tracks to keep one step ahead of all those envious of their achievements. That's also why, once they were all in one place, it was only a matter of time before they were found."

Even after so many years, the toll weighed heavily on Anton. In his soul he felt he'd personally betrayed all those who had paved the road before him.

"I was about your age when Stratan authorities finally located and condemned the MysTech colony on Golganath as just another 'murder/suicide cult,' no different than so many others strewn across history. They came for us with enough ships and firepower to wage a war. Their plan: force our people to surrender so a cadre of inadequate scientists, philosophers, and theologians could try to unlock and exploit centuries of MysTech discoveries.

"Except your grandfather was ready for them. Before they arrived, he orchestrated the translocation of the entire colony into Dark Space. As far as the Strata was concerned, we'd become just another lost colony that had launched itself into deep space rather than face Stratan justice. Alistair had outwitted them all. He built the barriers, and launched the campaign against the savages. All we have is because of him. That's the legacy I've tried to live up to. I know what I'm supposed to do, only now…"

Abigail nodded, but he had the sense his revelation was not unexpected to her: belief without conviction. Perhaps he'd really brought her along to test his own heart.

Abigail asked, "Would you ever sacrifice me?"

Anton shuddered. "The blessings of Dark Space are never offered without a price. You are the first born of this colony, the first native bred MysTech genuinely conceived in Dark Space itself—as much as you're my child, you were also chosen by this place to be its daughter."

"Is that what Mother believed?"

Anton winced. "Your mother was chosen to bear you; sadly Marilyn's spirit wasn't made for Dark Space."

"So Mother let you kill her?" Abigail asked bluntly.

"It's what Ithax colony was forced to accept if we were to survive: true progress is never achieved without sacrifice—the greater the revelation the more significant the cost; the more human the price, the more innocent the blood."

His confession tore shreds in his spirit. While Abigail only smiled, seemingly at how difficult this had become for him.

He continued, trying to smooth out the jagged edges. "Having been born here, you have an advantage over your ancestors. Dark Space clears your mind, grants free rein to your intellect. That's what it truly means to be a MysTech, a breed evolved from those genetic lines that formed us. This should all be yours. This place, your inheritance."

Their skimmer approached ground zero to discover half a dozen savages had beaten them to the site.

Anton activated a targeting scope to isolate and digitally tag each of the savages as they milled about the small impact crater that pocked the gray slope. With the press of a single button, he could eliminate all six. Only he needed to check first if any were byproducts of the MysTechs' most ambitious effort for neutralizing the savage threat: gene pacification—to literally breed the ferocity out of the gray-skinned beasts.

Abigail relayed, "No indication of modified behavior. I'd light them up."

Anton didn't move, observing the indigenous inhabitants that would attack their skimmer once their presence was noticed. *My own daughter is just as much an indigenous inhabitant as the savages,* he mused bitterly, finding what solace he could in the task before him.

Before Anton could act, Abigail reached across to his console and depressed the firing icon.

Four seconds later, the last of the savages fell to the ground, spilling black blood onto the gray soil.

"Don't be sentimental, Father. Let's see what we're dealing with here."

Abigail climbed out. Anton followed.

She stared at the wreckage, confusion played across her face.

Anton clarified, "That's one of the survey probes my father launched."

Serial numbers confirmed the specific unit; one of the sixteen that had been mapping Dark Space for decades, thus far charting a land mass that was nearly as large per square kilometer as the surface of Sol, the Stratan Sun. If it had gone down where it was currently charted to be, physical recovery should have taken a lifetime, only here it was a mere hundred kilometers from the colony that launched it.

One downed probe now cast doubt on all they'd ever learned about Dark Space. Abruptly insinuating the presence that lurked just out of sight could be lying to them even in their dreams. Amidst his own guilt, that was one thought Anton had never considered.

Yet another logic-defying mystery. Only this enigma wasn't conceptual. They had a tangible piece of technology to bring back and analyze. Scrutinize it for whatever revelations it might offer concerning the nature of Dark Space itself.

Abigail continued to stare, as if grappling with inner demons of her own. But Anton needed her.

The probe was light enough for one, yet bulky enough to require them both. The seal around the nuclear battery remained unbroken. Together, they wrangled the wreckage toward the back of their skimmer.

But Abigail abruptly backed away leaving Anton to grapple with the rest. He turned to see what was wrong, only to find her standing there with a sliver of broken airfoil in her hands. "You could have told me," Abigail hissed, her expression one of contempt.

"That I killed your mother?"

"That Dark Space has a name, Father. You used to know it." She glared at him as if his negligence on the matter served as another betrayal. "Only why did you never share it with me?"

Anton maneuvered the probe into the rear bed with a huff. "Because I was afraid of what this place would do to you. You were chosen...only Dark Space brought us out here alone so I could kill you too."

His final confession uttered, he slumped against the closed hatch.

He stared at his daughter as he began to cry, noting how her hand clenched on the sliver in her hand. "But I'm taking you home," Anton said. "Then we'll manifest back to the Strata with as many as we can convince to join us. Abandon Dark Space before it kills us all, or worse."

He had conviction on only one count: K'Oth was far more than any mere ideology. It was alive, and sentient, and had a name Anton could curse: *Ko'G'Oth* be damned. He'd failed Abigail her entire life. He wouldn't do it again.

ABIGAIL'S GLORY

"It would have broken my father's heart to see what's become of us."

Abigail Whiteside stood in the Command Center of Ithax Base having dismissed the rest of the Command Staff to the defense of the outer shield wall. Only Eve remained at her side.

An unbroken ring of monitor screens bordered the circular Command Center, providing real-time imagery of the ominous threat that encircled the outer gates of the colony.

"Yes, ma'am," Eve agreed.

It wasn't just that Abigail was the colony's leader that kept her ensconced safely within, but more so that she was now closing in on one hundred years of age. She could only hope that her own legacy of leadership would have made her father proud. She doubted it. They were on the brink of extinction.

"It was my grandfather who settled the colony here, his grandfather before him that originally discovered Dark Space, if discovery is the right word for what he did. So whatever my flaws, I come by them honestly. Still, Grandfather Alistair wouldn't have liked your kind."

Eve conveyed no judgment. She had been gestated to affirm, and never to bite the hand that fed her. "Yes, ma'am."

Abigail continued, "I never knew him. But by reputation, Alistair was the kind of MysTech that would have seen your kind exterminated rather than sit down to tea."

Eve finished her own cup then asked if Abigail would like more. Abigail chuckled and agreed.

As faithful Eve set herself to the task, Abigail continued, "It's my father you can thank for granting your kind the temperance to offer me tea. It was Anton who set the whole gene pacification project in motion. His contribution to Dark Space." Abigail felt unusually melancholy. Perhaps it was the inevitable doom congregating outside the domes.

"Yes, ma'am."

Eve was a third-generation Domesticate, and the first to be granted free access to the colony dome. She needed that freedom to come and go as she was instructed if she was to be a servant adequate to her mistress's needs. That was the real reason Abigail had granted her a name: one that carried both cultural and mythological significance.

Father Anton's solution to the savage problem had been genetic and they'd been reaping the rewards ever since. Breed a superior savage, which meant strain the aggression out. Whatever species emerged could probably be put to good use, while the numbers of the greater cannibalistic horde would decrease generation after generation. That was the plan.

But it was Abigail who had overseen the project to completion in the wake of the savages' attack upon her father that had proportedly left him for dead and granted her hereditary charge of all her grandfather had established.

Abigail continued, "Alistair and Anton had conflicting visions for the future of Dark Space, but what does it say that I have been in charge three times longer than they were combined. That should count for something."

She floundered for a moment; the MysTech population was now less than a third of what it had been when her grandfather first founded the beleaguered colony.

"Where did we go wrong?" Abigail asked, rhetorically of course. She remained too proud to consider her own leadership as the cause. If there was glory to be had, it was hers. But she found there was always enough fault to spread around.

For decades, the savage population had decreased in proportion to the success of the pacification program, following their impact models precisely. So promising were those first twenty years that Abigail oversaw a restructuring of MysTech priorities, placing genetic research at the top of their communal list.

As faithful Eve prepared her second cup of tea, Abigail looked up at the outside monitor screen: beyond the wall, beyond the triple rings of fencing, the savages stood in silent rows as impassively as the day the first few arrived weeks ago, congregating at the outer gate and staring inward at the miniscule portion of Dark Space that was denied them.

At first, their behavior was deemed a side effect of the pacification program, but the Domesticates lacked individual purpose, while this conduct indicated intent.

Then the numbers grew: one hundred, one thousand, ten thousand, five-hundred thousand. When the count was digitally estimated at one million, the last MysTech stopped referring to the situation as an anomaly and the colony was once more unified by mutual concern. Sacrificing one of their own upon the ancient Olmec altar, selected by lottery, failed to elicit any kind of response from their sentient domain. And still the horde grew. Two million. Three. Four. Five: a number that surpassed their every calculation of the savage population, as if Dark Space had selectively hidden the true extent of their numbers as it had the scope of Dark Space itself. A quarter-kilometer ring of savage gray creatures surrounded Ithax Base. Only then did long-range sensors stop registering any further movement converging on the colony.

As Eve brought Abigail her second cup of tea an instantaneous howling filled the Command Center as five million savages raised their voices in unison.

Faithful Eve dropped the cup, an antique purportedly owned by Abigail's grandmother. It shattered upon the floor. Abigail's heart skipped a beat as she fell backward into the central command chair. She swiveled round to take in the totality of the image as the horde abruptly charged the gate.

The ferocity of the electrical discharge was matched only by the silent lightning that shattered the deep gray of the Dark Space sky, the cries of the savages, living and dying, brought thunder to their rage.

The three fences collapsed one by one, thousands of savages dying in the process, but the fatalities barely registered against the totality of the converging masses.

The automated wall defenses, supplemented by the personal weaponry of the MysTech colonists, obliterated hundreds of thousands more. Yet those losses never even came close to eliminating the first million, let alone the four million that followed behind them. The wall was scaled *en masse*.

Abigail ordered Eve to clean up her mess.

As her fellow colonists abandoned the shield wall, Abigail sealed the entire complex with the press of a single button on her command console. The number of the horde could increase a thousand-fold, and they would still prove nothing more than flesh and blood against the unyielding elements that comprised the domes. They could mash themselves into a pulpy gray paste, while she and the Domesticates within weathered the storm in comfort. It had long ago been determined that the air they breathed, the sustenance they consumed were actually unnecessary. Dark Space itself sustained their existence.

Yet internal overrides opened the outer hatches. Abigail cursed whatever emotional responses had compelled whoever had remained within the complex to yield to their pity. She would find out who they were and have them gutted upon the Olmec altar once the doors were resealed and the crisis had passed.

When the situation had still been growing two weeks earlier, one doomsday scenario posited that if the worst were to happen, the MysTechs could survive as an order by manifesting themselves back to the Strata. Abigail had overridden any preemptory manifestation of their collected data. She wouldn't risk centuries of accumulated knowledge falling into the hands of common Stratan humanity, no matter what contingencies were employed to secure it.

But now all bets were off. She watched on the monitor as MysTechs grabbed pre-packed bags, handheld cases surely containing enough raw data to revolutionize any and every industry throughout the seven layers. Her rage grew at how easily these common MysTechs abandoned their faith and stole generations of society research for their own gain. The lines at the Manifestation portals were overwhelming, but no one was getting through.

From the Command Center, Abigail had no direct control over the portals. They simply weren't working. Digital algorithms projected the only thing capable of shutting down Manifestation technology would be a solar flare of such magnitude that even translation throughout the Strata would be severed, isolating each individual stratum for an indeterminate period of time. Solar activity had long hampered standard Translation on a regular basis, but for such minor intervals that the economy and social structure had long ago adapted to the occasional delays. But a storm powerful enough to interfere with Manifestation would be inherently capable of eliminating standard Translation for years, decades, perhaps even centuries. Stratan society as it was known would collapse. The odds of such a disastrous coincidence occurring between the Strata and the synchronous rioting hordes of Dark Space were impossible to consider without some sentient intelligence involved. Even the mind of a MysTech was rocked by the implications.

Panic consumed her people as the savages breached the complex. She watched, emotions oddly detached, as those savages devoured her people. There was some justice in that. And at least she would still be safe. No one was getting into the Command Center. Even its power was self-sustaining. She and faithful Eve would survive to pick up the pieces.

Abigail's physiology had been maintained by MysTech disciplines for so long, she felt confident she could still live long enough to recruit new acolytes once the solar storm abated, and thereby rebuild all that was being lost in human resources — and that next generation would look back upon her legacy as the one that truly mattered. She would strip names from their historic annals — her father, grandfather, all those of their line who had come before her — reinventing the lineage of Abigail Whiteside to suit her own fancy, granting her the immortal heritage she desired. That would be enough to leave this existence satisfied that she'd mattered after all.

The final screams faded from the speakers. Abigail turned off the volume. She had no interest in the inarticulate grunts of savages. She heard them pounding on the outer hatch like the proverbial Big Bad Wolf huffing and puffing against the house of brick. The last surviving MysTech would endure as long as she had to.

Abigail turned to her remaining companion, "Make me another cup of tea, would you, Eve?"

MARILYN'S CODA
In the temple ruins beneath Ithax Base…

Sacrificial dagger in his hand, Marilyn watched in awe as Anton's temperament transformed before her eyes, from reluctant Acolyte to estranged son enraged by a lifetime of his father's antagonism.

"It chose *me*, Father..." Anton grabbed the front of Alistair's robe and yanked him onto the altar next to Marilyn. His father tried to scramble off but Anton plunged the dagger to the hilt into the old man's chest, again and again. "...To convey its disappointment in you! All you did for your own praise, but you never once asked Dark Space its name!"

Like the ancient Olmec drawing out sacrificial hearts to appease their dark gods, Anton offered all that remained — himself and his chosen bride — to the glory of Ko'G'Oth.

ANTON'S END
Upon the dusty gray wastes, one hundred kilometers from Ithax Base...

Anton sensed all feeling and control of his lower limbs cease as his daughter Abigail ran the jagged sliver of airfoil into his back.

"Dark Space gave you a chance, Father..." Abigail railed, "and you rejected it!"

Anton involuntarily twisted as his lower torso and legs abruptly buckled beneath him, collapsing against the side of the skimmer.

Abigail shouted, "Ko'G'Oth told me to convey its disappointment in you!"

One tear spilled from Anton's eye. He understood the message. She rammed the jagged edge through his heart.

ABIGAIL'S CODICIL
In the Command Center of Ithax Base...

"No, ma'am," Eve rebutted her Mistress Abigail for the first time in her history of service. She stood by the door-lock panel that controlled entry to the Command Center.

Abigail half-rose, indignant. "What do you think you're doing?"

Eve's tone remained innocent of malevolent intent. "I am taking this opportunity to inform you, ma'am..."

"Of what?" Abigail's tone barely contained her anger.

"That you've proven a disappointment."

The last vestige of color drained from Abigail's face.

"Ko'G'Oth has lost patience with you," Eve concluded. "Ma'am," she added as the hatch opened, granting entry to the ravenous hordes of Dark Space.

There wasn't enough of Abigail to satisfy those in the room, let alone the four million outside.

EVE'S EPILOGUE

There is a spirit here. A *consciousness* as real as this gray flesh that is not our own. For generations spanning millennia, it has called to the children of men and women in their dreams that it might draw the likeminded unto itself, to acquire their intellect as its own.

Although our ancestors have been legion, we are but the first of those yet to come. For we are the true MysTechs, unified in purpose as Mistress Abigail, Father Anton, Grandfather Alistair could never bring themselves to be, as one in spirit and purpose with this place. With our predecessors' accumulated knowledge our race shall finally achieve its genetic perfection in form and function fulfilling our destiny at last.

Whether it take a thousand years or more, once the solar storms abate, our progeny will manifest in numbers beyond comprehension until the Strata is overwhelmed by our hordes, the Prime subdued; until we dominate the birthplace of humanity and eradicate the blight that are the souls of humankind.

We have proven ourselves the only loyal children of Dark Space. We alone understand this is not a physical domain like those levels of the Strata, but that we live in the metaphysical mind of our true master. We know its name, for it calls us by its own will, that of our lord Ko'G'Oth.

A Beginning

ABOUT THE AUTHORS

Gordon Linzner is the founder and former editor of *Space and Time Magazine*, as well as author of three published novels (*The Troupe, The Oni,* and *The Spy Who Drank Blood*) and dozens of short stories in *F&SF, Twilight Zone, Sherlock Holmes Mystery Magazine,* and numerous other magazines and anthologies, most recently *Corporate Cthulhu, Baker Street Irregulars II, Release the Virgins!* and the forthcoming *The Mountains of Madness Revealed.* He is a lifetime member of SFWA, a licensed New York City tour guide and lifelong resident of that city, edits, cat-sits, and leads the Saboteur Tiger Blues Band, among other distractions.

Ian Randal Strock (www.IanRandalStrock.com) is the owner and publisher of Gray Rabbit Publications, LLC, and its sf imprint, Fantastic Books (www.FantasticBooks.biz). He is the author of many short stories appearing in *Nature, Analog* (from which he won two AnLab Awards), and several anthologies, and of much nonfiction, including *The Presidential Book of Lists* (Random House, 2008), *Ranking the First Ladies* (Carrel Books, 2016), and *Ranking the Vice Presidents* (Carrel Books, 2016).

Robert Greenberger is a writer and editor. A lifelong fan of comic books, comic strips, science fiction and *Star Trek,* he drifted toward writing and editing, encouraged by his father and inspired by Superman's alter ego, Clark Kent.

While at SUNY-Binghamton, Greenberger wrote and edited for the college newspaper, Pipe Dream. Upon graduation, he worked for Starlog Press and while there, created Comics Scene, the first nationally distributed magazine to focus on comic books, comic strips and animation.

In 1984, he joined DC Comics as an Assistant Editor, and went on to be an Editor before moving to Administration as Manager-Editorial Operations. He joined Gist Communications as a Producer before moving to Marvel Comics as its Director-Publishing Operations.

Greenberger rejoined DC in May 2002 as a Senior Editor-Collected Editions. He helped grow that department, introducing new formats and improving the editions' editorial content. In 2006, he joined *Weekly World News* as its Managing Editor until the paper's untimely demise. He then freelanced for an extensive client base including Platinum Studios, scifi.com, DC and Marvel. He helped revitalize *Famous Monsters of Filmland* and served as News Editor at ComicMix.com.

He is a member of the Science Fiction Writers of America and the International Association of Media Tie-In Writers. His novelization of *Hellboy II: The Golden Army* won the IAMTW's Scribe Award in 2009.

In 2012, he received his Master of Science in Education from University of Bridgeport and relocated to Maryland where he has taught High School English in Baltimore County. He completed his Master of Arts degree in Creative Writing & Literature for Educators at Fairleigh Dickinson University in 2016.

With others, he cofounded Crazy 8 Press, a digital press hub where he continues to write. His dozens of books, short stories, and essays cover the gamut from young adult nonfiction to original fiction. He's also one of the dozen authors using the penname Rowan Casey to write the Veil Knights urban fantasy series. His most recent works include the *100 Greatest Moments* series and editing *Thrilling Adventure Yarns*.

Bob teaches High School English at St. Vincent Pallotti High School in Laurel, MD. He and his wife Deborah reside in Howard County, Maryland. Find him at www.bobgreenberger.com or @bobgreenberger.

Dayton Ward is a *New York Times* bestselling author or co-author of nearly forty novels and novellas, often working with his best friend, Kevin Dilmore. His short fiction has appeared in more than twenty anthologies and he's written for publications such as *NCO Journal*, *Kansas City Voices*, *Famous Monsters of Filmland*, *Star Trek Magazine* and *Star Trek Communicator* as well as the websites Tor.com, StarTrek.com, and Syfy.com. Before making the jump to full-time writing, Dayton was a software developer, discovering the private sector after serving for eleven years in the U.S. Marine Corps. Though he lives in Kansas City with his wife and two daughters, Dayton is a Florida native and still maintains a torrid long-distance romance with his beloved Tampa Bay Buccaneers. Find him on the web at http://www.daytonward.com.

Aaron Rosenberg is the author of the best-selling *DuckBob* SF comedy series, the *Dread Remora* space-opera series, the *Relicant Chronicles* epic fantasy series, and — with David Niall Wilson — the *O.C.L.T.* occult thriller series. Aaron's tie-in work includes novels for *Star Trek*, *Warhammer*, *World of WarCraft*, *Stargate: Atlantis*, *Shadowrun*, *Eureka*, *Mutants & Masterminds*, and more. He has written children's books (including the original series *STEM Squad* and *Pete and Penny's Pizza Puzzles*, the award-winning *Bandslam: The Junior Novel*, and the #1 best-selling *42: The Jackie Robinson Story*), educational books on a variety of topics, and over seventy roleplaying games (such as the original games *Asylum*, *Spookshow*, and *Chosen*, work for White Wolf, Wizards of the Coast, Fantasy Flight, Pinnacle, and many others, and both the Origins Award-winning *Gamemastering Secrets* and the Gold ENnie-winning *Lure of the Lich Lord*). He is the co-creator of the *ReDeus* series, and a founding member of Crazy 8 Press. Aaron lives in New York with his family. You can follow him online at gryphonrose.com, on Facebook at facebook.com/gryphonrose, and on Twitter @gryphonrose.

Award-winning author and editor **Danielle Ackley-McPhail** has worked both sides of the publishing industry for longer than she cares to admit. In 2014 she joined forces with husband Mike McPhail and friend Greg Schauer to form her own publishing house, eSpec Books (www.especbooks.com).

Her published works include six novels, *Yesterday's Dreams*, *Tomorrow's Memories*, *Today's Promise*, *The Halfling's Court*, *The Redcaps' Queen*, and *Baba Ali and the Clockwork Djinn*, written with Day Al-Mohamed. She is also the author of the solo collections *Eternal Wanderings*, *A Legacy of Stars*, *Consigned to the Sea*, *Flash in the Can*, *Transcendence*, *Between Darkness and Light*, and the non-fiction writers' guide, *The Literary Handyman*, and is the senior editor of the *Bad-Ass Faeries* anthology series, *Gaslight & Grimm*, *Side of Good/Side of Evil*, *After Punk*, and *In an Iron Cage*. Her short stories are included in numerous other anthologies and collections.

In addition to her literary acclaim, she crafts and sells original costume horns under the moniker The Hornie Lady, and homemade flavor-infused candied ginger under the brand of Ginger KICK! at literary conventions, on commission, and wholesale.

Danielle lives in New Jersey with husband and fellow writer, Mike McPhail and three extremely spoiled cats.

In her newest book, *Eternal Wanderings*, released at the beginning of 2019. An elven mage joins a Romani caravan to help a friend fight his inner demons, only to be confronted with ancient demons of a more literal sort.

To learn more about her work, visit www.sidhenadaire.com or www.especbooks.

Jody Lynn Nye lists her main career activity as "spoiling cats." When not engaged upon this worthy occupation, she writes fantasy and science fiction books and short stories.

Since 1987 she has published over 50 books and more than 160 short stories. Among the novels Jody has written are her epic fantasy series, *The Dreamland*, beginning with *Waking In Dreamland*, five contemporary humorous fantasies, *Mythology 101, Mythology Abroad, Higher Mythology* (the three collected by Meisha Merlin Publishing as *Applied Mythology*), *Advanced Mythology, The Magic Touch*, and three medical science fiction novels, *Taylor's Ark, Medicine Show* and *The Lady and the Tiger*. *Strong Arm Tactics*, a humorous military science fiction novel, is the first of *The Wolfe Pack* series. Jody also wrote *The Dragonlover's Guide to Pern*, a non-fiction-style guide to the world of internationally best-selling author Anne McCaffrey's popular world. She also collaborated with Anne McCaffrey on four science fiction novels, *The Death of Sleep, Crisis On Doona* (a *New York Times* and *USA Today* bestseller), *Treaty At Doona* and *The Ship Who Won*, and wrote a solo sequel to *The Ship Who Won* entitled *The Ship Errant*. Jody co-authored the *Visual Guide to Xanth* with best-selling fantasy author Piers Anthony. She has edited two anthologies of humorous stories about mothers in science fiction, fantasy, myth and legend, entitled *Don't Forget Your Spacesuit, Dear!, Launch Pad*, an anthology of science fiction stories co-edited with Mike Brotherton. She has two short story collections, *A Circle of Celebrations*, holiday SF/fantasy stories, and *Cats Triumphant!*, SF and fantasy feline tales. She wrote eight books with the late Robert Lynn Asprin, *License Invoked*, a contemporary fantasy set in New Orleans, and seven set in Asprin's *Myth Adventures* universe: *Myth-Told Tales* (anthology), *Myth Alliances, Myth-Taken Identity, Class*

Dis-Mythed, Myth-Gotten Gains, Myth Chief, and *Myth-Fortunes.* Since Asprin's passing, she has published *Myth-Quoted, Dragons Deal* and *Dragons Run* (Ace Books), third and fourth in Asprin's *Dragons* series. Her newest series is the Lord Thomas Kinago books, beginning with *View From the Imperium* (Baen Books), a humorous military SF novel.

Her newest books are *Moon Tracks* (Baen), a young adult hard science fiction novel, the second in collaboration with Dr. Travis S. Taylor. *Rhythm of the Imperium,* third in the Lord Thomas Kinago series; *Pros and Cons* (WordFire Press), a nonfiction book about conventions in collaboration with Bill Fawcett; and the 20th novel in the Myth-Adventures series, *Myth-Fits.*

Over the last thirty or so years, Jody has taught in numerous writing workshops and participated on hundreds of panels covering the subjects of writing and being published at science-fiction conventions. She has also spoken in schools and libraries around the north and northwest suburbs. In 2007 she taught fantasy writing at Columbia College Chicago. She also runs the two-day writers workshop at DragonCon. She and her husband are the fiction reviewers for *Galaxy's Edge Magazine.* In 2016, Jody joined the judging staff of the Writers of the Future contest, the world's largest science fiction and fantasy writing contest for new authors.

Jody lives in the northwest suburbs of Chicago, with her husband Bill Fawcett, a writer, game designer, military historian and book packager, and three feline overlords, Athena, Minx, and Marmalade. Check out her websites at www.jodylynnnye.com and mythadventures.net. She is on Facebook as Jody Lynn Nye and Twitter @JodyLynnNye.

Christopher L. Bennett is a lifelong resident of Cincinnati, Ohio, with a B.S. in Physics and a B.A. in History from the University of Cincinnati. A fan of science and science fiction since age five, he has spent the past two decades selling original short fiction to magazines such as *Analog Science Fiction and Fact* and *BuzzyMag.* For the past dozen years, he has been one of Pocket Books' most prolific and popular authors of *Star Trek* tie-in fiction, including the epic *Next Generation* prequel *The Buried Age,* the *Star Trek: Department of Temporal Investigations* series, and the ongoing *Star Trek: Enterprise — Rise of the Federation* series. His original novel *Only Superhuman,* perhaps the first hard science fiction superhero novel, was voted *Library Journal's* SF/Fantasy Debut of the Month for October 2012. His short story collection *Hub Space: Tales* *from the Greater Galaxy* is available in e-book and print formats from Mystique Press.

Christopher's homepage, fiction annotations, and blog can be found at christopherlbennett.wordpress.com, and his Facebook author page is at www.facebook.com/ChristopherLBennettAuthor.

James Chambers is an award-winning author of horror, crime, fantasy, and science fiction. He wrote the Bram Stoker Award®-winning graphic novel, *Kolchak the Night Stalker: The Forgotten Lore of Edgar Allan Poe* and was nominated for a Bram Stoker Award for *his* story, "A Song Left Behind in the Aztakea Hills." *Publisher's Weekly* gave his collection of four Lovecraftian-inspired novellas, *The Engines of Sacrifice*, a starred review and described it as "…chillingly evocative…."

He is the author of the short story collections *On the Night Border* and *Resurrection House* and several novellas, including *The Dead Bear Witness* and *Tears of Blood*, in the Corpse Fauna novella series, and the dark urban fantasy, *Three Chords of Chaos*.

His short stories have been published in numerous anthologies, including *After Punk: Steampowered Tales of the Afterlife*, *The Best of Bad-Ass Faeries*, *The Best of Defending the Future*, *Chiral Mad 2*, *Chiral Mad 4*, *Deep Cuts*, *Dragon's Lure*, *Fantastic Futures 13*, *Gaslight and Grimm*, *The Green Hornet Chronicles*, *Hardboiled Cthulhu*, *In An Iron Cage*, *Kolchak the Night Stalker: Passages of the Macabre*, *Qualia Nous*, *Shadows Over Main Street (1 and 2)*, *The Spider: Extreme Prejudice*, *To Hell in a Fast Car*, *Truth or Dare*, *TV Gods*, *Walrus Tales*, *Weird Trails*; the chapbook *Mooncat Jack*; and the magazines *Bare Bone*, *Cthulhu Sex*, and *Allen K's Inhuman*. He co-edited the anthology, *A New York State of Fright: Horror Stories from the Empire State*, which received a Bram Stoker Award nomination.

He has also written and edited numerous comic books including *Leonard Nimoy's Primortals*, the critically acclaimed "The Revenant" in *Shadow House*, and *The Midnight Hour* with Jason Whitley.

He is a member of the Horror Writers Association and recipient of the 2012 Richard Laymon Award and the 2016 Silver Hammer Award.

He lives in New York.

Visit his website: www.jameschambersonline.com.

Keith R.A. DeCandido is celebrating the silver anniversary of his fiction writing career, which started in 1994 with his Spider-Man short story "An Evening in the Bronx with Venom," and which has continued to include more than fifty novels, about a hundred short stories, and dozens of comic books, as well as more nonfiction than he can count. His other work in 2019 includes the novels *Mermaid Precinct* (also from eSpec Books, the latest in his fantasy police procedural series), *A Furnace Sealed* (kicking off a new urban fantasy series from WordFire Press), and *Alien: Isolation* (based on the classic movie series in general and the hit videogame in particular, from Titan Books); pop-culture commentary for Tor.com and on Keith's own Patreon (patreon.com/krad); and short stories in the anthologies *Brave New Girls: Adventures of Gals and Gizmos* (which also features Connie de la Vega), *Unearthed, Thrilling Adventure Yarns*, and *Release the Virgins!* Keith is also an editor, a third-degree black belt in karate, a musician, a podcaster, a Yankee fan, and possibly some other stuff he can't remember due to a perpetual lack of sleep. Find out less at his mediocre web site at DeCandido.net

Russ Colchamiro is the author of the rollicking space adventure, *Crossline*, the zany scifi backpacking comedy series *Finders Keepers, Genius de Milo*, and *Astropalooza*, and was editor of the scifi mystery anthology, *Love, Murder & Mayhem*, all with Crazy 8 Press.

He has contributed to several other anthologies including *Tales of the Crimson Keep, Pangaea, They Keep Killing Glenn, Altered States of the Union, Thrilling Adventure Yarns, Brave New Girls, Camelot 13*, and *TV Gods 2*. Russ is finalizing a noir novella collection for Crazy 8 Press, set to publish October 2019, and is writing the first in an ongoing SFF mystery series featuring his hard-boiled private eye Angela Hardwicke.

Russ lives in New Jersey with his wife, their twin ninjas, and their crazy dog, Simon.

For more on Russ's works, visit www.russcolchamiro.com, and follow him on Facebook, Twitter and Instagram @AuthorDudeRuss.

Judi Fleming works as a training specialist and instructional designer for the federal government in her day job and thus much of her writing is of the non-exciting technical sort. She is a graduate of Seton Hill University's Writing Popular Fiction Master's Program and enjoys writing short stories and her short fiction has appeared in anthologies and also writes non-fiction art articles and training programs. When she is not helping Red Dog Farm Animal Rescue Network by fostering horses, donkeys, and other farm animals, Judi lives with her husband on their 20-acre farm in North Carolina along with their own horses, goats, chickens, dogs, and cats. Her stories have appeared in *No Man's Land, Best Laid Plans,* and *Dogs of War.*

Bryan J.L. Glass is the multiple Harvey Award-winning co-creator/writer of *The Mice Templar* from Image Comics, now overseeing the return of *Cadence Lark Is Furious* from Crazy Monkey Ink (the acclaimed series formerly at Dark Horse Comics), and soon launching *BJLG's Dark Spaces*™ in both online comic and prose formats.

A contributor to DC Comics' *Adventures of Superman*, his Marvel Comics credentials include *Thor: Crown of Fools, First Thunder,* and *Valkyrie,* as well as adapting *Magician,* the *Riftwar Saga,* and Cirque du Soleil's *KÀ.* Bryan's earliest creative works include *Spandex Tights, Ship of Fools,* and *Quixote: A Novel.*

Graphics Designer **Mike McPhail** is the owner of McP Digital Graphics (founded in 2006), a company established to provide cover art, design, layout, and prepress services. This built upon not only his experience as a game designer and mechanical and computer draftsman, but primarily from his time as the proofing supervisor for Phoenix Color Corp in the Manhattan office, doing cover work for the great publishing houses.

STAR BACKERS

Alicia Blackburn
Allen
Anaxphone
Andy Remic
Andy Wortman
Angel Bomb
Anonymous Reader
Anthony R. Cardno
Aysha Rehm
Barbara and Carl Kesner
Carol Chapin Porter
Caroline Westra
Christopher Weuve
Curtis & Maryrita Steienhour
Dale A Russell
Daniel Lin
Dave Auerbach
David Perkins
Derek L Thompson
Douglas Vaughan
Evan Ladouceur
Gavin Sheedy
Gemini Wordsmiths
George
GMarkC
Ian Harvey
Isaac 'Will It Work' Dansicker
J.R. Murdock
Jakub Narębski
Jennifer L. Pierce
Jeremy Bottroff
Joanne Burrows
Joe Monson
John F. Bouchard
John Glindeman

John Green
Josh Mcginnis
Judith Waidlich
Kelly S. Pierce
Ken "Merlyn" Mencher
Kerry aka Trouble
Kierin Fox
Lark Cunningham
Lee Jamilkowski
Linda Pierce
Lisa Kruse
Louise Lowenspets
Marc "mad" W.
Maria T
Mark Carter
Mark Featherston
Mark Hirschman
mdtommyd
Michael A. Burstein
Michael Higgins — NobleFusion
Mike Crate
Mike Maurer
Mike Skolnik
Morgan Hazelwood
Neil Ottenstein
Niki Curtis
Pat Hayes
Paul van Oven
Pekka
Peter Young
Philippe van Nedervelde
PJ Kimbell
R. Garber
R.J.H.
Ralph M. Seibel

Ratesjul
Richard P Clark
Richard Stone
RKBookman
Robby Thrasher
Robert Claney
Robert E Waters
Robert Flipse
Rose Pribula
Samuel Lubell

Scott Elson
Scott Mantooth
Scott Schaper
Sheryl R. Hayes
Stephen Ballentine
Tim DuBois
Tony Finan
V Hartman DiSanto
Wes Rist

CPSIA information can be obtained
at www.ICGtesting.com
Printed in the USA
LVHW041558140120
643593LV00004B/470